Starpeople

Mankind Gets A Second Chance

The Sirian Redemption

a novel by

Linda Tuck-Jenkins

Inspirational Fiction
New Smyrna Beach, Florida

Published by Inspirational Fiction
P. O. Box 2509
New Smyrna Beach, FL 32170-2509
www.inspirationalfiction.com

Cover Design: Peri Poloni, www.knockoutbooks.com

This is a work of fiction. All places, names and characters are either invented or used fictitiously. The events described are purely imaginary.

ISBN: 0-9710429-9-3

Library of Congress Control Number: 2001090701

Printed in the United States of America

For Chris, Mary, and Mary Jo

Thanks to my readers for encouragement and constructive criticism: Bonnie, Cliff, David, Jerry, Jude, Iona, Kelly, Larry, Mary, Pam, Paul, Rachel, and Ronnie. Special thanks to: Chris Jenkins, my best friend and biggest supporter; Cathy Woolcott Edwards for editorial expertise and good humor; Rosemary Stevens for literary advice; and Susan Hayward and Malcolm Cohan for permission to quote *A Guide for the Advanced Soul.* Finally, I am indebted to Jerry Jampolsky, a this-world Reese, for introducing me to *A Course In Miracles.*

Part One

The Awakening

Prologue

MacDill Air Force Base, Florida
June 7, 11:56 A.M. EDT

I've got something, major." Lieutenant Norville called the officer standing at a console a few feet away. The flight control center was a flurry of activity. Every station was staffed as the crew struggled to keep up with a half dozen tropical waves, depressions, storms, and Ervin, a full-fledged, level two hurricane that was running up the Florida Gulf Coast.

Major Travis Collins leaned over Norville's shoulder, peering across the top of half-moon glasses at the computer display. "What do you have?"

Norville pointed to a flashing entry on the right of the screen. "These are the last pressure readings from the Sanibel station. Look at this drop."

"It's just a tornado."

Norville stroked the keypad, bringing up another display. "But sir—the pressure dropped below twenty-two, then shot up to thirty-five inches minutes later. Isn't this something we should report?"

Breathing hard and muttering to himself, Collins ran his index finger down the list of numbers on the computer terminal. He didn't like what he saw. The phenomenon wasn't natural; it happened too fast. Winds were off, magnetics wrong. Collins' mouth went dry. *Omagod.* They had one: a bogey.

Chapter 1

Come to the edge, he said.
They said, We are afraid.
Come to the edge, he said.
They came.
He pushed them ... and they flew.
Guillaume Apollinaire

Sanibel, Florida
June 7, 12:05 P.M. EDT

She'd thought the hurricane would skirt the coast. It didn't. The deluge struck in the middle of the Sanibel Causeway Bridge. The normally solid Mercedes was no match for Hurricane Ervin. A swirling blast rocked the car.

Kelly Saunders hit the brakes and hydroplaned sideways into the raised sidewalk. Luckily no one was following. No one else was stupid enough to be on the road during a hurricane, much less going on vacation. Idiocy. Why hadn't she waited another day? Kelly wondered as she sat in the car, wedged against the bridge, knees shaking too violently for her to press the accelerator.

Cheapness? Perhaps, she was an economist. The condo was paid for; it was a shame it let it go to waste. But it was more than that. Captiva was her favorite place on the planet.

Hawaii without a volcano, she always said, and Kelly was ready for a rest. She'd worked twelve-hour days for weeks and deserved a vacation—she just hadn't bargained for breaking her neck in the process.

A screeching gust caught the driver's side from below, lifting the car, teetering it on two wheels. Adrenaline surged, quashing Kelly's fear. She stomped the gas pedal. The Mercedes smacked down on all fours and lurched ahead.

Kelly made it across the bridge and took a right on the only road to Captiva Island. Her first inclination was to stop and wait out the storm, but every pull-off and parking lot was flooded. So she kept moving. Figuring some motion was better than none, she plowed through standing water and dodged downed trees. It was slow going—visibility was zilch. Just as well, the brakes were waterlogged, making stopping a risky maneuver at best.

The rain finally subsided when she reached the straight stretch of road beside the Ding Darling Wildlife Refuge. Her head pounded, shoulder muscles seizing with each frantic slap of the windshield wiper. Only a few more miles she told herself. She'd be at the resort in thirty minutes if the storm's hiatus lasted.

Kelly sped up, eager to reach the safety of the condo and get some medicine for her head. Relief was in sight if she could hold out for a little while longer. She rolled along, water spewing from either side of the car, when a *log* appeared directly ahead. Kelly slammed on brakes and the wheels locked, sending the car into a spiraling skid. The Mercedes twirled lazily, eventually coming to rest beside an enormous alligator. She slumped across the steering wheel, her heart racing.

It was then that the man jumped into the car. "Thanks for stopping," he said, shaking water from his hair.

Kelly's throat clenched. Where did this guy come from? "Wha-a-a—," she croaked, breathless with surprise. "W-what do you want?"

The man grinned meekly and clasped his hands, prayer fashion. "You're the only person who's been by in the last hour. Please don't put me out."

Kelly's mind raced. Was this a carjacking? It happened all the time in Atlanta and Miami, but on Sanibel, a sleepy barrier island, in the middle of a hurricane? Mike, her old boyfriend, always told her to ram another car if she were ever hijacked. "Gets other people involved so you don't have to fight alone." Good advice under normal circumstances, but there was no one around now. She had to get away.

Kelly grabbed the keys and swung her door open, ... into the upraised snout of the alligator which had walked around from the front of the car. Now what? She glanced from the intruder to the alligator. Not much of a choice: mauled by a giant reptile or robbed and raped by a twerpy guy.

"I'm not going to hurt you." The man held his palms up and smiled soothingly.

She set her jaw, sizing him up. He had a deep tan, wiry build, and piercing green eyes. His sandy hair was streaked gray, indicating he was in his fifties, although his face was unlined and smooth with an impish, boyish quality. He wasn't very tall: five foot four, five foot five. Standing, he'd barely come to her shoulder. He was trim and fit, which didn't bother Kelly since she worked out and was in good shape herself. On dry land, Kelly was confident she could thwart an attack from him, though the outcome wasn't so certain in the tight confines of the car.

In any event, he didn't seem to have a weapon— *Weapon!* Kelly glanced at the tube on her key ring and grinned. She'd completely forgotten the pepper spray. She angled the canister in his direction, her finger poised on the trigger. "Okay, what do you want?" she demanded, shutting the door in the big reptile's face.

"A ride. My vehicle was ... flooded."

Kelly looked around; there was no car in sight. "Oh? Where *is* your *vehicle?*"

The stranger raked back dripping hair. "Back there." He motioned over his shoulder toward the refuge.

Right. He must think she was a fool. "What are you doing out in this storm?"

He leaned against the passenger door, arms folded across his chest. "Field work," he said quietly. "I am a scientist. What brings you out in weather like this?"

Kelly leaned back, too, trying to look confident, all the while keeping the spray trained in his direction. "I'm on my way to South Seas Plantation."

His brows shot up. "So am I," he said, holding his hand out gingerly. "Reese."

Hurricane Ervin chose that moment to reassert its presence. The sky flashed and thunder boomed, unleashing a fresh torrent. She studied the intruder, his hand suspended futilely in midair. The guy seemed harmless; perhaps he was telling the truth. "Kelly," she said finally, accepting his hand. A bolt of lightning split the sky. She was wasting time. Kelly started the car and inched past the gator.

Reese sank into his seat, looking relieved. Kelly tuned the radio. Although the broadcast was broken and laced with static, one phrase got through loud and clear: . . . *tornado sighted on Sanibel Island.* "Uh, I think I was in it," Kelly exclaimed.

Reese sat up, clearly interested. "Really?"

"On the causeway bridge. The wind lifted the car right off the ground."

"Did you hear anything?" Reese asked eagerly.

Kelly was puzzled by the comment. "The wind."

"No conversations?"

Conversations? Was this guy on drugs or something? Kelly squeezed the steering wheel, wondering if she should have taken her chances with the alligator after all.

"Cross-talk; dimensional bleed-through," Reese added quickly.

"I don't know what you mean."

"The cyclone effect, the high energy rotation of a hurri-cane —tornadoes, too—are doorways to other dimensions. If you listen closely, sometimes you can pick up impressions, even snatches of conversations, from other places and times."

"Other dimensions?" Kelly asked testily, "You really believe that?"

"The fast rotation of a tornado causes time and space to merge. How else do you explain the piece of straw found embedded in an unbroken pane of glass after a tornado passes or the twig that penetrated a solid piece of steel? The tornado's vortex warped space and time, so the straw melted into the glass and the twig merged with the steel."

The straw melted into the glass and a twig merged with steel. Uh huh. Reese sounded like a kook Kelly'd seen on a talk show a few nights earlier. "What kind of a scientist are you?" she asked skeptically.

"Archaeologist, anthropologist, ... philosopher, ... a little bit of everything."

"That's quite a combination. What exactly do you study?"

"Ancient civilizations. Ever heard of Atlantis?" he said matter-of-factly.

Kelly was stunned. Of all the things he could have said, there was nothing more intriguing. She'd always been fasci-nated by the legend of the ancient continent that sank into the sea.

He continued, "I know where it is."

Kelly turned down the windshield wipers. "Where?" she asked, braking gently for a puddle covering the road.

"In the Atlantic, off the coast of Florida," Reese replied.

"How do you know that?" she demanded.

"I've been there."

He'd been to Atlantis? Kelly frowned skeptically. That was a tad much to swallow. "Why hasn't this made the news? The discovery of Atlantis would be a story as big as extrater-restrials landing on the White House lawn."

"That *is* why," Reese said, his emerald eyes flashing.

"What does that mean?"

Reese folded his arms, defensively, Kelly thought. "Some people like things the way they are. The truth about Atlantis would ... what is the saying? ... upset the apple cart."

Now Kelly felt anxious; his last comment gave her the creeps. Reese looked American, didn't have an accent, yet, *...what is the saying?* ...that was a strange way of talking. "So, what did you find? What was Atlantis really like?"

"The stuff of legend at its height, in many ways more advanced than your present society. There was no poverty or hunger like you have today—"

Like you have? There it was again.

"—the arts flourished," he continued. "Poetry, sculpture, music—modern man's greatest works are like cheap copies in comparison. And science, ... much of their knowledge has yet to be rediscovered."

"You could tell all of that from some underwater ruins?"

"There are records," he said.

Kelly didn't reply immediately because they'd reached the resort. She gave her name at the guard station then guided the car through the gate, tree limbs and debris covering the usually perfectly manicured grounds. "It's hard to believe that an advanced civilization could vanish. Surely, someone got away; somebody remembered it," she said, pulling into a parking space in front of the resort office.

"There were many survivors; however, people believe the stories—their memories—are supernatural fantasies," Reese said, making no move to get out of the car.

"You're talking about the tales of Greek gods and celestial warfare? Do you believe those myths were true accounts of Atlantis?" Kelly gathered her purse and keys, preparing to leave. Yet Reese didn't move. He was not taking the hint.

Reese gestured emphatically. "Yes, but it's not only the Greeks. Even your Bible talks about flying ships, pillars of fire, and visitors from on high. Although everyone assumes the passages are poetic references, maybe they are authentic memories of an ancient civilization."

She chewed her bottom lip nervously and studied Reese. *My Bible.* There was something strange, almost hypnotic, about this little man. Remarkably, he acted as if he could talk all day. And under different circumstances she might have obliged; he was hitting on some of her pet theories. But not today, not now. All she wanted at that moment was to get some aspirin for her pounding head.

Kelly opened the door. "You may be right," she said, "but this is the end of the line." She held out her hand. "It was nice meeting you."

Reese took her hand mechanically, then nodded and got out of the car.

What's that about? Kelly wondered. Surely he didn't expect her to spend the afternoon talking. Or maybe he did. "Hope I see you again," Kelly called after him, feeling guilty.

"I, too," he replied over his shoulder without looking back.

Kelly went straight to the condo after checking in and unpacked in record time, all the while thinking about Reese. Their encounter ranked among—no, *was* unequivocally— the most bizarre experience of her life. Far from timid, Kelly still wasn't in the habit of picking up strangers or having them jump into her car uninvited. That she didn't squirt Reese with pepper spray and dump him in the street was a wonder.

What possessed her to let him stay? Normally cautious and level-headed, her reaction to Reese was completely out of character. And of all the topics that would peak her interest, Atlantis was the one. It was almost as if Reese could read her mind, knew exactly what button to push.

Kelly went to the back window and studied the sky. A low-hanging layer of steel gray vapor was rushing in from the east. No doubt she was making too much of it all. Desperation can make people do funny things, even jump into a stranger's car, she told herself. And Reese said he'd been stranded for over an hour. The stuff about Atlantis didn't mean anything either; the lost continent seemed to be on everyone's mind lately.

Scholars in Greece claimed to have found it on a sunken island in the Mediterranean, a television special put it on a mountaintop in South America, while her friends in Lauderdale pointed to the Bimini Road as proof of its whereabouts. Still ... could Reese be on the level?

Kelly took an address book from her purse. Her friend Cara would know if Atlantis had been found. Cara traveled in West Coast circles and purported to know an expert in every field. Besides, Kelly owed her former neighbor a call.

Kelly chuckled as she dialed the number. Cara Stevens was a true original who'd try almost anything if she thought it would bring enlightenment. Geez, she'd done some silly things. Like sitting on a magnet to align her body's energy centers or sleeping with a crystal under her pillow to stimulate prophetic dreams. And the colors! Kelly snickered at the thought. Convinced that her lower energy centers were blocked, Cara once had switched all the light bulbs in her house to orange ones. She wore orange-colored clothes and only ate carrots, apricots, oranges, and cantaloupe. And if she hadn't gotten a terrible case of diarrhea, she'd never have stopped.

"A good cleansing," Cara had said. "Shows my second chakra's been freed up." Naturally, the fiber and acidic content of the food were irrelevant—"the color's energy did the trick."

Kelly gazed out the back window as she waited for Cara to pick up the phone. Another swirling tendril of the hurricane had come ashore. The palms and oleanders stretched in the wind, bobbing spastically as updrafts caught from below. She was on the verge of hanging up when Cara answered.

"Yes? Talk to me," Cara commanded breathlessly.

Kelly recognized the tone and could almost see the exasperated look on Cara's face. "Hey, lady. Am I interrupting something important?"

"Kelly, where the heck are you? I thought you'd fallen off the face of the earth."

"Still here; I'm on vacation. Captiva; this is my time share week."

"Isn't there a hurricane down there?"

"Ervin. The eye missed us. It's moving into the Gulf, but we're getting some pretty good squalls." Kelly watched as a man in a suit struggled along a sidewalk outside. His tie flapped sideways, waving like a flag. He held his hat on with one hand and a briefcase with the other, using the leather satchel to shield his face from the driving rain.

"Sorry I'm not there. Great energy, I'm sure." She let out a long breath, and Kelly knew Cara had just lit a cigarette.

"Say, do you know anything about Atlantis?" Kelly asked.

"Atlantis?" Cara's voice whistled as she exhaled. "An ancient civilization that sank into the sea. Some people think it was a space colony. You know, the same guys that built the pyramids on Mars."

Kelly knew about the Martian monuments. Viking or Mariner or one of the unmanned probes had taken pictures of them. Although NASA dismissed the notion that the strange formations were anything but natural, Kelly'd met a man who'd seen the actual photographs. Robert said the monuments looked manmade, much like the pyramids in Egypt. He'd appeared reasonably normal to Kelly, not a UFO fanatic or anything.

Cara continued, "The language guy, er, Berlitz, wrote a book on it. Why in the world are you interested in Atlantis?"

"I picked up a man who claims to have found it."

"Picked up? Getting desperate?" Cara giggled.

Kelly sighed. She'd walked into that one. Ever since Kelly broke her engagement with Mike, Kelly's love life or lack thereof had been Cara's favorite subject. "You said I needed to meet some men," Kelly threw back. "But seriously, the guy said he'd seen records—their science was far advanced to ours."

"Really?"

"A strange bird, he also talked about tornadoes, uh ... vortexes ... being interdimensional gateways."

"Whoa, I've heard that, and just recently," Cara said, sounding serious. "I met a lady, a friend of a friend, who said the same thing. Only, dear heart, the woman claims to be a reincarnated space person."

Kelly laughed. "Do her feet touch the ground?"

"The lady isn't as crazy as you'd imagine—she's a business executive here in Las Vegas. Apparently there are a lot of people who believe the same thing; in fact, they recently had a convention in California."

"Please."

"Yeah, the lady went."

Kelly started to pace. The extra long cord let her get all the way to the fireplace in the living room. The condo had most of the comforts of home, which was surprising for a vacation unit. The kitchen and living room were on the top floor of the three-story structure, giving a spectacular view of Bryan's Bayou from the back window and the Gulf of Mexico from the front. Stretching the cord to its full length, Kelly could see across the back porch to the rain that was no longer falling, but flying—horizontally—in great, gray sheets.

"The woman's name is Betty," Cara went on. "Would you like to talk to her? She may know something about Atlantis since she just got back from the conference. In any event, she knows about vortices."

Kelly paused to consider the offer. Although she believed in UFOs, herbal medicine, and the power of the mind, there were certain things that were a stretch even for her and a reincarnated space woman definitely fell in that category.

"I could ask her to give you a call," Cara prodded.

Kelly swept back her chin length brown hair and stared at the floor. What could it hurt? Talk to the woman, that's all she had to do. Kelly didn't have to believe her. "Sure, if Betty will. Ask her to call tonight."

They went on to discuss Cara's catering business, mutual friends, and the shows Cara had seen. As always, her friend begged Kelly to come for a visit—get away for a little gambling and a meditation or two in Red Rock Canyon. Kelly promised to try, knowing full well it would be impossible before the end of the year.

"Kelly, the stuff about Atlantis is fascinating. You need to track down that man and get the details."

"I'll see what I can do." Kelly grinned, realizing Cara wouldn't rest until she had all the particulars. "I'll look for him, promise."

"Call me immediately when you do."

"I will, swear."

▼▲▼

Cheyenne Mountain, Colorado
June 7, 1:00 P.M. MDT

The fax had come over the secured line; he could tell from the texture of the glossy paper that couldn't be copied. The images would only last about twenty-four hours—supposedly enough time for the old-fashioned purists who hated computers to assimilate the information. The paperless office was a must for protecting sensitive data, or so the security experts said. In practice it never worked that way. The paper would go blank all right; that much of the system operated as promised. The problem was that field operatives almost always kept handwritten notes lying around. A draft of the memo could be on top of someone's desk at that very instant. Since it was around noon on the West Coast, the office might well be empty, an easy target for anyone snooping around. That's why no one was allowed to stay on the project very long—the security risks were too great.

Colonel Stanley Houston perused the list of attendees at the UFO conference in California, then handed the fax message back to the aide standing before his desk. "Put it into the system. It's probably nothing, but I guess we should follow up. Have their phones monitored for a week or two."

"Court order?"

"Use the satellites; this is most likely a wild goose chase. We don't want to get Justice involved."

"What should we look for?" Captain John Persman asked as he rolled the page into a tight cylinder.

"The usual. Sammy knows." Houston grinned and waved dismissively, signaling an end to the conversation.

Persman was fishing. Houston guessed it was time to have him transferred out. A shame—he liked John. They'd had dinner on a few occasions and even driven over to Cripple Creek once to do some gambling. A fair golfer, too. They'd played a couple of times and were evenly matched. Although twenty years his junior, Persman played with finesse. In his early forties, the younger officer had grown beyond trying to muscle the ball, concentrating on his short game instead. Lethal within fifty yards, Houston discovered—he didn't bet Persman anymore.

Houston would be sorry to see Persman go, but it couldn't be helped. He was getting curious, like everyone did eventually. Houston would try to have him transferred to a warm post close to a bunch of golf courses, like in California, Florida, or Arizona; it was the least he could do.

Houston laced his fingers behind his head and leaned back. A Navaho rug hung on the wall in front of him, next to the door. He'd put it there on purpose. For some inexplicable reason, the coarsely woven runner made him feel peaceful. A backdrop for anyone standing on the other side of his desk,

Houston could look at the rug instead of the visitor, and no one was the wiser. Everyone marveled at his even disposition, were amazed that he could stay cool in the midst of disaster. Little did they know that a magic carpet was responsible—a common black and red geometric print he'd purchased in Colorado Springs.

For an East Coast city boy Houston had grown remarkably fond of the mountains. Of course, it felt like home now. He'd been stationed inside a mountain most of his working life. Granite, thousands of tons and miles and miles of it, had always stood between him and civilization. Most people would find it confining, feel cut off from the world. He'd felt that way in the old days, before the satellites, computers, and all the marvelous technology. But things had turned one-hundred-eighty degrees. Now he could sit at his desk and watch a parade in Moscow, troop movements in Iran, or storms brewing in the Atlantic. Today Houston felt isolated when he had to go outside.

The telephone buzzed; Houston checked his watch. That would be Washington. Time for his daily report.

"General Brandt for the colonel, sir," Persman's voice came over the line.

"Stall a minute," Houston instructed as he flipped the switch to his computer. The screen flashed blue. He typed in his password and waited as a beach ball bounced across the screen. "Cute," he mumbled sarcastically. What fool would put a beach ball in a security program? The logic escaped him. When the ball reached the bottom of the display, the words *Caution: This Is A Restricted File* flashed in bold, red letters. Another entry and *Project: Night Sky* appeared.

He pushed a button on his telephone. "Good afternoon, general." Houston stroked the keyboard, bringing up a list of information.

"Colonel."

Although he and Brandt had worked together for almost ten years, their communications always had a formal air.

Nominally assigned to Air Force Intelligence for budget purposes, Houston had to report to someone, and Brandt was the logical choice. Yet it had become clear, early on, that the assignment was far more than an ordinary security job and Brandt was little more than a front man for the real decision makers.

"There have been a half dozen incidents over the last twenty-four hours," Brandt continued. "Here, Australia, France."

"I know, sir. It seems to be increasing."

"What do the guys in Alaska say?"

"They're working on a theory involving high frequency radio waves but are afraid they won't have enough power to seal them all," Houston replied. "Any chance for help from other installations? What about the Europeans or Russians?"

"We're pursuing it—too soon to tell. We've got to do something; they're popping up all over. What about the California thing?"

"I don't think there's anything to worry about there. We're going to eavesdrop for a while. Purely a precaution. I don't expect to uncover much."

"Stan, we've got to find a solution. We can't wait for the skullcaps."

Houston glanced at the Navaho rug and sighed. He wasn't feeling peaceful. "I know. I've got an idea to discuss with Stack."

"Good. Keep me posted," Brandt instructed.

Houston logged off the computer and headed down the hall. His office was tucked at the back of the intelligence department, a few doors away from his old friend and section chief, Colonel Doug Stack. The door to the office was open and Houston caught sight of his buddy with his feet resting on the credenza.

"Good thing I'm not conducting an inspection tour," Houston barked at his unsuspecting colleague. "Don't you know to keep your door closed?"

Stack swung around, then realizing it was only Houston, scowled and propped his feet up again. "Too damned hot, something's wrong with the blower in this office. Besides, there are fifty of my men between here and the elevator. I'd know someone was coming before they got ten feet."

Houston dropped into a green and blue wing back chair. "My, my, rank does have its privileges."

"You'd know too if you had a regular post with a normal staff," Stack snapped.

Houston stretched out lazily, clasping his hands behind his head. "Yeah, but I don't have to do budgets and all of that administrative crap."

"Right, I do it for you. So, what do you want? If you're here for more money, forget it—the well is dry."

Houston cocked his head innocently. "I want to talk about AWACS and Blackhawk EH-60A helicopters—the ones with all the electronics."

"You can't have any."

"Come on, Doug, tell me about their jamming capabilities."

Stack eyed Houston suspiciously. "They can do it. Why are you interested?"

"I'm involved in some weather experiments."

"Uh huh."

"Really. Scientists think you might stop a hurricane or tornado by blasting its center with radio waves. Could an AWACS or Blackhawk do that?"

"Probably." Stack leaned forward, searching Houston's face. "Weather? I can't see you chasing cold fronts."

"I'm serious—one hundred percent."

Stack laughed. "Bullshit."

Chapter 2

Charlotte, North Carolina
June 7, 7:00 A.M. EDT

Neal pulled the strap of her nightgown away with his teeth and ran his tongue across her freckled shoulder, stopping to nibble her neck.

"Honey, I don't have time." She rolled onto her back, squashing his arm.

"Ouch," he complained, pulling himself free. "Come on, Al, we don't need much time." He stroked her flat abdomen and resumed licking her shoulder.

She grabbed his hand and held it still. "I'm not in the mood, hon. I've got to get to work early. Faults all over the electric grid yesterday. We'd get one line up and another would go down. It's the weirdest thing I've ever seen."

He pressed his swollen groin against her thigh. "You poor baby. But I've got a line without any faults; a charged, energized, pulsing line—"

"No-o-o-o." Allison Winters rolled away and bounced to the floor. "I've seen that charged line before; that hot, throbbing, overloaded line ... and we definitely don't have time." She pulled on her robe and headed for the bathroom.

"Damn, ... damn, my own wife, a heartless wench," Neal whined pitifully to the ceiling. "I didn't even get to talk to you last night—you were asleep when I got home."

"And why is that?" she asked sarcastically. "I went to bed at eleven o'clock, my normal time."

Neal heard water running in the background and knew he had no chance of changing her mind. "Babe, it wasn't my fault. The city council meeting ran over. They passed the gun control ordinance, so I had to go back to the office to write the story. For once they did something that mattered. It couldn't wait until today."

"If you're not first with the story, it's too late. I've heard that before."

"It's true," Neal said as he pulled on his boxer shorts. "Old news is no news. I am a reporter."

"How could I forget? Story, interview, deadline, that's all you ever talk about. You're not the only person in the world with problems, you know."

Not that tired old argument again, he thought. Then he heard the door to the shower clink shut. *No good luvin' this mornin'. Damn.* Neal trudged to the kitchen feeling sorry for himself. Alternately sighing and mumbling, he scooped coffee into a dented percolator.

Allison had a good job, a career path, good benefits... and she made more money than he did. Why did he let that bother him? Engineers made more than virtually every other discipline, and she worked for an electric utility. Everyone knew the power companies could afford to pay more; they were rolling in money.

Journalism was different. It was a lot more than facts and figures. It was a craft, it took talent, and you had to pay your dues. But there was an intangible factor too—luck. Like Woodward and Bernstein who became famous for Watergate, you had to be at the right place at the right time. Once you got the big story under your belt you could go anywhere, do anything, and make a lot of money. It would even out in the long run, he told himself. Allison made more now, he'd make the big bucks later. All he needed was a break.

Allison was out of the shower by the time he came back with the coffee. He slid the cup with cream and sugar in front of her and sat on the edge of the bathtub. "Yesterday was tough?" he asked.

Allison talked to his reflection in the mirror as she stroked on mascara. "It was bizarre. Even the old-timers couldn't figure out what was going on. Transformers were popping like corn. While there were only a few localized outages, the system came within a gnat's lash of collapsing."

"The entire Southeast blacking out? Not a pretty picture," Neal commented.

"We had to scramble two nukes. I guess they're buying power from the Midwest today to make up for it. It'll probably cost millions, and the state commission will launch an investigation."

Neal blew on the steaming brew before gingerly tasting the liquid. "What's the big deal? Why does the government care?"

Allison frowned. "You can't turn nuclear units on and off like a car engine. Once they go down, it takes time to bring them back. When you lose one like we did yesterday, you've got to buy power from somewhere to make up for the lost generation. Nine times out of ten the replacement energy is more expensive; that's when the regulators get excited. If the plants were shut down because of an avoidable problem, they won't let the company recover the additional costs."

"But you couldn't help it, right?"

"We had to do something—the transmission system in Georgia became unstable and was on the verge of collapse. But the commission will want to know why that happened. Was it because the company bought cheap, defective transformers? Or maybe a lineman made a mistake. If that's the case, the government won't let the company recover the costs."

"What do you think?" Neal asked.

Allison paused to find her rouge. "I don't have a clue. Massoud believes it's the transformers. We've recently started buying from the Japanese. He thinks the new equipment is defective."

Neal sipped his coffee and thought. Competitive bidding, low cost foreign providers, defective equipment, the prospect of a widespread blackout—it might be a good story. "This could be a great article. Mind if I snoop around?"

"Yes, I mind. It will jeopardize my job."

Neal set his coffee down and pulled her close. "I wouldn't do anything that could harm you. Hey, I like your income, too. This isn't like the electromagnetic field story; everyone knows the power's going out. The state commission is going to investigate, you said so yourself." He stroked her back and buttocks sensuously.

She pushed him away. "No. Charm won't change my mind."

He leaned against the counter facing her. Gawd, she was good looking, even when she was angry. "Al, this is different. The electromagnetic field thing was speculative; I understand why you didn't want me to pursue it. But the power failure is a fact; everyone knows it happened. There's no surprise here except for the reason, and I might be an asset on that count. Let's say the cause was unavoidable. If I publicize it, the state won't be in a position to come down on the company. Public opinion will be against them—they'll look like a bunch of jerks."

She nodded pensively. Neal could see she was wavering. "Anyway, you use your maiden name at work. No one will even know we're related."

"A lot of people know you're a reporter," Allison countered.

"No one knows my last name is Winters."

"Human resources does."

"Forget human resources. They'll never make the connection. Babe, this could be my big break. A good, meaty story might spring me free from the local government dribble."

"I don't know …."

Allison leaned against the counter, arms folded, chin tilted provocatively. Her slender throat seemed to scream for a caress, but Neal held back, not daring to break the mood. He was winning. "I won't use your name."

"What if the problem actually stems from a company error? Then what?"

He brushed her cheek with the back of his hand and whispered, "I'll drop the story. Promise. Allison, your job ... and happiness ... are important to me."

"I don't think you appreciate what a closed little network the electric utility industry is," she managed softly. "Disloyalty is a sin, a cardinal sin. Heads have rolled and careers been ruined for much less."

"I know that, but this is one story where I have an edge. Someone is going to report it and the yokels who do won't have an appreciation for the problem. I do. I've learned that from you. I can give the story balance. I need a chance, that's all," Neal pleaded.

Allison turned back to the mirror and resumed putting on make-up. "It's too dangerous. I don't want you to get involved."

Neal cursed inwardly; he'd almost had her convinced. He was close—he could feel it. Just a little more .... He sat on the counter, putting himself between Allison and the mirror. "Believe me, I won't do anything to jeopardize your job. A chance, that's all I want. If I discover that the situation is controversial, I'll back away."

Allison rolled her eyes. "When did you ever back away from a story?"

"I dropped the electromagnetic field thing and I'll do it again. So, who can I call for a statement about what's going on?"

She snorted with exasperation. "Grayson, corporate communications."

Grayson proved to be a smooth talking *spin doctor* who knew very little about utility operations. Neal was familiar with the type, encountering them daily in dealings with government officials, and knew the conversation was worthless unless he obtained a referral to a person in the trenches who actually did some work. As frustrating as Grayson's transparent gibberish was, Neal was sympathetic to the man's plight. Electric utilities had innumerable government agencies breathing down their necks; and a news report, no matter how benign, could usher in round after round of pointless investigations and hearings. Having listened patiently to Grayson's whitewashed prattle for close to ten minutes, Neal decided to push for the referral by asking a technical question. An inquiry about transformers got what he wanted—an entrée to the director of transmission planning.

"Will Carne? This is Neal Winters, I'm a reporter with the *Charlotte Sentinel.* Tom Grayson referred me to you. Do you have a couple of minutes?"

"A few."

"I hear y'all had some problems yesterday, had to shut down two nuclear units."

"Correct."

A few; correct? Another paranoid utility employee. If Neal was going to get anything out of Carne, he'd have to put the man at ease. "Grayson explained that the outages were freak occurrences and that stuff like that happens from time to time. It has to do with weather, sunspots, or something. That's what I hoped you could help with—for background."

"Sure, I could do that."

Neal could hear the relief in Carne's voice. Weather and sunspots were non-controversial territory.

"How much do you know about electromagnetism?" Carne asked.

"Almost nothing." Neal had actually picked up a fair amount from Allison over the years, but he didn't want to explain where he'd gotten his knowledge, so it was best to plead ignorance. Besides, he'd learned long ago that he could get more information from an interview by playing dumb. Knowledge seemed to threaten most people.

"Without getting too technical, the sun is a giant inferno with violent storms and eruptions that spew electrons into space," Carne said. "You've probably heard of solar wind. It's nothing but the charged particles and radiation thrown off by solar storms."

"I never knew that," Neal said.

"Yeah. The particles flow through space and eventually reach Earth. Most of them are deflected by the Earth's magnetic field, but some get through and interact with the atmosphere, creating an aurora like the northern lights. If the sun's storms are particularly strong, the solar wind can distort the planet's magnetic field which plays havoc with electric systems. It's rare to have a problem this far south, although I saw a lot of it when I worked in Canada. Back in 1989 an Auroral storm caused a blackout throughout the entire province of Quebec."

"You mean the atmosphere can cause power outages?" Neal asked.

"During intense solar activity everything can be disrupted —television, communications, power. Of course, NOAA— the National Oceanic and Atmospheric Administration— monitors solar activity, so we typically have some warning."

"You think a solar wind was responsible for the problems yesterday?"

"It's a possibility."

"Any chance of faulty equipment?"

Carne hesitated, institutional paranoia taking hold, and Neal knew the interview was over.

"Equipment is always a possibility, and we're checking that," Carne allowed defensively.

"Sure," Neal brushed off the comment as nonchalantly as he could. "I'm intrigued by the solar wind angle."

"I'm not an expert on that, but a Professor at Colorado Tech delivered a paper on it not long ago. Let's see ...."

Neal could hear papers rustling in the background.

"Here it is. Evans, Dr. Jonathan Evans."

▼▲▼

Charlotte, North Carolina
June 7, 12:10 P.M. EDT

Eyes glued to a monitor suspended from the ceiling of the WSTV newsroom, Neal pretended he didn't hear the row. It was all he could do to stay focused on the rotating red blob the newscaster labeled Ervin, since Ben Miller, his best friend and lunch partner, was being verbally assaulted less than four feet away. Neal had already waited five minutes, listening to an old man rage about government plots and mind control experiments. As the station's health reporter, it was Ben's duty to do something, the senior citizen lectured.

Neal had sometimes envied his fraternity brother's success. Best friends throughout college, they'd taken the same classes and earned identical grades. Both interviewed for a position at the station after graduation and were ranked so closely, the human resources director confided over drinks one day, that he'd eventually flipped a coin. At times like this Neal was happy he worked for a newspaper. Studies showed that readers ignored by-lines—which Neal rarely got anyway—unless the article addressed a pet peeve. Few subscribers knew his name, making chances virtually nil that he'd encounter an irate reader.

Television was a different game altogether. News people weren't reporters—they were personalities. Although celebrity status had its perks—good tables in restaurants and invitations to movie premieres and charity events—there was a dark side, too. Going on-camera made television reporters prime targets for grandstanding weirdoes and misfits.

Spleen apparently vented, the old man offered his hand. Ben took it, camera smile waning as he watched the feeble critic waddle out. "Come on," Ben said, motioning toward the rear door.

"What was that about?" Neal asked.

"Dr. Simmons thinks the Russians and Chinese control the FCC and are plotting to take over the country. He says secret messages are embedded in radio and television broadcasts that are inciting violence and slowly driving people crazy. Once everyone goes nuts the bad guys will waltz in and take over."

The two men stepped out of the building into a wall of hot, humid air. Sticky even by Deep South standards, the atmosphere was like a wet plasma that mocked hair spray and dissolved starch in shirts. They threaded along the crowded sidewalk toward a small restaurant a block away. The Magic Mushroom was a hole-in-the-wall frequented by young professionals, especially journalists. Specializing in shredded meat and vegetables stuffed into pita bread, the restaurant was cheap and played pop music. A booth at the back of the room was being vacated when they entered.

"Dr. Simmons may be on to something," Neal said as he perused the menu. "Violence is definitely increasing, and everyone seems to be crazy."

"Including him," Ben said emphatically.

"I give you credit—you displayed amazing patience. Gawd, he was shouting in your face. Didn't you want to deck him?"

"At first," Ben replied, "then I realized he's hard-of-hearing. Anyway, he's a friend of one of the owners. Grandston's father's doctor, I think that's the way it goes."

"Not still practicing, I hope."

"Right-o, he's a few bricks shy of a load."

Sandy, an attractive waitress in her early twenties, greeted Ben with an affectionate smile. Single and good looking, he was considered quite a catch. Most of Allison's unmarried friends wanted to date him. She'd even fixed Ben up with a few, though nothing ever came of it.

"Not interested in anything serious," Ben always said. "Concentrating on my career until I'm thirty-five, then I'll think about marriage."

Aside from their looks—Neal was a typical redhead while Ben had dark hair and olive skin—Ben's aversion to settling down was about the only difference between the two men. Neal and Allison dated all through college and were married a year after graduation. Coming up on their fifth anniversary, Neal couldn't imagine life without her.

Ben winked at the waitress and bantered flirtatiously. The woman beamed at Ben, obviously infatuated, and Neal felt a pang of sorrow. He'd heard Ben's lines a million times and knew they didn't mean a thing, yet Sandy was clearly smitten. Neal interrupted, ordering the garden-chicken special, in a valiant effort to save her from certain disappointment. Sandy didn't appreciate Neal's chivalry. She scribbled his order peevishly and left in huff.

Twice in one day, Neal thought, as he watched the angry woman stalk off. Such good intentions, so misunderstood. Anxious to change the subject, he turned to Ben. "So, what about the doctor?"

Ben chuckled. "He said our bodies are more than a bag of chemicals. The brain and all bodily functions depend on electric pulses traveling through the nerves and the current running through our bodies can be affected by radio waves. He says the Russians or Chinese—he's not sure which or if they're working together—have figured this out and are broadcasting signals to drive us insane. He said that's why there's so much crime and mental illness is at an all-time high."

Neal shrugged. "Who could argue about that? There are more psychologists and therapists than at any time in history, yet people are nuttier than ever."

"Of course, supply creates demand."

"I think that's demand creates supply," Neal corrected.

Ben smiled indulgently. "You must have slept through Econ class, good buddy. Henry Ford didn't build the Model T because people were beating down his door to get one. He built one, then convinced the people they needed it. That's what the doctors, psychologists, and lawyers are doing. Marketing. Mass marketing."

"I'm not going to quibble," Neal said, suddenly feeling weary of arguments and misunderstandings. "Let's go back to the old man. How does the FCC fit into his scheme?"

Ben leaned forward, shielding his mouth from the rest of the room. "He says they control the radio and television frequencies and are involved in a conspiracy to put secret codes in the broadcasts."

"And how did the bad communists get control of the FCC?"

"Spies and mind control," Ben said, grinning.

"I should have guessed. I suppose there's a wave generator in the basement of the Federal Communications Commission that turns the employees into pliant zombies."

"He wasn't clear on that point."

"What does he expect you to do?" Neal asked.

"He wants me to do a story which will *awaken the people*. He claims everything he said, except for the foreign connection, can be verified."

Sandy arrived with the food and talking stopped temporarily. The waitress hovered over Ben throughout the meal, refilling his glass after practically every sip while Neal's glass sat empty most of the time. When Neal finally brought the oversight to her attention, Sandy was conveniently out of tea. Ben snickered and lit a cigarette. Neal smirked and took Ben's tea.

"You going to do anything about the good doctor?" Neal asked, leisurely sipping Ben's drink.

"I've got to do something because he's Grandston, Sr.'s friend. After all, it took connections to get past the receptionist at the station. I'll have one of the interns go to the library and look something up. Then I'll send the doctor a letter saying we're working on it but can't go public until we get all the facts. I'll throw in a tidbit the intern uncovered so he'll know we're sincere, after which I'll forget the whole thing."

Neal looked around guiltily before speaking. "Allison would kill me for telling you this: some people believe electric power lines' electromagnetic fields cause health problems. While nothing's been proven, it might be the tidbit you need to satisfy the old guy. It's not radio waves, but it shows you're looking at the effect of electromagnetism on humans." Neal was understating it slightly; he knew there was an enormous body of research on the subject, and he was pushing his luck by telling Ben. He could hardly believe Allison agreed to let him look into the power outages; she'd kill him if she found out he'd informed Ben about transmission line fields.

"I've heard about that. Good idea, that's exactly what I'll do."

"Don't tell Allison I said anything."

Ben snuffed out his cigarette. "Sure, power lines and electromagnetism, I won't say a word."

Neal hurried back to the office, cursing himself for telling Ben about electromagnetic fields. But it was too late—the deed was done. He'd just have to trust Ben to keep his word.

The newsroom was almost empty when Neal arrived. He checked the wire service for breaking stories, and finding nothing except the usual political quibbles, fired up his computer to continue the power outage investigation.

He called Dr. Jonathan Evans several times before getting through. Catching him between classes, Neal was surprised by the professor's candor. Quite a change from Carne at the electric utility or most other corporate employees who were shell-shocked from layoffs and downsizings. Academics, at least the tenured ones, could afford to be open. They didn't have to worry about a misstatement costing their jobs. Academic freedom it was called; Neal learned about it first-hand when he taught a course at the community college.

"I didn't know there'd been trouble in Georgia," Evans said. "That's Atlantergy's territory. Quite a transmission system—covers everything from Indiana down to the Florida panhandle. That utility was formed by the merger of four electric companies, it's the biggest in the country."

Neal knew that. Allison made a tidy profit on her retirement account when the stock was swapped for the new shares. "The company says sunspots or solar wind could have caused the outage. What do you think?"

"Possible. Radiation can do some pretty funny things. Your contact didn't say anything about shooting balls of light, did he?" Evans asked, laughing.

"No, why?"

"A local joke. Spacemen. Haven't you heard that UFOs hover over nuclear plants and high voltage transmission lines?"

Neal cradled the telephone receiver against his shoulder and typed into the computer. "That's the first I've heard of it."

"Here in Colorado, we actually have a fair number of electrical problems accompanied by strange lights and balls of fire. I've seen the lights myself, and there was a power interruption a couple of weeks ago."

"You think it was caused by UFOs?" Neal asked.

"Naw, I think it was caused by the government. There are a lot of Air Force facilities around here. They're probably testing a new weapon or airplane. You know, all that experimental technology could turn out to be a real problem for this country's electric supply, communications, and who knows what else. There are so many satellites circling the Earth, it's amazing we ever see the sun.

"And Reagan's Strategic Defense Initiative proposed some bizarre technology—science fiction stuff like death rays and space-based electromagnetic guns. Although SDI is supposedly dead, research is still going on. A friend at the San Francisco Institute of Technology says half of his physics department is working at a military installation in Alaska, and I don't think they're up there worrying over the environment. That's the troubling part: today their experiments cause a few localized outages and some communications problems—no big deal. But tomorrow? Whole species could be wiped out."

"Uh huh." Environment. Neal's fingers flew across the keys. This was great stuff; there might be a good article after all. "You think the power problems in Georgia could have been caused by government experiments?"

"I'm not saying that, although there is a big Air Force base around Atlanta. As I tell my students, alternating current is tricky stuff. Any number of things can go wrong. I'm sure the utility has their best people working on it."

"Undoubtedly," Neal replied, stalling for time as he finished typing. "Say, that Alaska project sounds interesting. Could you refer me to someone who could supply details?"

"My friend doesn't work on it directly, but he could probably put you in touch with someone who does. His name is Peter Rourke, electrical engineering."

With the time differential between Charlotte and the West Coast, Neal decided to call Rourke from home. Neal sat at the kitchen table, laptop computer open and ready for action. "Dr. Rourke, this is Neal Winters from the *Charlotte Sentinel*. Professor Jonathan Evans suggested I give you a call. He's been helping me with a story about electric problems in the Southeast. Evans thinks that the military's high tech experiments could be a threat to our electric and communications systems. He said you knew about a big government project in Alaska."

"Good old Jonathan, still at it I see."

"Excuse me?" Neal asked, bewildered.

"He's a raving environmentalist. We'd all be living in caves if Jonathan had his way. He was a perfectly normal guy until he moved to Colorado. People say Californians are strange; Coloradans are every bit as bad, especially when it comes to the environment."

"You don't think his concerns about military experiments are valid?"

"I didn't say that. Jonathan may be fanatical, but he's not stupid. In fact he's one of the best researchers I've ever known.

He makes good points; I simply don't wring my hands as much as he does."

"He seemed concerned about the Alaska project. Do you know what's going on up there?" Neal asked.

"Not really, although a number of my colleagues work on it from time to time. It's called HAIR. I think they're doing experiments on the Auroral electrojet."

Neal typed the information into his terminal. "Auroral electrojet, that's a new one on me. Can you translate?"

"You've heard of the aurora borealis?" Dr. Rourke inquired in typical pedagoguish fashion.

"Sure, the northern lights."

"It's basically the same thing. They're studying the impact of radio waves on the upper atmosphere."

Radio waves, Neal thought. That made twice in one day. Ben's old doctor, now Rourke. "What are they trying to achieve?"

"There must be a weapons application or the military wouldn't be involved," Rourke replied.

"Could it affect electric systems?"

"If they pumped enough energy into the ionosphere, a whole lot of strange things could happen. Although I've never said anything to Jonathan, I've wondered if it could be the cause of mysterious flashes that have started appearing in the Midwest. Mini-auroras have been popping up above thunderstorms and no one has a good explanation."

Neal typed as fast as he could. He wasn't sure where all of this was headed, but it was interesting. "Who would know about those mini-auroras?"

"I heard about it from a plasma physicist at Stanford University. Carter. Sally Carter. You could try giving her a call."

Chapter 3

Life is like a wild tiger.
You can either lie down and let it
Lay its paw on your head—
Or sit on its back and ride it.
    Ride the Wild Tiger

South Seas Plantation, Captiva, Florida
June 7, 9:00 P.M. EDT

Kelly absently sipped cold tea and snuggled into the crook of the floral print sofa. She'd stopped at a book store on the way to the grocery on Sanibel. Arriving minutes before it closed, she'd asked for the first thing that came to mind, Berlitz's *Atlantis*, the book Cara had mentioned. The shopkeeper recognized the title and led her down a narrow aisle at the back of the shop. Standing on tiptoe, the petite woman pulled a hardback volume from a shelf overhead, sending a paperback sailing. Bouncing off Kelly's chest, a slim purple book fell into her hands: *The Fellowship. Spiritual Contact Between Humans and Outer Space Beings.* "I'll take this, too," Kelly'd said, remembering the New Age adage: there are no accidents.

She'd purchased provisions from Jerry's Supermarket, then headed home and watched the Weather Channel long enough to learn the hurricane had gained strength and was heading for New Orleans. Relieved the sky would clear before the vacation ended, she'd decided to wait out the storm. So she'd read. And read.

In a terrible night Atlantis vanished beneath the sea ... , so said Plato. A wondrous civilization with great palaces, gold-roofed temples, and crystal pyramids. Legend said the rulers were descended from gods, springing from the union of Poseidon, god of the sea, and Ceito, a mortal. The couple had five sets of twin sons, and Poseidon divided the land into ten portions, giving one to each. Atlas, the first born, became ruler of Poseidia, the great capital city built among seven concentric channels.

Many believed the continent was the seed culture for the world's great civilizations, and Edgar Cayce, the famous clairvoyant, put the city near Bimini, off the coast of Florida. The location was consistent with Reese's claims, and a shiver shot up Kelly's spine when she read of Cayce's prediction that it would be discovered.

Atlantis seemed to be synonymous with strange phenomena. Kelly learned of expeditions, aircraft sightings, strange force fields, wildly spinning compasses, lost ships, and eerie fogs. And she was just reading about a 1978 Greek expedition in search of underwater pyramids when the telephone rang.

"Kelly Saunders?"

"Speaking." Kelly laid the book aside and swung her legs to the floor.

"My name is Betty. Cara asked me to phone."

Kelly cradled the receiver on her shoulder and stood up. "Thanks for calling."

"Cara said you've met an archaeologist who claims to have found Atlantis and talks about energy vortices and higher dimensions?"

"That's right."

"What can I do for you?" Betty sounded guarded.

Kelly pulled the cord into the kitchen and fired up the tea pot. "I'm not sure. Cara thought your recent experiences might be connected in some way. She said you've had an encounter with … a, a UFO?"

Betty took a deep breath before answering. "I don't broadcast it—they'd lock me up. Let's just say I've been in contact with beings from another realm. And I'm not the only one; people from all over the world are having similar experiences.

"You see, mankind is approaching a crucial juncture—so important our choices will affect the whole galaxy, the entire universe. Because this is such a critical time, entities from other places are coming in to help us. I don't have all the answers, but I can tell you this much: the world we see is merely a sliver of the entire picture. It's akin to being color blind and not perceiving certain shades, like red or green. We don't see everything that's going on."

"Going on? Like what?" Kelly dropped a tea bag into a mug.

"I'm not an expert, but it has to do with vibrations." Betty hesitated. "You're not a Star Trek fan, are you?"

Kelly laughed out loud. "Yes, one of the worst."

Betty's tone brightened. "Do you remember the episode in the old series, with Captain Kirk and Spock, where people from an advanced race hijacked the ship? The people had a higher vibration and moved so fast the crew couldn't see them."

"I remember that," Kelly said, laughing. "Captain Kirk, sly dog that he was, seduced the queen and saved the ship."

"Standard operating procedure for the captain, always chasing a skirt," Betty quipped, the wary edge gone from her voice. "Anyway, that's the way it truly works. Not Kirk seducing women, but vibrations. There are other beings all around us, except they're living at higher frequencies so we don't see them. In fact, whole societies live in the same place at the same time, only at different levels."

Multidimensional reality. "I've heard that before, but have a hard time relating to it," Kelly said.

"I felt the same way until a few weeks ago."

The statement sent another chill up Kelly's spine. "What happened?"

"I'd rather not talk about it. Nothing bad, just hard to explain. Anyway, as people progress—which we all are—some are touching these other realms."

"Reese, the man I met, called it cross-talk. He said storms like tornadoes are gateways to other dimensions and he could see stuff, even hear conversations, from other times and places."

"Precisely, and a lot of people are getting information—advice—from other-dimensional entities."

"What sort of advice?" Kelly asked.

"It's highly individualized, though basically aimed at moving humanity forward."

"How?"

Betty paused as if trying to decide how much to divulge. Although the air of secrecy annoyed Kelly, Betty could hardly be faulted for being cautious with a complete stranger. "Toward a more peaceful existence," Betty finally said. "I know it sounds like a sappy cliché."

"It's a nice thought. I guess humanity is messing up royally."

"Not as bad as you might think, although we're approaching an important milestone. They wouldn't waste their time if we were totally hopeless."

"Why are they interested in us?"

"Why not?" Betty shot back.

Kelly's cheeks flushed. The lady wasn't on trial. "Sorry, I didn't mean to come on so strong. The concept is just difficult to grasp."

"You'll get it when the time is right. There are no accidents."

"Yeah." Kelly smiled weakly at the statement. She used the phrase all the time. The mantra of the New Age crowd, it was an affirmation of humanity's place in a grand, benevolent plan. Yet somehow it sounded trite when Betty used it. After all, they were talking about a turning point for mankind with aid coming from otherworldly beings. In that context, *there are no accidents* seemed hollow and thin.

"I'd like to hear what you learn about Atlantis."

"Sure. Cara issued strict instructions that I pump the guy for all he's worth. If I get any good information, I'll set up a conference call between the three of us. Thanks for calling."

"No problem," Betty said. "Good luck."

Kelly replaced the receiver. Luck, she thought. I hope I don't need it.

▼▲▼

Cheyenne Mountain, Colorado
June 7, 8:00 P.M. MDT

Colonel Houston stared at the Navaho rug, searching for answers. Freak storms and whirlwinds were popping up all over the country with a surprising number in the Southeast. The area around Fort Myers and Sanibel, Florida was especially active. The High-frequency Advanced Ionospheric Research Project (HAIR), or skullcaps as General Brandt preferred to call them, thought they might be able to create counter-resonance to cancel out the disturbances. Unfortunately, their equipment was still being tested—hardly ready for a precision exercise. Using aircraft to disrupt the anomalies was a long shot, Houston knew that, but was having an AWACS and a couple of Blackhawks flown down to MacDill Air Force Base in Florida anyway.

As much as Houston hated to admit it, the U.S. couldn't handle this one alone. Brandt said he'd talk to the big guys. They'd lose face and it would cause political problems, yet it had to be done. The situation was simply too big to handle and too important to screw up.

Chapter 4

Richmond, Virginia
June 8, 8:00 A.M. EDT

Frank Scortino gazed out the window, drinking coffee from a squat, Styrofoam cup. The stuff tasted awful, like it had been brewed through an old dirty sock; nevertheless it was hot and better than nothing.

He let the cup linger at his lips and its vapor rise toward his forehead. It felt good to his dry, scratchy eyes. They always bothered him after long flights. He'd flown all night and come directly to the office from the airport. He usually carried eye drops, but lost them on the plane from Anchorage to Los Angeles. For now, the steam would have to do; Frank had a meeting in thirty minutes.

He took another sip of the nasty brew and watched the cars crawl on the street below. Rush hour—it was always that way in Richmond. Most of the Secret Service agents were housed on the lower floors. Only he and three or four others were graced with quarters near the top, in the *stratosphere*. Frank usually loved the view; being up so high conferred a sense of power, wisdom, and ... control. He rubbed his eyes and dropped into a high-backed chair. Control of a bed was about all he wanted at that moment.

His assignment to HAIR had come as quite a surprise. After all, he'd been close to nabbing counterfeiters he'd tracked for over a year. But HAIR took precedence, his boss said. They needed Frank because of his background in physics.

Sure, he held a bachelor's and master's degree in astrophysics; however, it had been twenty years since he'd cracked a science book, and most of the stuff he'd studied probably wasn't valid anymore. Yet his protests had fallen on deaf ears. They'd given him two hours to go home, pack a bag, and get on a flight to Alaska.

He drained the cup of now-cold coffee and laughed to himself, remembering the trip. What a bunch of screw-ups. They should rename the project HAIR BRAIN, he thought. Frank pulled a blue blazer over his slept-in shirt and headed down the hall to Conference Room B. Carl, his boss, and a stranger in military garb were waiting.

"Was it good?" Carl asked sarcastically as Frank sank into a chair at the far end of the table.

"A complete waste of my time and taxpayers' dollars."

"I heard. Shit happens."

"You'll get no argument from me." Frank had been to Alaska and back for nothing. An Air Force lieutenant had met his plane and driven him to a remote installation in the middle of a forest. The three-hour trip had netted one piece of useful information: he was attached to a Special Investigation Team (SPIT) for HAIR which was meeting at the base that morning. Every other question had elicited a sterile "I'm not authorized to divulge that information."

Things hadn't gotten any better when he arrived at the base. Since the computers weren't working, his security clearance couldn't be verified and he hadn't been allowed to attend the meeting. A whole installation of antennas, the biggest damned antennas he'd ever seen, and no one could contact Washington to get his clearance. What a bureaucratic crock. He'd cooled his heels in a waiting room until eleven o'clock, when the authorization finally came through. By then, the meeting was over and everyone, including the team leader, had left. The mindless twerps had forgotten he was there.

He'd been too angry to speak on his trip back to the air-port. "Never speak in anger," his father always said. "Hold your tongue, bide your time. When you're ready, look your opponent in the eye and speak softly, all the while planning how you'll stab him in the heart." The old ways, the ways of the *familia*, had a simple elegance that always worked. On the flight to L.A., Frank made a vow to educate the team leader in Old World etiquette as soon as he saw him.

The memory of the HAIR fiasco made Frank mad all over again, and he caught himself glaring at the man in military garb.

Carl retrieved a thin document from a folder, flipped through it quickly, then slid it across the table to Frank. "Maybe this will help."

Frank glanced at the memo. The letterhead said Phillips Laboratory, Hanscom AFB, and he noted the document didn't have classified markings. "Should I read it now?"

"Later. This is Major Walker Clark. He came down from the Pentagon this morning to give the briefing you should have gotten in Alaska."

Frank half-rose, extending his hand. "A pleasure."

Clark hesitated, scowling, before returning the courtesy. "What do you know about HAIR?"

"Nothing except it's name." Frank looked Clark in the eye.

"HAIR is a joint effort of the Air Force and Navy. We're studying the effect of radio waves on the upper atmosphere and testing new technology for surveillance and long-range communications. The goal is to improve the performance of the military's command and control systems."

"Star Wars?" Frank asked.

"The idea was hatched in the Reagan era, though it has evolved beyond that. Anyway, we know that our efforts are not unique. Similar installations, albeit on a smaller scale, are operated by other governments."

"How does the special investigation team fit into the scheme?"

The major cleared his throat and shifted with a jerky motion. Experience told Frank that the words to follow were not entirely true.

"We've recently detected a large number of anomalous atmospheric events. Sudden increases and decreases in pressure, temperature, that kind of thing. These quirks could be caused by another country's high frequency experiments. That's what we need to find out. Under the guise of cracking down on equipment malfunctions and contractor fraud, NOAA has been instructed to report extraordinary weather incidents. The task force will investigate them."

"Isn't that a job for scientists?" Frank asked.

"You're part of a multi-pronged effort. The scientists are working on it, too, but we believe foreign operatives are in this country. That's where you come in. Small squads of agents and scientists will be dispatched to investigate suspicious events."

"I'm going along to nab foreign agents? Isn't that CIA?"

Clark cleared his throat and shifted again. "It's an inter-agency effort. The CIA is participating. We want you because of your science background."

Frank didn't buy it—the guy was giving him a line. "I'm pretty rusty; you realize that, don't you?"

"It'll come back fast," Carl said with an insincere smile.

Frank glanced at the memo and considered what he'd heard. Maybe the assignment wouldn't be bad after all. He was sorry he wouldn't be around to nab Jimmy or "Jerky" Johnson, as he preferred to call the counterfeiter he'd tailed for the better part of a year; still, international intrigue was a good substitute. "Where do we go from here?"

Clark and Carl exchanged a conspiratorial look. "There's a 12:45 flight to Fort Myers. Be on it. Your contact's name is T. J. Morrow."

▼▲▼

Charlotte, North Carolina
June 8, 11:30 A.M. EDT

Neal squeezed Allison's hand and drew it to his lips. Five good years. According to Emily Post it was their wooden anniversary, so the Chinese restaurant seemed appropriate. Although neither could handle chopsticks worth a darn, it was the thought that counted, Allison said.

"We should do this more often," Neal said as he nibbled her fingertips.

She glanced around self-consciously.

"No one cares about us," Neal reassured as he started to suck her thumb. "I didn't get enough to eat."

"Hm-m-m," she cooed, pushing her thumb across the gap between his front teeth and arching her back playfully. "I could go for some dessert myself."

Neal's eyes grew wide as he felt her foot brush against his crotch. She was calling his bluff, right there in the restaurant. He dropped her hand and grinned foolishly. His groin was starting to ache. Gawd, she was hot. Yet this wasn't the time or place; he had to get back to work. "Can I have a rain check?"

"Why wait? I could just duck under the table—"

Oh, she was brazen. He shifted uncomfortably, groin screaming now. "Tonight."

"What happened to that charged, throbbing line?"

"You're driving me crazy, Al. I'm meeting with a councilman in two hours." There, she'd won; he was the one backing off this time. She giggled triumphantly. "I probably won't get home until after eight, the council's holding a special session on annexation," he said. "We could go to the Club for a sandwich, it's blues night."

"Sounds good, I need to work late myself. Massoud and I are trying to correlate data on the outages."

"Come up with anything?"

"Nothing concrete. It's strange. Transformers are tripping off for no apparent reason. We thought it was the system that monitors the electric grid until we heard from Fort Myers Electric in Florida. They're having similar problems and hoped we could help them."

"Why is that important?"

"They use a different monitoring system and another brand of transformers, consequently the problem appears to be broader than we thought."

"Hmph. Fort Myers?" That sounded familiar. Neal pulled a notebook from his briefcase. "I've been talking to a bunch of professors about your outages. A couple of them think government experiments on the upper atmosphere may be the cause."

"That's a stretch," Allison said. "Stuff like this is rare, but not unheard-of."

Neal flipped through the notebook. "Here, Dr. Sally Carter. She's a specialist in plasma physics at Stanford and working on a project for the Air Force. Guess what? She was unexpectedly called away to Captiva Island, which is next to Fort Myers."

Allison regarded her husband skeptically. "How do you know that?"

"I called her. She wasn't there, but I talked to a nice, help- ful graduate student. Strange coincidence, don't you think?"

"That *is* funny. What kind of experiment is the government doing?"

"Beaming radio waves at the ionosphere. A professor in San Francisco thinks they may be responsible for auroras that have started appearing over thunderstorms in the Midwest."

"I've heard about that and there *have* been a number of electric disruptions," Allison allowed.

Neal leaned forward excitedly. "I'm on to something, Al. Don't tell anyone. I can smell a Pulitzer."

"Don't tell anyone? It's my job to keep the lights on. I have to inform Massoud."

"You can tell him, but no one else. This is a big story, I can feel it in my bones."

Chapter 5

All the world's a stage.
And all the men and women, merely players;
They have their exits and their entrances,
And one man in his time plays many parts.
                                    Shakespeare

South Seas Plantation, Captiva, Florida
June 8, 11:30 A.M. EDT

The sun felt good on Kelly's face. Eyes squeezed tight, she let her mind drift on swirling afterimages from the bright light. She'd stayed up most of the night reading, and it hadn't gotten her anywhere. Overload. Spacemen, tidal waves, pyramids; none of it made any sense.

She longed for sleep, yet her mind would not cooperate and as the drifting images started to churn, Kelly stopped trying. She pulled the chair's back upright and flipped through the Atlantis book. The author's picture caught her eye. Clad in a black wet suit, Charles Berlitz looked like a knight, or maybe a penguin. She chastised herself for harboring such a ridiculous thought—the man was brilliant, spoke twenty-five languages. What impudence. How could she liken him to a tuxedo-clad bird? No, ...definitely not a penguin, she thought, ...a walrus. She laughed out loud.

"Good book?" A thirtyish man was sitting a few yards away.

"No, ... yes," she stuttered, cheeks growing hot. "It *is* a good book, but I was laughing at the author's picture. It struck me funny."

"Atlantis?" The man rolled his eyes. "I suppose the author claims to have found it."

"Naturally," she tossed her head with exaggerated sass and smiled back. The guy was attractive, a *hunk* by most standards. Dark hair, deep tan, and tall enough—a solidly built six-foot-plus. She caught herself looking at his naked ring finger. At another time she might have batted her lashes and turned on the charm, but today she wasn't interested. Actually, she hadn't been drawn to any relationship since she'd broken up with Mike. What was the use? She was different, too different, always had been.

As a child, Kelly entertained herself with chemistry sets while her friends played with dolls. Later she wrote books and plays as the other girls chased boys. And today, as an economist, she was still bucking the feminine stereotype. Although she'd made many friends over the years, she'd felt a real kinship with only a handful of people. Mike was one, her soul mate, she thought. Yet, in the end he couldn't accept who she truly was. A few weeks from the altar, it became clear that he wanted a mate who baked pies, kept a clean house and played golf with the ladies' league. Kelly couldn't handle that. Breaking up with Mike was the hardest thing she ever did. Three years had passed, and it still hurt.

Kelly glanced at her handsome companion. Well, heck, there was nothing wrong with a friendly chat. "It's intriguing," she said, flipping the book toward him. He caught it just before it hit the sand.

He fanned the pages and scanned the inside cover. "The guy sort of looks like a ... a ... walrus, doesn't he? Berlitz, I've read his book on the Bermuda Triangle. It was pretty good. By the way, I'm Jake."

"Kelly." She stuffed the book in her beach bag and settled back.

She learned Jake was at the resort for a conference that started in a couple of days. He'd been on a fast track with his job and was taking a little time off before the seminar. Jake said he was in electronics, and although he didn't elaborate, Kelly gleaned that he was associated with the government in some fashion. He'd also traveled all over the world.

Jake was a nice, easy guy. Not pushy or macho, more like the fellow next door. Kelly found herself telling him about Cara—he howled at the magnet episode—and even about Betty, the reincarnated alien. He took it all in stride, reacting far better than Mike would have. While Kelly didn't think Jake agreed with everything she said, he didn't put it down, either. He was a friendly sort and she was having a great time talking with him. Unfortunately his beeper sounded about one o'clock, bringing their conversation to an abrupt end.

Energized by the encounter, Kelly suddenly felt famished and headed up the beach for a hot dog. She wolfed down a foot-long in no time flat and was licking mustard from her fingers when Reese appeared.

"Ha-all-o." Reese sauntered up, hands clasped behind his back. He was barefooted, bare chested and had on the same faded shorts from the day before. "There are some great shells down on the point," he said, motioning toward the end of the island.

"I'll bet, … the storm, … I didn't think of it. How are you today? I was hoping I'd see you," Kelly said.

"I, too." The little man nodded stiffly and started down the beach. She bolted after him, almost running over him when he abruptly stopped to scoop up a sand dollar. He handed it back to Kelly.

"Thank-you," she muttered, turning the petal-etched disk over and over. An unbroken specimen was a rare find.

They walked in silence, Kelly scouring the ground for treasure. Pickings were slim until they reached the island's tip and the mother lode of sea shells. The ground was littered with molluscan remains of every type. Feeling like a kid in a candy store, Kelly pulled off her Nike cap and started filling it with shells. Reese perched on a rock and watched.

Hat nearly full, Kelly turned her attention back to Reese. "Tell me about Atlantis. How did an advanced society just disappear?"

Reese leaned forward eagerly, as if he'd been waiting for her to ask. "It didn't vanish overnight. There was a series of cataclysmic disasters, although the real destruction was one of spirit. The physical upheavals were the final blows; the true collapse had taken place much earlier."

"A destruction of spirit?"

"Atlantis was originally an entry station, like a port."

Kelly shrugged. So? Reese's body language said he expected her to be surprised, but what was so unusual? A port? Big deal.

"Earth was a seed planet, a proving ground for experimental races."

Kelly's jaw sagged. An unbelievable coincidence. Cara had said that Atlantis was a space colony. "Experimental races?" Kelly half-rose, eyes fixed on Reese. "You're not talking about space men, are you?"

He patted the air in a calming gesture. "Hear me out."

Her heart quickened as her mind shrieked *run away*, and Kelly had to clench her teeth to force down an unexpected wave of panic. Why was this frightening? It was merely a theory. The man was harmless, probably a lonely guy who'd read too much science fiction. She sat back, folding her arms defensively. "Okay."

Reese resumed in a professorial tone. "Life has existed on this planet far longer than scientists think. An intergalactic task force originally planted life here millions of years ago."

"Millions? Earth isn't that old, is it?"

"Actually billions. As I was saying, this planet was a laboratory, an incubator for experimental species. Atlantis was the entry point, the headquarters for the alien scientists."

"A *space* port?"

He stared at the horizon as if searching for words. "Of
sorts. Societies, civilizations, whole galaxies exist on many
levels simultaneously. Your visible universe is a tiny slice of
all that there is."

Kelly was dumbfounded; Betty said the same thing.
Vibrations. An image of Captain Kirk, Mr. Spock and the fast
moving aliens raced through her mind.

"You think we're alone right now, but we're not," Reese
went on. "This place is teeming with life—you just can't
perceive it. Take the shell you're holding. It looks dead,
doesn't it?"

Kelly glanced down at a lightning whelk. "Yeah."

Reese threw his head back and swept his arms wide. "That
seemingly dead shell is filled with life, energy, movement.
Its atoms move at dizzying speeds. Its electrons are spinning
and flipping around in their orbital shells so fast you couldn't
find one if you wanted to. All scientists can do is estimate where
they might be. Electrons are called subatomic particles, though
they're not solid. They're nothing but energy, potential."

"You mean Einstein, $E = mc^2$, and all that?"

"Exactly." A yellow-footed egret swooped down, landing
at Reese's feet. Cocking its head to one side, the bird stared at
Reese as if to say, "Go on." Reese held out his hand. Instead
of scurrying away as most birds would, the white fowl brushed
its beak across Reese's fingertips. Kelly watched with disbelief. Reese acted as if it were perfectly natural.

"Now, as civilizations progress and grow, their vibrations
increase," he continued. "The atoms that make up their
bodies and everything in their world ascend—jump—to
higher energy potentials. This is what the mystics call the
journey back home, because at the highest level of perfection
vibrations become so rapid they blur into the exact opposite:
utter stillness or absolute peace." Reese lingered over the
last word as if its sound evoked the state.

Kelly wondered what he could feel. She'd heard about vibrations and other planes of reality, but had never equated peace with the upper limit of vibrations or frequency. When the shamans, yogis, and gurus talked about the peace of God, is that what they meant? She'd always regarded science and religion as two separate things; it hadn't occurred to her to consider scientific explanations for spiritual concepts.

The bird hopped up on the rock alongside Reese. "Every living thing has a spirit or soul."

"Everything?" she asked, looking from Reese to the egret.

"Everything. Regardless of outward form, all living things are a part of the divine essence."

She could buy that. Kelly'd always felt a connection with plants and animals, thought she could sense their feelings.

Reese kept on, "Spirits incarnate, enter physical form, to perfect themselves. The material realm is the grossest or slowest level. Everything on this plane takes a long time to accomplish; however, changes made here are the deepest and most lasting. That's why advanced spirits sometimes take material incarnations, to finish off, once and for all, the development of a character trait or talent. While the concept of place loses its importance at the highest frequencies, races tend to cluster around a planet or star system they use for gross incarnations.

"Although the levels appear separate to you, all frequency ranges are connected, with the lowest level anchoring the others. In other words, each race's progress depends on the growth of every other. You see?"

Kelly believed in reincarnation. The idea that a soul took on many bodily forms in order to develop its talents and progress toward perfection had always made sense to her. The notion was ridiculed by western pundits, but it was the majority view from a global perspective. Even so, the concept of levels of reality superimposed on each other was harder to swallow. "I'm not sure I understand the levels. Are you saying that other beings are here now, just at higher vibrations so we can't see them?"

"Correct."

Kelly shook her head incredulously. It was one thing to believe the shell was alive and quite another to accept that invisible people were running around the beach.

"Let's go back to Atlantis," he suggested, noticing her skepticism. "There are many other life forms in the universe. Millions of years ago this planet reached the point where it was ready to sustain life. As I said, physical incarnations are desirable for spiritual development, but a suitable form is required. A number of races from this galaxy were working on new species. They agreed to use Earth as the proving ground, and an intergalactic task force was dispatched to oversee the process.

"Two great centers were established. One was created by the Sirians in what is now the Pacific Ocean; that was the legendary Lemuria. The Sirians along with other races also built an encampment in the Atlantic; that was Atlantis."

"The Syrians?" Kelly asked, thinking of Iraq and the Persian Gulf War. "S-y-r-i-a-n-s?"

He looked puzzled. "No, S-i-r—the Sirius star cluster. As I was saying, races from throughout the galaxy established bases on this planet. The original task forces retained their high vibrations and, in your terms, were only semisolid."

"Like a ghost?" Kelly asked.

"It might appear that way to an untrained observer. Anyway, in many cases the experimental species had been engineered to promote procreation. To that end, powerful pleasure responses were preprogrammed. Regrettably, the scientists monitoring the experiments became fascinated by the sensual pleasures."

Kelly sat up stiffly, looking repulsed. "You mean the ethereal scientists were sneaking around watching people make love? That's disgusting."

Reese shrugged. "They *were* scientists. In any event, their curiosity coupled with the deceleratory friction from constant contact with the slower vibrations drew them down into this plane of existence. Unfortunately, as their energies fell, the scientists lost their high level memories and became trapped."

"Trapped?"

"Perhaps lost is a better word. The scientists were trapped or lost because they had forgotten their source. Without the memory of their origin or purpose, many became enmeshed in the Earth plane, their lives a relentless quest for feelings and pleasure. Of course, their true essence was unchanged, and they immediately saw their errors when they made their transition, or died in your terms. Because of the law of cause and effect, transgressions committed on Earth, against its people, must be rectified here. Thus the fallen Starpeople were forced to reincarnate on Earth. That group was responsible for the excesses and eventual destruction of first Lemuria, then Atlantis."

"What's the law of cause and effect?"

"Simply that everything is joined—whatever one gives out will eventually come back to the sender."

"What goes around, comes around," Kelly mused. "It sounds like karma."

"It is the basis for your concept of karma. Yet the term is commonly interpreted to mean retribution for some wrong. It can mean that, but with an important distinction. There is no great power judging your actions and meting out punishment. You judge yourself and choose your own experiences so as to raise your vibrations and progress to the next level."

Kelly stretched out, letting the tide lap around her. She agreed with the concept which was basically the same as the New Age adage: *You create your own reality*. She'd adamantly opposed the idea when she first heard it a decade earlier, but the ensuing years provided numerous examples of its truth. Over and over she'd seen competent people hold themselves back through self-doubt while others with far less training and experience succeeded on the strength of confidence and a positive view of the future.

"You said the observers were trapped by their fascination with sensual pleasures. Why were they so enthralled? Didn't they have feelings of their own?"

"You have to understand that existence at higher dimensions doesn't contain the extremes of pleasure and pain that you experience down here. Life is more ... even ... tranquil. When the intergalactic scientists witnessed their creations' potent responses to stimuli like the sex act, they became curious and wanted to experience the pleasure themselves. Also, a number of the scientists became enamored with their charges, much as you would love an artistic creation. The descent into matter took thousands and thousands of years, the result being that the observers became participants by mating with their wards."

Kelly remembered the story of Atlantis' inception. "Legend says that Atlantis was founded by the union of Poseidon, god of the sea, and a mortal woman. You're saying that's factual?"

"The Starpeople were not gods," Reese objected instantly. "Nevertheless that was the source of many cultures' stories about gods mating with humans."

Kelly considered what she'd heard. "I suppose your theory makes sense," she allowed.

He hopped down from his perch, the egret followed. Reese waded knee-deep into the water, then turned back, splashing Kelly as he retreated. She sat up with a start.

"It's not just a theory," he said quietly.

"Yeah? Well, how can you prove it?"

He flashed a silly grin. "I'm from outer space."

Kelly slapped the water with her palm, hitting him with a fine spray. "Right, and so am I."

He stopped beside her and stared into her eyes. "Yes, you are."

Kelly was nonplused. Sure, she'd questioned her existence before, but Reese's words stung like a slap in the face. Kelly sprung to her feet and squared her shoulders defiantly. She'd had enough. The guy had crossed the line, and she was getting out of there. Eyes riveted on Reese, she stooped to retrieve her shells. He caught her forearm as she reached for the cap and clamped down hard.

"You can't leave."

She tried to twist away, but her diminutive companion held fast. The guy was surprisingly strong for his size. "Let me go," she shouted, glaring down at him with clenched teeth. She dug her toes into the sand and swung with her free arm, catching him on the shoulder. It felt like hitting a wall.

"I won't hurt you. Give me a few more minutes, and I'll never bother you again. Please, *meloria*."

And Kelly went limp. Was it the word? It meant something, it was familiar. She thought she'd heard it before, but where? In any event, Kelly couldn't think. It was as if she'd been doused with a bucket of warm syrup. She had to sit down. Her muscles quivered as Reese guided her to a sitting position at the edge of the surf.

He kneeled beside her. "It's time to wake up, Kelly. I've come to help you remember. Look into my eyes. Think. Remember Sirius? Remember your mission? Think."

His eyes were like magnets, pulsing, probing, sucking at her very soul. There was something hazy and dark at the back of her mind and he was pulling on it. She could feel it ooze forth. Stretching, twisting, squirting through any small opening, it spewed out from the core of her being. She was terrified and relieved all at the same time.

"Listen to the universe, Kelly. The message, you know it. It's always playing. Listen." He shook her and peered into her mind.

It was moving, growing. She could feel *it* flowing up toward awareness.

"What's going on here?" A man's deep voice sliced through her consciousness and broke Reese's spell. Kelly whirled toward the sound. A heavyset man holding a golf club—he looked like a linebacker—stood a few feet away.

"Are you okay?" the man asked Kelly, brandishing his club.

Reese straightened to face the intruder. "She felt faint. Probably too much sun."

The man eyed Reese suspiciously and squatted beside Kelly. "Are you sick?"

"Lightheaded. I can't think," she said.

The man called over his shoulder, "Syd, bring the cart. Come, give me a hand." He swung a massive arm around her waist and pulled Kelly to her feet. A golf cart with a South Seas Plantation emblem skidded to a halt as they reached the edge of the beach. "Sunstroke, take her to the clubhouse."

The beefy hands steered her into the cart and folded her fingers around a handhold on the edge of the seat. Kelly whipped back as the vehicle started forward.

Reese and the egret were the last things she saw. They were standing on the beach side-by-side, the linebacker looming over them ominously.

Chapter 6

Fort Myers, Florida
June 8, 2:15 P.M. EDT

Frank eyed the shapely blonde at the end of the jetway and let out an appreciative sigh. Although conservatively attired by anyone's standards, the khaki culottes and starched sleeveless blouse did absolutely nothing to hide a traffic stopping, bronzed, hourglass figure. Could this be T. J. Morrow? Frank wondered as he made his way toward the petite woman holding the placard with his name.

"I'm Frank Scortino."

"Sally. Sally Carter." She offered her hand.

Her grip was firm and the skin soft. Frank liked that. "I was expecting someone else."

"I know, Morrow. He's tied up."

Frank followed her down the hallway toward baggage claim, enjoying the way her hips swayed. Frank knew he should ask for her credentials, and he would, but for now he would indulge in the view. A good looking female agent was a rarity.

Surely, she couldn't be FBI; the white-shirted crew cuts would have driven her crazy. As far as Frank was concerned Feebies were only a few steps up the evolutionary ladder from Neanderthals. They would have harassed a looker like her to death. The Bureau had offices in the same building back in Richmond, and Frank ran into them all the time. They were always strutting around, pounding their chests like John Wayne. No, she had to be CIA. On the whole they were a classier lot, and a striking blond would be an asset for dealing with Middle Easterners.

He retrieved his bag from the luggage carousel and followed her to a white Dodge Caravan parked at the curb. "I guess I should see some identification."

"Me too," Sally said.

Frank handed over his badge and studied the blue-rimmed card she offered. The picture didn't do her justice. Sally Jane Carter, Ph.D., Stanford University. He'd been wrong, she was working under contract to the Air Force. "You're our scientist?" he asked, handing back the badge.

"Plasma physics."

"And Morrow?"

"FBI Special Operations. He's an electronics expert."

Sally guided the van out of the airport and followed the route marked *To Beaches.*

"So, what's the deal?" Frank asked.

"NOAA's picking up strange pressure readings from Sanibel. They plummet, then shoot through the roof a few minutes later. That's the usual pattern. I'm trying to get a fix on the source. I'm not sure what Morrow's doing. He just paged and asked me to fetch you."

Frank closed his eyes. He'd tried to sleep on the plane but caught little more than a catnap. Now he was dead tired, weary to the bone. "Where are we headed?"

"Captiva, a small island north of Sanibel. We have a condo in a resort."

"As long as there's a bed, I don't care if it's in the middle of the street." He folded his arms across his chest and leaned back against the headrest.

"Hard night?" Sally asked.

"You could say that—I was in Alaska."

"You went to HAIR?"

"You've been there?" Frank replied, surprised.

"Worked at the facility last summer."

"What the heck are they doing?"

"Broadcasting, big time." Sally broke off to pay a toll, resuming as they started across the causeway to the islands. "They're beaming radio waves at the upper atmosphere. By altering frequency and dispersion, they can heat the ionosphere to focus and reflect radio waves."

"What does that do for us?"

"We can use it to monitor communications, detect missiles or peer beneath the surface of the earth. The technology could even affect the weather, like kick up a hurricane or tornado over your enemy's territory."

The memo Carl gave him referred to all those applications, but something else was going on. Major Clark had been lying, Frank would stake his reputation on it. "That's the sanitized party line. You worked there—what's really happening?"

Sally shrugged and looked at him from the corner of her eye. "What makes you think there's anything else?"

"Gut feeling."

"You realize that other countries are working on the same technology, don't you? They may have used it to conjure up these storms and hurricanes, even El Nino."

Frank nodded. "It crossed my mind. Weather warfare could certainly make guns and missiles obsolete."

"You don't believe that's a big deal? Global warming, melting the polar ice caps, all of that is possible with this technology. What could be more important than planetary weather patterns?"

Frank leaned back and closed his eyes wearily. "Beats me, but I think there's more to it than that."

▼▲▼

Charlotte, North Carolina
June 8, 4:00 P.M. EDT

Neal was finishing the annexation piece when Allison called.

"Hon, you're right," she said in a hushed voice.

He stiffened at her serious tone. "Right about what?"

"Government experiments causing the electric problems. I just got off the phone with Lisa Anderson at Fort Myers Electric. We went to school together. They're having major problems on Sanibel Island. Freak weather—sudden downpours, mini-tornadoes—and the circuits are tripping off for no good reason. Her husband's a ranger at the wildlife refuge on Sanibel. He says the Air Force has been flying over the area on a regular basis."

"Air Force? Is he sure?"

"Steve's a reserve pilot. He knows what he's talking about."

"Did you tell her about my theory?"

"I didn't have to. *She* brought it up; her husband thinks the same thing."

This was it, the opening Neal had hoped for; he had to get down there. So far his evidence was purely circumstantial. Neal needed something concrete to tie things together. Suspicious air operations might be the perfect angle for the story, his ticket to wire service fame. His boss would never approve the trip; he'd have to take vacation. And the money? Neal could drive down—that was no problem—but lodging could cost a fortune. Sanibel was a world class resort.

Aunt Tillie. Neal almost shouted her name aloud. No one in the family liked his father's sister, and she wasn't his favorite, either; but she owned a condo on Sanibel. He'd call her as soon as he hung up. If that didn't work, Neal vowed to camp out or sleep in the car. He couldn't let this opportunity slip away. "I'm going down there. Can you set me up with your friend's husband?"

"Have you lost your mind? The paper will never let you go."

"I'll use vacation and drive."

Allison protested, "It's our anniversary. You said we'd go to the Club for dinner."

"I'll make it up to you, promise. Will you set up the appointment?" Neal asked in a pleading tone. He'd been doing a lot of that lately.

"For when?"

"Tomorrow afternoon."

Neal hung up the phone, mind racing. He had to submit the article, call Tillie, talk to his boss, stop by an ATM for cash, run home for clothes ... what else? Allison. She'd be alone on their anniversary. But, it couldn't be helped—this might be the break of a lifetime. Still ... he had an idea. Neal picked up the telephone and dialed. Ben answered on the third ring. "Hey, buddy."

"I was just thinking of you. The old doctor—Simmons, remember?—is on target. Nerve pulses really are electrical and can be influenced by electric fields and radio waves. My intern found a whole book on it at the library. Some physicians think you might even regenerate lost limbs by stimulating tissue with electric currents. They've already done it on frogs. Isn't that wild?"

"Do these doctors wear black, pointy hats?" Neal quipped.

"We're talking major hospitals and medical professionals with tons of credentials. Granted, they're on the cutting edge— eh, precipice—of accepted practice, but it's happening."

"Good, I guess you didn't need the transmission line angle," Neal said, relieved Allison would never find out that he had told Ben about electromagnetic fields.

"Are you kidding, if this stuff is true, it lends credence to the controversy over electric lines."

Terrific, Neal thought. Allison would give him the silent treatment for a year if Ben made that connection. "I need a favor," he said, anxious to change the subject.

"I'm not going to cut off an arm to see if electricity can regenerate limbs."

"Don't worry, there'll be no pain; in fact, you'll probably enjoy it."

Ben said, "Shoot."

"Take Allison to the Club tonight; it's our anniversary."

"I know we're best friends, but ..."

"I've got a hot story and need to go out of town. I hate to leave her alone. She's such a trooper; she deserves better than sitting home with a microwave dinner."

"No problem. You know I love Allison. But what would lure you away from your lovely bride on such a special day?"

Neal knew he could trust Ben. They'd been through a lot together, and Ben would do anything for him. Next to his mother, Allison and Ben were the most important people in Neal's life. "I'm following a lead about the power outages. Military experiments may be responsible."

Ben whistled. "That *is* hot. What's your source?"

"Academics at major universities and a reserve officer in Florida who's witnessed suspicious Air Force operations. I'm going down to Sanibel tonight to pursue the Air Force slant."

"Interesting," Ben commented. "Well, don't worry about Allison; she's in good hands."

"I owe you one," Neal said.

"Good hunting."

▼▲▼

Cheyenne Mountain, Colorado
June 8, 3:00 P.M. MDT

Colonel Houston slammed the cup down. The coffee tasted like reprocessed sewage. "Doesn't anyone ever wash the damned pot?" he spat the words angrily. Probably not. Captain was the lowest rank assigned to the area, and no self-respecting officer would stoop to doing dishes without a direct order.

He hated coffee anyway, only drank it when he needed a boost. But it wasn't working; in fact, nothing was going right.

Maelstroms were popping up all over the Southeast. As if that weren't enough, Intelligence had turned up a handful of contacts between *unidentifieds* and people attending the California conference. That wasn't good, not good at all. The trend seemed to be accelerating. They were all being monitored, and a special team had been dispatched to Las Vegas. A half dozen this week, a dozen next week? Resources were already stretched thin. How could he keep it quiet? If it spread much further, he couldn't. It had to be stopped, that's all there was to it.

Brandt had persuaded the Europeans and Peruvians to cooperate and HAIR Command had started coordinating the effort. The Russians were playing hard to get. The general thought they'd eventually come around, especially if he could sweeten the deal with a little foreign exchange. For some unknown reason they weren't being targeted, ... yet. Brandt said it was simply a matter of time, and his Russian counterparts agreed. Nevertheless they played games.

Anything for a buck, Houston thought. The world was about to go down the tubes and the Russians were holding out for pocket change. Unbelievable. It was just wall-punching unbelievable.

Chapter 7

The difference between a flower
And a weed is a judgment.
Unknown

South Seas Plantation, Captiva, Florida
June 8, 7:30 P.M. EDT

Kelly peeked over the top of the oversized menu and scanned the crowd one more time. No sign of Reese or anyone else she knew for that matter. A waiter appeared with a glass of chardonnay. She watched the server move away before lowering the menu. Had he detected her puffy eyes? Crying always made her eyes swell. Just a few tears and her sockets puffed up like marshmallows. Allergies, she'd say, if anyone noticed. She took a drink of the wine and hoped it would help her relax.

Although she'd quit smoking long ago, Kelly had specifically asked for a seat in the sinners' section, as she and her friends used to call it. From years-gone-by she knew that area of Chadwick's was on an elevated platform at the rear of the restaurant. Seated with her back to the wall, she was strategically placed to ward off a sneak attack.

The incident with Reese had thrown her for a loop. For some unknown reason, his wacky pronouncement had scared her to death. Oh, she was probably being silly. She'd been

around and around all afternoon, one minute thinking Reese
was a dangerous psychopath, the next believing he was a
harmless guy with a vivid imagination. But, he had grabbed
her arm, and she had punched him. She'd never done that
before, hit someone. She could hardly believe it had happened.
Yet, the man had triggered something in her, something hidden,
and big and . . . and . . . crucial.

Kelly gulped the chardonnay and let its warm glow ripple
through her body. No more thinking tonight, it was getting
her nowhere. Tomorrow Cara would help her sort through
the events of the last few days and everything would look
different. She drained the glass and held it up for her waiter
to see.

The server reappeared in a couple of minutes. He swapped
the glasses with practiced ease, then tilted his head politely,
poised to receive her order. She chose the grouper. He bowed
from the waist and backed away,…directly into Jake. The men
fumbled in an awkward dance. Kelly watched the spectacle
with a mixture of amusement and dread, dabbing self-consciously at her eyes.

Finally extricating himself from his gangling partner, Jake
straightened his golf shirt and grinned. "I missed you on the
beach this afternoon. I thought you'd come out to watch the
sunset."

Kelly pointed toward her face. "Too much sun, figured I
should lay low for a while."

He scrutinized her face. "Must be sun poisoning."

"Happens every now and again." Kelly smiled weakly,
wishing she could sink through the floor. "How was the
sunset?"

"Average by Captiva standards. May I join you?" Jake asked.

"Please." Kelly took a gulp of air and a swig of wine. The
evening was not going as planned. All she wanted was a change
of scenery and some good food; pleasant conversation was
the last thing on her mind. Reese had killed any yearning for

company and she was mentally drained from thinking about Reese, Atlantis, and spacemen. Stimulating small talk was simply not a possibility.

Yet Jake fooled her. He had a smooth, easy wit and before she knew it dinner was finished, two hours had passed, and they were still chatting between nips of Kahlua and Bailey's Irish Cream. The shock of her encounter with Reese forgotten, Kelly relaxed into the crook of the overstuffed chair.

"Tell me about Atlantis," Jake said playfully.

Kelly paused to study the ice bobbing in her milky brown drink. Looking up through long lashes, she responded slowly in a husky tone. "What do you want to know?"

"Anything, everything."

She cupped the glass with both hands and stared at the liquid as if gazing into a crystal ball. "It's very strange, I'm not sure you can handle it."

"I'm tough."

Kelly grinned impishly, feeling giddy from the night's libations. "I don't know-w-w...." She purposely let the last word draw out for effect. "What ... if... I told you Atlantis was pop-p-ulated by people from outer space?"

"I'd agree."

"You would?"

"Sure. Earth is only one of millions, billions of planets. I'm not so arrogant as to think that this is the only one that developed intelligent life. I believe the laws of probability say there are at least one or two others. Anyway, there are too many unexplained anomalies in our ancient history."

She was startled by his response. "Anomalies... ?"

"UFOs for one thing. Even President Carter saw one. Then, there are the ancient monuments like the pyramids, Stonehenge, and the monoliths on Easter Island. All those ancient ruins took some pretty advanced engineering and construction techniques. And many ancient civilizations had a staggering understanding of astronomy. In fact, many of their ancient beliefs have only been verified in this century, like the Dogon."

"The Dogon?" Kelly blurted, stunned. She'd just read about them in the Atlantis book.

Jake continued, "A primitive African tribe whose secret tradition includes the knowledge that our planets revolve around the sun, our moon is dry as a bone, Jupiter has four moons, and Saturn has a ring around it. If that isn't enough to get your attention, they also have an intimate understanding of the Sirius star cluster which is light-years away."

Kelly almost choked at the mention of Sirius.

Jake went on, not noticing her reaction. "Their ancient legends assert that Sirius, the Dog Star, has a small, invisible companion orbiting it. Lo and behold, astronomers in this century have discovered a white dwarf orbiting Sirius. Sirius B, the tiny new discovery, is absolutely invisible to the naked eye.

"The Dogon claim to have gotten their knowledge from the Nommos, beings from the Sirius system who founded society on Earth."

Kelly couldn't believe what she was hearing. In all the years she'd dabbled in New Age teachings, she'd never heard anything about Sirius until the last two days. She'd thought Reese was loony, now ... ? "So, you believe Earth has been visited by people from outer space?"

Jake paused while the waiter replaced their empty glasses with full ones. "I've traveled a lot, seen a lot of things, and learned to keep an open mind. There is no good explanation for the Dogon's knowledge." He took a sip of the liqueur and leaned back. "We were talking about aliens. Have you ever seen one?"

Kelly thought of Reese. Could his wild story be true after all? As nice as Jake seemed, she feared he'd laugh hysterically if she told him about her encounter. "I once met a man who claimed to be from outer space."

"What did he look like?"

"Oh, an average, nutty human." Her wine-soaked brain was beginning to spin, and Kelly knew she'd better leave before she made a fool of herself. "It's getting late, I think I'd better go."

"As do I." Jake scribbled his name and room number on the check and circled the table to pull out her chair.

The full force of the alcohol descended when Kelly stood up. For a brief moment she felt woozy, but sucked up her fortitude and headed uncertainly toward the door. Jake followed a half step behind, his hand lightly touching the small of her back. She felt the pressure of his fingers with each step. At first just a warm touch, his fingertips gained power, pumping a current up her spine which obliterated all thoughts of Reese, Atlantis, and star systems. She smiled to herself, reveling in the pleasurable sensation.

A resort trolley was parked in front of the restaurant. Jake sat next to her on the narrow bench, his arm across the back of the seat. Kelly leaned into the wind as the open-air vehicle made a stop and start journey through the resort. Was Jake coming on to her, she wondered? His touch had aroused something in her that had lain dormant a long time. Too long. If he walked her to the door, should she invite him in? Logic said no—after all they'd just met—though the alcohol said yes.

"This is my stop."

The statement came from nowhere. "What?" Kelly asked hazily.

"It's been a great evening. Hope I'll see you tomorrow." Jake squeezed her hand and started down the aisle.

He was leaving; she had to say something now or .... "Me too," Kelly stammered. "Thanks for dinner." She watched him cross the street and disappear into a parking lot. "Darn," she cursed herself, "how could you let him get away?"

▼▲▼

South Seas Plantation, Captiva, Florida
June 9, 12:30 A.M. EDT

"What is going on?" Kelly asked, a little too loudly. It was well after midnight, and although the euphoric cloud had lifted, she could still feel the effects of the wine. Putting a coherent thought together was an effort that took her full attention. Yet she needed to think and ... clearly.

The telephone's red message light had been on when she got home. A cryptic message from Cara instructed Kelly to call as soon as possible. But, when Kelly did as directed, Cara refused to talk—said she had to ring back. Now, here Cara was, calling from a phone booth.

"Betty thinks her telephone is tapped, and she's pretty sure she's being followed."

"What?"

"It's because of the space thing. She wouldn't tell me all the details, but her contact with aliens was apparently not a one-shot deal. She's had an ongoing relationship with the ... whoever they are, and now the government—or someone— has gotten wind of it. A lot of the people she met at the California conference are also under surveillance. If they were listening to our conversations with Betty, we may be next."

"Oh no, give me your phone number." Pulling the telephone's cord to its full length, Kelly rifled the coffee table for a pen. Finally finding a chewed-up ball-point, but no paper, she abandoned the search and wrote on her hand. "Are you in a safe place?"

"A grocery store."

"I'll call you back."

Kelly stared at the telephone, trying to gather her thoughts. Where could she find a public phone on Captiva? On an island with a population of maybe a thousand, there certainly weren't any all-night grocery stores. Figuring the convenience mart across from the Bubble Room was her best bet, she slipped the room key into the pocket of her shorts—this was no time to fumble for it—and headed out the door.

The windows were dark in the market and no moon shone overhead. A street lamp across the road provided the only light, which illuminated the public telephone hung on the side of a clapboard building. The air was wet and still with a faint fishy smell. She extinguished the lights on her Mercedes and took a long look up and down the street. Nothing, not even a dog, was in sight.

Holding the pepper spray, Kelly punched in the number to the Las Vegas grocery. The telephone rang a dozen times before Cara answered.

"I was playing a slot machine and had to gather my winnings," Cara said brightly.

"A slot machine? At a time like this?"

"It was better than twiddling my thumbs."

Kelly glanced around nervously. "I'm standing in the middle of nowhere, so let's get on with it. The Atlantis man I told you about, Reese, says he's an alien from a planet in the Sirius star cluster."

"Sirius? That rings a bell—"

"Wait, you haven't heard the rest of it. He says I'm an alien too."

"Holy cow—"

"There's more. I met a guy on the beach today, who joined me for dinner—"

"You didn't tell him about Reese, did you?"

"No. But we talked about Atlantis and UFOs—he'd seen me reading Berlitz' book. Out of the clear blue he starts telling me about an African tribe with amazing astronomical knowledge, knowledge of Sirius. These primitive tribesmen claim Earth's civilization was founded by aliens from there. Exactly what Reese said."

"What a synchronicity."

Kelly shook her head and sighed. Synchronicity: the mysterious coincidences that shape one's life. The advice, the person, the money, the experience that appears out of nowhere when you need it most. The benevolent universe nudging humans along, New Age pundits said. Jake's statement was hardly a nudge. Kelly felt as though she'd been pushed off a cliff.

Cara chattered on, oblivious to Kelly's distress. "I saw Betty this afternoon—that's when she told me about the phone tapping. She's freaked about being followed. I had to meet her at the slot machines in the Luxor casino."

"Cara, please get to the point. I'm alone in the middle of nowhere."

"Although Betty didn't tell you, she thought Reese probably was an alien. Your encounter fit the pattern, she said. The world is approaching some important date or . . . juncture, that's what she called it. Anyway, this was preordained and a bunch of alien spirits took incarnations in this generation specifically to help mankind through the critical phase. Most Starpeople wake up on their own. One day a light goes off in their head, they remember who they are, and why they came. Other space spirits have missed their cues. They haven't awakened or remembered what they're supposed to do. That's why extraterrestrials like Reese are coming in now, to help them remember."

As Cara spoke, the THING, the black seed in Kelly's mind started to stir. It was moving, tugging, twisting again. A wave of terror shot through her. Kelly's hand went limp and the pepper spray rolled across the wooden deck. She leaned against the market's wall as her knees turned to goo.

Kelly's voice was barely above a whisper. "That's what Reese said: I had to remember my mission." She burst into tears, chest heaving uncontrollably. "Cara, I'm scared. There's something in my mind, I can feel it."

"Calm down. What's wrong with your mind?"

Kelly sniffed back tears. "There's something there that I should know, but can't recall. I'm afraid; it's too scary. I think I'm losing my mind."

"Kelly, there's nothing to fear. Thoughts can't hurt you. You know that, don't you?"

Kelly wiped her eyes with the back of her hand. "Uh huh."

"It's your resistance to the memory that causes pain. Allow yourself to remember. What could be so bad? I always thought there was something special about you. I wish I were in your shoes, I'd love to meet an ET."

"You would, wouldn't you?"

"Absolutely. If there's ever an invasion I'm going to jump up and down, whistle and shout 'Hey, boys, over here.'"

Kelly smiled into the receiver. "You may have met one already."

"Huh?" Cara said slowly. "Oh, you," she finally shrieked with delight.

Chapter 8

> *The course of human life is like that of a great*
> *river which, by the force of its own swiftness,*
> *takes quite new and unforeseen channels where*
> *before there was no current—such varied*
> *currents and unpremeditated changes are part*
> *of God's purpose for our lives.*
>
> *Rabindranath Tagore*

South Seas Plantation, Captiva, Florida
June 9, 8:00 A.M. EDT

Kelly closed the book and stared at its faded cover. *A Guide for the Advanced Soul. Hold a problem in your mind,* the book jacket instructed. *Open this book to any page and there will be your answer.* Unforeseen channels? Unpremeditated changes? The book was uncanny, bordering on magic. She laid the slim volume down and stared out over the Gulf. The water was quiet, faint undulations sparkling in the early morning sun. Clumps of seaweed, still wet and foamy, marked the limit of the tide's assault from the night before.

A strange calm had settled in Kelly. Perhaps it was the early hour—morning was her favorite time of day—or maybe she'd cried and thought herself into a daze. In any event, Kelly had awakened feeling better. Like always, 3:00 A.M. and she'd had *the dream*; the same one she'd had over and over since childhood. Invariably, Kelly saw herself sitting in a classroom with a lot of other people, ... That was it. She could never remember anything else. Yet, this morning she awoke determined to push her fears aside, see Reese again, and get to the truth.

A blue heron swooped down on ragged wings, gliding to the ground a few yards away. One foot dangled limply as the stately bird pecked at a clump of seaweed. Kelly winced at the sight of the injured bird and looked away. A figure approaching in the distance caught her eye. It was definitely a man and, though too distant to discern his features, she instinctively knew it was Jake. Her heart flipped at the realization and she headed down the beach to meet him.

"Well, you're up early," she said, falling into step.

"Got to go to work today."

"Ah." She wanted to talk about Reese, about wiretapping, and all the things she'd never have discussed with Mike. Did she dare? Jake seemed to be open, but .... "I didn't sleep very well, had a distressing call from a girl friend. I think I mentioned her to you, the reincarnated space spirit?"

"Sure, I remember."

"We laughed about it, but she's serious," Kelly said. "At dinner last night, you mentioned the Dogon, the tribe that claims to be descendants of aliens from Sirius."

"Yeah."

"My friend met a man who says he's a visitor from that very star system ... and maintains she is, too. The whole thing threw her for a loop, and she asked for my advice."

Jake's brows drew together doubtfully. "Advice on what?"

"Whether she should talk to him again. He told her she was here—on Earth—to do a mission, but they were interrupted before he could finish. At the time she thought he was insane, now she wonders if it could be true, especially after I told her what you said about the Dogon. What do you think?"

"I'm not sure I believe in reincarnation. Alien beings? That I might buy. I read about the Dogon and Sirius in a magazine article. It's no big secret. If I were going to play a prank, I'd base it on a fact or plausible situation. What did the alien look like? Did it speak English? Have a spaceship?"

Kelly averted her eyes; she'd never been good at lying. "She met him ... uh, in the desert. She didn't see a ship, and he looked like a normal human being."

"That's too farfetched. Someone's pulling her leg," Jake said crisply.

Kelly tensed her lips; she was not making herself clear. "She thought he was trying to communicate telepathically. She got strange feelings from him."

"People who've had alien encounters say they communicate mind-to-mind. Did she lose track of time?"

"No, but he said a foreign word that struck a profound chord in her."

Jake stopped and glanced at his watch. "She should be careful. There are a lot of sick people in this world. I've got to head back," he jerked his head in the direction they'd come, "walk with me."

They did an about-face, retracing their steps. The sun had finally cleared the roof lines and the beach was coming to life. Joggers clumped along at intervals while bent-over shellers scrounged through seaweed and dredged the Gulf's floor with stubby nets.

"Why is this an issue?" he asked.

Because it's me! I'm the alien, Kelly wanted to scream but didn't dare. "Curiosity. She'd like to know what the mission was, wonders if it would sound familiar. I guess she thinks the story might be true."

"That's a favorite con, you know."

"What?"

"Telling someone they're special or famous. Like the rich dowager who died without any heirs. It just so happens you may be related, and for a small fee, a genealogist will trace your family tree. And why is it that everyone who's reincarnated was someone famous? No one was ever a plain old servant or sheep herder."

Kelly laughed. "There's a lot of that, for sure. It's amazing how many people were high priests or priestesses in ancient Egypt. I've met three priests plus two Nefertitis."

"My point exactly. Most of that stuff comes from pseudo psychics and self-styled gurus who need followers to sponge off. Don't get me wrong—I believe there are true spiritual beings on this planet. Yet, as with anything, there are charlatans out there, too. Your friend needs to be careful, that's all." His pace had slowed until Jake finally stopped in front of apricot-colored condos. "This is where I get off." He grinned mischievously and raised his wrist watch to his mouth. "Transporter room, beam me up."

Kelly slapped his arm playfully. "You're making fun of me."

"Sorry, I couldn't resist. Hope I'll see you again, but if I don't, it's been a pleasure." He smiled into her eyes.

Kelly felt sad. She wanted to talk; tell him about Reese, Atlantis, about everything, but couldn't. "Me, too. It's been fun."

He winked and headed up a path flanked by vines and sea oats. Kelly looked after him. Alone again, she thought, then sighed and walked away.

▼▲▼

South Seas Plantation, Captiva, Florida
June 9, 9:00 A.M. EDT

Frank whirled at the sound of the front door clicking shut. He instinctively tensed as a shadowy figure made its way down the hallway toward the living room.

"You must be Francis R. Scortino," a masculine voice said from the corridor.

Muscles steeled for action, Frank strained to bring the intruder into focus. Outwardly nonchalant, he responded with his best imitation of an English accent, "Morrow, I presume."

The man chuckled. "Quite right, old chap. It's Jake, T. Jake Morrow at your service."

A tall male stepped from the shadows. A little younger than Frank was, mid- to late-thirties, he guessed. Clad in a bright green swimsuit, Jake was the epitome of a yuppie on holiday.

"Good disguise," Frank said, shaking Jake's hand. "I thought white shirts were mandatory for Feebies."

"Times have changed, this is the new FBI. The bureau even issued a surf board for this assignment," Jake shot back.

Sally appeared on the stairs from the second floor. "The agencies meet. No fireworks yet?"

"Give us a few minutes." Frank waited as Jake and Sally poured coffee and joined him in the living room. "What's up, gang?" Frank asked. "I understand we're SPIT—the special investigation team—for HAIR. Damn, you'd think they could have come up with better names. Are we sure this is a real project and not someone's idea of a joke?"

"It's real all right," Sally said.

Frank had his doubts, though that was another matter. "Sally's tracking strange atmospheric readings. What are you up to, Jake?"

"Not much so far. Our truck was flown into MacDill last night and is en route as we speak."

"Our truck?"

"Yeah, with the equipment: scientific instruments and surveillance gear. Major Travis Collins from Air Force Intelligence is driving it down."

"I take it you've both been involved for a while."

Sally answered first. "As I said yesterday, I worked at HAIR last summer and have been on one investigation with a field team. It was down in the Keys. Same peculiar pressure readings; we never turned up anything."

Jake drained his coffee. "I've done two assignments. One off the coast of California, up by San Francisco. The Navy had picked up odd sounds underwater and air pressure spiked up and down for three days. We never found the cause. The second set-up was near Taos, New Mexico. We chased weird signals, electromagnetic disturbances, and dust devils across four counties."

"Any sign of foreign operatives?" Frank asked.

Jake said no while Sally shrugged.

"Since that's why I'm involved, something must have happened to ratchet up the project," Frank said.

"Maybe," Sally replied. "I noticed a couple of things while I was at HAIR. First, there's almost no interaction between sections. One hand doesn't know what the other is doing. Also, they rotate people in and out of the field quite a bit. Too much, really. About the time a person gets a feel for his job, gains proficiency and starts to see patterns—you know, the things scientists are trained to do—they transfer him out. Everyone jokes about it, call it quantum leaping. There one minute, gone the next."

"Sounds like they don't want anyone to see the big picture," Frank observed.

"Aw, come on," Jake said.

"Seriously, what do we know about this assignment? The briefing papers I received were hardly more than a press release and it wasn't even classified. HAIR has four functions: peering below the surface of the earth, tracking missiles, communicating with submarines, and my personal favorite, controlling the weather. Did I leave anything out?" Frank looked to Sally.

"That covers it."

Frank continued. "The memo talked about creating lenses in the ionosphere to focus and disperse radio beams. How the heck do they do that?"

"It's like a microwave oven," Sally explained. "By beaming radio waves into the ionosphere, they can excite the ions and molecules and heat up a patch of sky. Because the hot area has a lower density than surrounding space, radio waves can pass through it. Radio waves are normally scattered by the lower ionosphere. However, the heated area creates an opening which allows them to reach higher altitudes. That's how they can extend the range of communications."

"How can they tell if a missile has a nuclear warhead? The memo said it could do that, too."

"Use the same procedure to excite electrons in the path of an incoming missile. You could then determine the missile's composition from its electromagnetic signature. In fact, you could even make the missile explode or short out its circuitry—that was the Reagan-era concept of Star Wars."

Frank looked out the window, rubbing the back of his neck. "I assume they affect the weather by heating up the atmosphere in the same way. Makes you think, doesn't it? This has been a record year for hurricanes."

"That's why we're here. It's possible a foreign government is using their facility against us," Sally said.

"It's a frightening scenario. With this new technology, conventional wars may soon be a thing of the past. In the future countries will whip up hurricanes—flood cities, ruin crops, destroy the infrastructure. Very effective—and no nuclear fallout."

"But weather takes lots of power, more energy than we thought the other facilities possessed," Jake argued.

"Can't the Air Force track it down with satellites?" Frank asked.

"I'm sure they're working on it, if they don't already know. The problem is stopping it."

"Bomb the facility," Frank said.

"Which facility?" Sally countered. "We need proof. All that stuff about manipulating the weather is speculative. The U.S. can't go off bombing countries on the basis of conjecture."

Frank folded his arms and stared at the lapping sea. Sally and Jake were too trusting. Sally's naiveté was understandable;

she was an academic. But Jake? Ten bucks said he was more of an office jock than a field operative. If that were the case, Jake was likely afflicted—stricken—by *staff infection*, the scourge of bureaucracies everywhere.

Yet, it was a beautiful day in paradise. The project was squirrely, riddled with holes, but there was nothing Frank could do about it. Maybe he should just relax and enjoy the scenery—his eyes followed a statuesque brunette wading in the surf. It was certainly better than hanging out in Alaska.

Chapter 9

The fates lead him who will—
Him who won't, they drag.
                              Seneca

South Seas Plantation, Captiva, Florida
June 9, 12:30 P.M. EDT

Kelly clutched the book to her chest and looked across the channel at Upper Captiva. The two islands had been joined until 1921 when a hurricane dug Redfish Pass, separating their fates forever. Now the southern part was the home of a famous resort while the northern island remained largely unpopulated, little changed from its sleepy past. Unconnected to anything, it had simply stopped in time.

Storms or vortices were portals to other dimensions, Reese had said. Hurricane Ervin had certainly changed her fate; yet which would it be? Would she progress upward, transforming into something wonderful or wither and stagnate like Upper Captiva? Kelly wasn't sure, but she had to find out.

Thunderheads rolled across the sky, and a jagged bolt of lightning flashed. Sitting on the rock where Reese had perched the previous afternoon, she'd waited all morning, hoping to see him again. Her fear was largely gone, replaced by a gnawing curiosity. "Remember your mission. Listen to the universe—the message is always playing." Reese's words danced in her mind, over and over like a mantra. What was her mission? What was the message?

Thunder sounded, and a curtain of rain drew nearer. Rolling her books in a towel, Kelly sprinted down the beach toward the condo. The downpour hit just as she reached the parking lot.

At exactly two-thirty Kelly dropped a quarter into a telephone at Chadwick's Square and dialed the number of the Las Vegas grocery. The line was busy. Leaning against the wall, she pulled her shorts up for the tenth time. Her pockets bulged with quarters—twenty dollars worth. She'd used a credit card for the call from the convenience mart the night before. A dumb mistake, yet there wasn't anything she could do about it.

A dozen men rounded the corner from the reception center, heading toward Chadwick's Restaurant. Dressed in slacks and casual shirts, the group looked like typical conventioneers. Maybe this was Jake's seminar, she thought. She searched the crowd, but didn't find him.

Kelly tried the phone again. Eight, twelve, fourteen rings.

"Hello." It was Cara.

"I was about to give up on you."

"A teenager was on the phone so I sat down. Have you seen Reese?"

Kelly replied, "I waited at the point all morning; he didn't show up."

"You've decided to see him again?"

"I can't put him out of my mind. The situation is bizarre, yet at some level I wonder if it could be true. I won't find out unless I talk to him."

"No argument from me," Cara said.

"I'm reading another book about extraterrestrials. It literally flew off the shelf when I was buying *Atlantis*. Guess what it's about?"

"Sirius?"

"Close—communiqués from outer space. From the earliest times people have been getting messages—high, universal truths—from other realms. The book speculates the information, which is usually attributed to gods or angels, is actually coming from extraterrestrials. In fact, most of the account echoes the stuff Reese said. Ever heard of the Sumerians?"

Cara gasped. "This is too spooky. I learned about them hardly an hour ago. They're an ancient Babylonian race that achieved an advanced civilization well before anyone else. Their creation legends say gods came from the sky to show them how to live."

A recording broke in requesting more money and Kelly pumped in a handful of quarters. "Yes. Overnight the animalistic nomads developed cuneiform writing, acquired vast scientific knowledge—like the planets revolve around the sun—and became master mathematicians."

Cara cleared her throat. "The Sumerians also claimed the gods from the stars were amphibians. Ties in with the story of Atlantis, don't you think? You know, Poseidon, god of the sea, mating with a mortal."

"I read about that in the Atlantis book," Kelly said.

"The Sumerians weren't the only ancient people who knew about Sirius. The early Egyptians' religion centered on it."

Cara explained that the air shafts in the Great Pyramid were aligned to Sirius and the constellation Orion, while the placement of the Giza pyramids themselves mirrored the layout of the stars. In addition, the Egyptian calendar was based on the rise of Sirius and the temple of Isis at Denderah was situated so that Sirius' light would illuminate the altar.

"American Indians like the Hopi also have similar beliefs," Cara added.

"How do you know so much?" Kelly asked.

"I've been asking around. Although I've never paid much attention to UFO stuff before, it turns out that a guy I've known for years is an expert on alien visitation lore. Funny how things can be right under your nose, yet you don't notice them until you need it."

"What's truly amazing is that there are so many different legends about Sirius and ancestors coming from the stars, yet modern scientists dismiss it all as imagination and coincidence. How can they be so blind?" Kelly asked.

"Ego."

"What do you mean?"

"If they acknowledge the existence of extraterrestrials, they're no longer the top dogs. It's a big ego trip. The status quo, the self-proclaimed saviors of humanity in government, science and business would lose their power base, because ETs are one thing they can't control. And if they can't control it, they have to deny it—otherwise they lose their god-like status."

Kelly bit her lip. "You think the government knows about extraterrestrials, but is suppressing it?"

"I don't rule it out. New revelations about government cover-ups surface every day. What about the MIAs in Vietnam, nuclear experiments on service men, the CIA's research on psychics? The authorities denied each, and those stories turned out to be true."

For the first time that day, Kelly felt a pang of fear. "Yeah, and there's more at stake here."

"Some people think the military has captured flying saucers and is testing them here in Nevada. They say the aliens came from Zeta Reticuli, and they're short little people."

"With gray skin and big heads? That's not Reese; he looks like us."

"A bunch of alien races supposedly visit the planet, some more benevolent than others."

"Huh?"

"You've heard the stuff about alien abductions and animal mutilations. Several of the alien races, especially the short gray ones, are fairly sinister. Others are completely benevolent," Cara said.

"Does anyone talk about visitors from Sirius?"

"No one's mentioned them yet."

The telephone signaled it was hungry again, and Kelly stuffed in more silver. "What about Betty?"

"I was on her doorstep at seven, got her out of bed."

"Well?"

"She said your experience fit the pattern. You're not losing your mind. The feelings you described—and the lump or blank spot in your mind—are normal. Relax and allow yourself to remember."

"Easier said than done. What is the mission? Didn't she tell you?"

"She wouldn't, couldn't, just said everyone plays a unique part. Your role is different from hers and everybody else's. But she cautioned you about getting hung up on Reese being an alien. You should focus on the message, not the messenger, she said."

"Damn—," Kelly cursed, then caught sight of a young boy standing in front of the gift shop. Turning her back to him, she continued in a subdued tone. "That doesn't help at all. Did she at least tell you how I can find Reese?"

"She said her contact always found her."

"What am I supposed to do, stand on the street corner?"

"I know you're frustrated—"

"You're darn right I am."

"He'll find you, I'm sure of it. Reese came all this way to wake you up, and you're not awake, are you? He won't quit until you recall whatever it is you're supposed to remember."

"I guess so." Kelly mouthed the words without conviction. "I've got to go—I'm running out of money."

They made arrangements to talk later that night. Hands stuffed in empty pockets, Kelly was lost in thought as she rounded the corner of the building.

"Feeling better?"

Kelly stopped dead in her tracks. Reese stepped from the shadow of the building and grinned.

▼▲▼

Ding Darling Refuge, Sanibel, Florida
June 9, 2:58 P.M. EDT

Neal checked his reflection in the rearview mirror. His eyes were bloodshot, and he looked like he hadn't shaved for days. Well, it had been about thirty hours. He'd driven all night, stopping only for gas. He was supposed to interview Steve Anderson at three o'clock. The time piece in the dash of his Toyota Celica said he'd made it.

He locked the car and looked around, tucking in his shirt tail. The Ding Darling Visitor's Center was a rustic building stuck in the middle of Florida jungle. Although it was a typically hot June day, the grounds were shaded and a good ten degrees cooler than the street. Only a handful of cars were parked in the lot. Neal was happy for that—unhurried interviews yielded the best information.

A senior citizen greeted him at the door and directed him toward a back office. Steve Anderson sat at a metal desk with his feet propped up.

"Anderson? Neal Winters from the *Charlotte Sentinel*. Our wives went to school together."

Steve motioned toward a battered wooden chair next to the door. "I've been expecting you. Right on time. You drove?" he asked, eyeing Neal's scruffy appearance.

Neal grinned sheepishly. "I'm doing this story on my own time. May submit it to a magazine or something."

The lights flickered just then. Steve said, "Queer power problems. Lisa says the utility doesn't know what to make of it."

"That's why she called Allison, my wife. Atlantergy's in the same predicament. I hear you have a theory."

"Not a theory—more like an observation," Steve said guardedly.

Neal held up his hands. "This is off the record, if you'd like."

"I'm in the Air Force reserves. I don't want to be accused of spreading false rumors."

"No problem. I won't use your name." Neal pulled out a notebook and waited.

"Why don't we take a walk?"

Neal followed Steve out a back door and down a dirt path. Dense foliage lined the trail on both sides. Thick, blunt cut stubs protruded at all angles, testifying to a recent assault from a machete. Steve resumed the conversation when they were safely out of sight of the building.

"The Air Force has shown a lot of interest in this area recently. I saw an A-7 flying up the coast the other day and believe it or not, I think I saw an AWACS."

"AWACS, that's the plane with all the electronics? Heard a lot about them in the Persian Gulf War."

Steve nodded. "Typically used for command and control of air campaigns. Fly at high altitudes."

"They don't normally cruise around here, I take it."

"Could have been a training mission from MacDill, I guess. But I saw a Blackhawk, too. It looked like the EH model, the one with all the antennas. They're used to monitor and scramble enemy communications. It flew over after one of those freak storms and power blackouts. Interesting coincidence, don't you think?"

Neal concentrated on his note taking, wondering how much he should divulge. A one-sided interrogation was usually a short interview. He needed to offer something to keep the discussion going without tipping his hand and leaking the story. "Maybe the Air Force is seeding clouds," Neal ventured.

Steve shrugged. "The weather this year has been queer enough. It's only June and we've already had five hurricanes.

According to the Weather Channel, three more are headed for Florida. Satellite photos of the Atlantic look like radar scopes during hub hour at Miami International. The storms are lined up like planes waiting for clearance to land.

"Of course, that's just the major storms. The climate has been unstable since Hurricane Ervin passed. Clear one minute, howling gale the next. I've seen two funnel clouds over the lakes out back. Damned strange, if you ask me."

"Do you think the military could be experimenting with something that causes the storms?"

"They can disrupt communications and electric systems if they want to—did it in the Persian Gulf."

A group of hikers overtook them from behind, and Steve stopped talking. The group passed, but the intrusion quashed the conversation. Neal tried to draw Steve out again to no avail.

"I'm staying on Sanibel." Neal scribbled the phone number on a page in his notebook and handed it to Steve. "If you think of anything we haven't covered, please call. By the way, where did you see those whirlwinds? I'd sure like to see one myself."

"Follow the road to the lakes. The last one was out by the observation tower."

Neal got a soft drink from the vending machine and drove into the park. The narrow, unpaved road wound through the wet lands, bulging out for tourists to park at especially picturesque spots. He was too tired to care about the scenery. Neal figured he'd take a quick tour, then head to Aunt Tillie's apartment for a shower and nap. He had the next two days to chase storms.

The observation tower was little more than an elevated gazebo. Well after three o'clock, the sun angled through the trees giving the area a magical quality. Neal parked the car and grabbed the camera. A couple of quick pictures, that's all, he vowed as he bounded up the steps.

Two men—the older one was short with sandy hair, the other a caramel-skinned black—were already present. They stopped talking when Neal appeared and eyed him warily. Neal canted his head as if to say "Sorry" and started lining up a picture. As a reporter, he was used to barging into places, most times uninvited, and it normally didn't bother him. But for some reason these guys made him feel uneasy. The white man seemed vaguely familiar, though Neal couldn't imagine how they could have met. He snapped two quick pictures and made a hasty retreat to his car, the older man watching him the whole time.

Peculiar, Neal thought. Then he threw the car into reverse, spinning its wheels, and headed down the road spewing a rooster tail of wet sand.

Chapter 10

South Seas Plantation, Captiva, Florida
June 9, 3:05 P.M. EDT

Frank, Jake, and Sally sat on stools at the back of the truck. Major Travis Collins stood in the aisle, silhouetted by the doorway to the front. Speaking in a loud monotone, the officer lectured on the vehicle's capabilities. In contrast to its name—WIMP—the weather/intelligence mobile post could do almost anything. Full weather gear, complete with electromagnetic (EM) sensors, were packed into one side of the compartment. The opposite wall contained sophisticated intelligence equipment: listening devices, infrared cameras, satellite hook-ups, motion detectors, and heat sensors.

Frank shifted uncomfortably on the hard metal seat and glanced at his colleagues. Seated closest to Collins, Sally listened intently. Jake appeared bored, intermittently fidgeting and drumming his fingers on the side of his stool. Frank just wanted to get on with the mission. The afternoon was nearly shot, and all they'd done was set up a command post in the condo. The way things were going, the anomalies would be over before they got started.

"...you'll drive, Carter will man the weather station, and Morrow will handle intelligence."

Frank perked up, happy something worthwhile was finally happening.

"I'll man the base station. My handle will be Papa Bear—you're Riding Hood."

Frank turned away, shaking his head. The project's name was bad enough, but fairy tale characters? And they couldn't keep the stories straight.

"That's it. Hop to." Collins jumped to the ground and swung the armored door shut.

Frank sunk into the driver's seat as Sally switched on her console. Multicolored displays sprang to life, illuminating her face.

Frank eased the van out of the parking lot, going slowly at first to feel out the truck's handling abilities, but was up to speed by the time they reached the guard station at the main gate. He stopped, waved to the sentry, and waited as a young woman crossed the street with a graying man. He watched the odd couple and wondered what their story was. Was the man her father? He looked old enough. Or was this a May-December marriage, a common sight at posh resorts? Aging men, terrified of losing their prowess, with a trophy wife hanging on their arm. Trying to buy time, stave off the Grim Reaper, Frank thought. After the couple crossed, the security guard motioned them on. Frank turned the van south. "Where to?"

Jake answered. "Stay on this road until you hit water at the end of Sanibel. I need to establish an electromagnetic base line for the area."

"Check." Frank turned up the air conditioner and relaxed into the bucket seat. He couldn't go much faster than twenty on the narrow road, and he was in no hurry, anyway. They drove in silence, Frank enjoying the peacefulness of the lush scenery, Jake and Sally intent on electronic meters and displays.

The road followed the coast at the island's narrowest part which was merely wide enough for a single row of buildings. Pine Island Sound peeked between gaps in the structures on the left while the Gulf stretched to the horizon on the right. A handful of tourists were still on the beach, some catching the late afternoon sun while others, dressed for dinner, walked lazily in the surf sipping from plastic cups. A little past the 'Tween Waters Inn the road curved inland, leading down the center of the island.

Venerable cypresses formed a canopy over the road, low-hanging branches lashing against the top of the bulky vehicle. Although the day was clear and bright, only occasional shards of sunlight shone through the verdant ceiling giving the scene a mysterious quality.

A piercing buzz sounded from the rear, breaking the seductive mood. "Riding Hood, here," Jake said mechanically.

The guy can't leave us alone, Frank thought. Gone less than thirty minutes, and Collins was already calling. The guy was a heel-clicking GI Joe. Everything by the book; what a bore. Frank guided the truck over a short bridge, noting a welcome sign for Sanibel Island.

Jake spoke in a string of one and two word sentences. "Differential? ... Coordinates? ... Geographic fix? ... We'll see what we can find."

"What's up?" Frank called over his shoulder.

"Satellites have picked up a drop in temperature."

Frank let out a low whistle. "Satellites? The big boys *are* watching."

"See anything, Sally?"

"I've got a pressure drop. Where are we?"

They were on a vacant stretch of road. Frank slowed down, looking for a landmark. A wooden sign gradually came into focus. "J. N. 'Ding' Darling National Wildlife Refuge," he announced.

"Slow down, slow down," Jake ordered. "I'm getting an EM surge. Any power lines or substations around?"

"Not that I see." Frank answered, pulling off on the shoulder of the road.

"Pressure's going back up," Sally reported.

"EM frequencies stabilizing," Jake said. "What the heck was that?"

"It's the usual pattern," Sally replied. "I'll bet a whirlwind set down close by."

"Why the EM surge?" Frank asked.

"Don't know. Pressure and temperature changes, even big ones, occur all the time. But massive electromagnetic fluctuations? That shouldn't be happening."

"Weather warfare," Frank mused to himself. "I guess we'd better locate the enemy."

At Sally's urging, they decided to add an EM sensor to the weather gear already stationed at the wildlife refuge. A quick flash of Jake's FBI badge gained them entry to the chain link enclosure that housed the park's electric substation and NOAA instruments.

"Ranger headed home?" Frank asked as he watched Jake connect the sensor to a junction box. Sally jotted notes on a small pad.

"He has to lock the front gate. Told us to let ourselves out and watch for alligators, they roam this time of year."

Frank glanced around dispassionately. "Going to be long?"

"Not if I can help it."

Sally snapped the notebook shut. "The ranger said they've had strange weather the last few days—two waterspouts, a lot of sudden storms. Electricity's been flashing on and off and the memory in his PC was wiped clean. A couple of transformers blew. No one knows what to make of it."

Jake wrapped electrical tape around a knot of wire and replaced the metal cover to the receptacle. "That should do it. Maybe this will give us some answers."

Sally went ahead to unlock the van. Frank and Jake gathered the tools, verbally jousting over the merits of their agencies, when Sally's shriek silenced their banter. Pulling a semiautomatic from an ankle holster, Frank raced toward the van. He found Sally looking down the snout of a ten foot alligator.

"Back up slowly," Frank instructed, targeting the reptile's eye. One step, two, … the alligator stared straight ahead. On the third step it blinked and waggled its massive tail.

Jake shoved the tools into the front of the truck. "The passenger door's open. Keep coming, Sally, nice and slow."

The gator's jaws parted.

She did as instructed, backing into Jake, then vaulting into the truck. Jake and Frank were close on her heels.

"Damn. They let those things run loose?" Jake asked.

Frank turned the key, bringing WIMP to life. "It's a wild-life refuge."

"That guy could eat a tourist."

"Judging from his size, I think he's already had a few."

Frank pulled away, watching the reptile in the rearview mirror.

They'd hardly gone a block when Sally called out, "Whoa, barometric pressure's falling."

"EM levels are going through the roof, again," Jake added.

Frank slowed the van to a crawl. Thick clouds rolled overhead, then darkness engulfed them. An eerie silence descended as if every bird, reptile, and insect had gone mute or vanished entirely. Although sunset was hours away, it seemed like the dead of night. Frank turned on the headlights and peered into the gloom. "Can you get a fix on the location?"

"Go forward," Jake ordered. "There's a heat differential between the front and back of the truck."

"What are we looking for?" Frank asked over his shoulder, not daring to take his eyes off the road.

"Usually a small tornado or whirlwind, maybe a water-spout. Don't get too close, if you see one."

"Don't worry." Frank had no desire whatsoever to find out if the truck could fly.

Mosquitoes danced in the headlights as Frank inched the van along the dirt road. He squinted at the darkness, searching the foliage for movement. Night vision goggles were encased in a pocket on the door; however, he might miss something in the time it took to put them on. He cursed himself for not planning ahead and vowed he would keep them on the passenger seat in the future.

"EM levels soaring, all frequencies," Jake called. "See anything?"

"No." The word was barely out of Frank's mouth when a man darted through the headlights. Frank slammed on brakes and grimaced at the grinding sounds emanating from Jake and Sally's telescoping stools. "Sorry. A guy came from nowhere. Ran directly in front of us—into the woods—barefooted, no less."

"Heat source ahead, eighty yards," Jake announced.

Two red lights blinked through the darkness. "It's a car, small, judging from the spacing of the tail lights. It's pulling out. Should I follow?" Frank gripped the steering wheel with both hands. He suddenly felt lightheaded, as if the top of his head were about to blow off.

"Pressure's down to twenty-six," Sally exclaimed.

Frank blinked, trying to clear his mind. A violet blaze exploded to his left, bathing the area with an unearthly purple glow. He fumbled with the latch holding the infrared goggles, then slammed on the brakes and jerked the glasses free. Slapping them over his eyes, Frank swung his face toward the light. He could make out the outline of a man. The guy who dashed into the woods. Then a brilliant flash blinded him. "Crap."

"Pressure's rising, temperature, too."

"EM stabilizing."

Frank gritted his teeth and forced his eyes open. He had to see what was going on. Tilting his head back, he peered through slitted eyes. Swirls of heat pulsed green, forming a writhing, twisting cone of energy. Where was the man? Frank glanced from side-to-side. The torrid spiral was dissipating, its tendrils dissolving. Clouds raced apart as if sucked up by a colossal vacuum cleaner. In less than a minute it was daylight again. Daylight, and the barefoot man was nowhere in sight.

▼▲▼

Ding Darling Refuge, Sanibel, Florida
June 9, 4:45 P.M. EDT

Frank was disgusted with himself. If only he'd had the goggles ready. If. If. He'd iffed the thing to death. But, who would expect to need them on a clear summer's day? He should have—he knew strange weather was a possibility. What if he'd been guarding the president?

The van bumped along the unpaved road toward the highway. They never found the man who'd run in front of the van though they used heat sensors and everything. The guy had vanished. Barefooted no less. Barefooted in a swampy, bush land filled with alligators. Jake thought he'd been picked up by the car. Frank guessed it was possible, things had become confused toward the end.

Shortly after the anomaly passed, Collins called and ordered them back to the resort. He said satellites had discovered another temperature spike and an AWACS had been dispatched from MacDill. AWACS meant they were looking for something on the ground, but what? And how did all of this fit into the HAIR project?

Frank turned onto the highway. "Sally, explain again how HAIR can create storms."

"Radio waves are used to heat the upper atmosphere. By rotating frequencies and focus, it's possible to create wind swirls and torrential rains or dissolve clouds to cause droughts."

"Would equipment have to be on the ground?"

Sally rubbed her temple thoughtfully. "Theoretically, no. A land-based beacon could be used to mark the target area or set up sympathetic waves, but it isn't necessary."

"What would an AWACS be looking for?"

Jake replied, "Could be anything. The modified version can monitor communications, read infrared, and detect virtually all known electronics."

"Doesn't it surprise you that one has been dispatched?"

"This project really bothers you, doesn't it?" Sally said.

Frank shook his head. "It doesn't add up. An interagency task force is a first in my experience, we haven't been adequately briefed, and now an AWACS is assigned to investigate a temperature aberration. You don't think that's odd even by government standards?"

But Jake didn't get a chance to comment. Papa Bear had buzzed him again.

Chapter 11

Man cannot discover new oceans
Until he has courage to lose sight of the shore.
Unknown

South Seas Plantation, Captiva, Florida
June 9, 3:35 P.M. EDT

Kelly was dying to know what Reese was thinking, but determined to let him speak first. They walked along the beach, frothy waves breaking at their feet. It was as if the water were breathing. A giant green lung rankled by disease, the Gulf gasped and sputtered, its life an endless series of congested heaves. Inhale: the viridescent chest expanded and the life-giving elixir sucked in. Exhale: spumy mucus spewed forth, coughed up from the depths of its being.

She glanced at Reese again. He's not going to say anything, she thought. The little man looked straight ahead, seemingly oblivious to her presence. "Who are you, honestly?" she asked finally.

"Exactly who I said I am."

"An alien from outer space? You expect me to believe that?"

"You believe it at some level; otherwise, you wouldn't discuss it with your friend Cara."

"You were eavesdropping on me." Kelly scowled. "You were hiding around the corner, listening."

He shook his head.

"Admit it—how else could you know I was talking to Cara?"

"This is not my natural state. Your concepts of time and space do not apply to me."

"What does that mean?"

He pointed at a flock of birds about twenty yards away. A knobby-kneed tern scurried across the sand, pecking at shells and seaweed. Sandpipers paraded in the tern's wake, stopping when it stopped, racing to keep up when the bird started out again. "What are they doing?"

"Doing? They're foraging for food."

"How do you know that?"

"I can see them."

"Correct, and you have a good vantage point. In fact, not only is that flock in view, so are the sea gulls over there." Reese pointed at three birds flying low over the water. "The sandpipers are oblivious to the gulls. From their perspective the sea gulls don't exist, they're beyond their field of vision. Yet you see them both, since you have a better vantage point."

"Okay, you're saying that you see more because you're from a higher dimension?"

"Correct."

"You'll forgive me if I don't swallow that hook, line, and sinker. You look pretty normal, and so far you haven't done anything a clever, this-dimensional human couldn't do."

"You sat at the point all morning."

Kelly gasped, but recovered quickly. "That just proves you're spying on me. If you saw me there, why didn't you show yourself?"

"Conditions weren't right."

She glared at him, hands on hips. "You must think I'm a dimwit. It's going to take more than a glib story to convince me you're from another world."

"It usually does." Reese turned away and gazed across the water. Black clouds were amassing in the distance. Like thick plasma, layers of moisture streamed together to form a churning whirlpool. "Take my hand," he said.

She hesitated, looking around self-consciously, yet did as he asked. Reese stood perfectly still, eyes blank and glassy. His grip, once so hot, now felt strangely cool. Her fingers encircled his, making his hand appear small and childlike. She noticed his nails had an iridescent sheen.

His palm started getting colder, and a chill shot up her arm. His fingertips throbbed and glowed and seemed to grow larger, their volume expanding with each pulse until his fingers looked like transparent, swollen sausages. She gaped at the spectacle and tried to pull away, but the tumid mass held fast—his hand was expanding, too. No longer fully solid, it flowed up and out, through her own, his substance passing through her flesh. Her skin crawled with the realization, while panic welled up in her chest. She twisted and pulled, frantically now.

Reese's eyes flew open, and he relaxed his grip.

"What was that?" she asked, rubbing her hand and backing away.

"My natural state, approximately."

"Approximately?"

"This plane is so heavy and the pressures are so great that it is impossible to expand fully."

Semisolid. He'd told her that before, though it hadn't fully registered.

Next he walked to the water's edge and raised his face to the sky. Clouds swirled overhead and rain started to fall, each fat globule leaving its print in the sand.

She stared at him, uncertain what to do. "Reese, it's raining. Let's go."

He didn't budge.

The rain pelted them savagely, each drop a painful projectile. "Come on," she called emphatically.

Reese remained immobile.

A roar like a freight train sounded in the distance. Shielding her eyes with both hands, Kelly strained to see through the gray curtain of rain. And then she saw it—at first a faint outline, finally coming into full view—a funnel of water was skipping across the sea, heading straight for them.

Kelly froze. The waterspout danced closer, ultimately stopping a few yards from Reese. Then as abruptly as it appeared, it vanished and ... there were two of them.

She blinked in disbelief. Two Reeses stood only a few yards away. Her pulse pounded in her ears, and she felt like running, but couldn't. *Omagosh.* Both Reeses were walking toward her.

The man on the left pointed at his twin. "This is ... my colleague. You can call him Joe."

"H-how?" Kelly stammered.

"Are you convinced?" Reese asked wearily. "Could a trickster do this?"

"I don't know ... I guess not, ... how?"

"The vortex," Joe said in a voice identical to Reese's.

"Well?" Reese looked exasperated.

Kelly nodded, too stunned to speak.

Joe inclined his head as if to say good-by and waded into the surf. He stopped about knee-deep and looked up at the sky. Reese pulled her back. The wind screeched, and another torrent descended. Then, in a swirl of water Joe disappeared.

▼▲▼

South Seas Plantation, Captiva, Florida
June 9, 4:45 P.M. EDT

Side-by-side on a bench overlooking the water, Kelly regarded Reese curiously. The rain had stopped almost immediately after Joe vanished, and sun worshipers descended. Kelly and Reese had headed north to escape the commotion, alighting on the first bench.

"Did your spaceship create the waterspout?"

"I don't have a spaceship as you know them."

"How did you get here?"

"As I told you before, it is a matter of frequency. We have technology which slows our vibratory rate and allows us to slip into your plane. The vortex of a waterspout is a gateway."

"Are all vortices portals or only the ones you create?"

"They are all potential doorways to other dimensions, the difficulty lies in controlling the destination."

"I can imagine. You said yesterday that a number of alien races planted life on this planet. You're from Sirius, but what about the other races? Do they use spaceships?"

"Some have vehicles."

"Flying saucers?"

Reese stared at her, and Kelly glanced away. He was trying to probe her mind; she could feel it. She could block him if she thought of something else. *One hundred, ninety-nine, ninety-eight,* ... she started counting backward in her head.

"You wonder about the aliens with the big eyes. You're afraid I might be deceiving you," Reese stated matter-of-factly.

That was exactly what she was thinking. Was his story a ploy, a prelude to abduction? Did his people do sex experiments on humans or mutilate animals? It hadn't occurred to her until Cara brought it up. Although Kelly didn't chase UFOs, she knew about aliens. Like Atlantis and the pyramids, she'd always been fascinated by reports of extraterrestrial visitors. But the shock of meeting Reese had driven all of that from her mind. She'd been so stunned by his story, the possibility of abduction had never occurred to her. "The little gray men are real, aren't they? You know about them."

"They exist, and they have been visiting your planet. We have known for some time, though did not interfere. Imposing our will on others is not our way. We committed that mistake in the early days and vowed not to make the same error again. That transgression has not only held back this planet's development but our own as well. We hoped the Neboki would see their errors without our intervention."

"You said *hoped*. Does that mean something has changed?"

"The larger universe has grown impatient with the delay. The Neboki's development, like yours, anchors the entire sector. We and the others who are ready to move on have intervened."

"What were the Neboki doing here?"

"They were among the original scientists who planted life. And they, like us, have monitored the planet's progress. Roughly a thousand years ago their species evolved to the point they lost their ability to reproduce. That is a natural stage in the evolutionary spiral. Unfortunately, they did not take the next step, the leap to a higher octave where procreation manifests in a different way. So they found themselves stuck, in a sense, between two worlds. They could not reproduce, yet they weren't ready to move to the next dimension. In desperation they turned to Earth to solve their dilemma, never realizing they were cementing themselves in the wrong place at the wrong time."

"The UFO people were right—the Neboki were actually doing sexual experiments on humans. Did our government know about it?"

"Some in Earth's governments have known for years."

His last statement had a sorrowful tone, which told Kelly that government's role was more than mere knowledge. "Were the Neboki trying to make a deal with our authorities?"

"An arrangement was made, but it is not your concern."

She grimaced. Government officials making deals with aliens who wanted to conduct experiments on their own people. A horrifying thought, although not much different from the slavery, genocide, and other cruelties that went on throughout the world. Man's inhumanity to man—was there no end? If humans were truly evolving, progressing toward a kinder, gentler state, it wasn't obvious. If change was occurring, it was murderously slow. Could an outside force speed up the process?

"What is your world like?"

Reese smiled and closed his eyes. "Not so different from yours, if you remove the need for survival and the desire for power."

"You've summed up human existence. What else is there?"

He chuckled. "The senses have been both a blessing and curse for your species. On one hand, the quest for pleasure and the fear of pain have spurred men to achieve, to attain new heights in medicine, the arts, ... everything. Yet, power is the absence of fear, and in its name the most grotesque atrocities have been committed. So the very thing humans seek has hurt you the most.

"We were much the same, eons ago. Our vibrations were lower, and we had feelings and emotions like you. Yet we were fortunate—the cruel edge of power never took hold. To us, knowledge has sovereignty. Since knowledge is unending, our quest conferred a sense of humility. No matter how much one knew, there was always more to learn. And even after we had mastered the visible universe, there were the facts beyond the facts, the levels beyond the obvious to be explored.

"The thought of subjugating anything—a person, a plant, a rock—without its permission is abhorrent. A sin against one is a sin against all. It simply does not happen in our society."

"How does that work? Humans think knowledge is power."

"You have not yet realized that minds are joined. A thought by anyone is accessible to all—it is merely a matter of alignment. Each of you have the capability, but only a few use or trust it. Everyone on Earth is getting information all the time, from us as well as other humans. They simply have not learned to sort it out, to listen."

"If that's true, the flood of information would be overwhelming. If I could hear everyone's thoughts, it would drive me crazy."

Reese agreed, "Indeed it would if you had no way of filtering extraneous material. You see, like attracts like. Haven't you ever had a problem or wondered about something, then suddenly stumbled across a book or person that provided the answer?"

Like attracts like was another way of saying synchronicity— the very thing Kelly and Cara had been talking about only hours earlier. Everything was going in circles, the same things coming up over and over. Her situation was wilder than any dream. The universe was absolutely beating her over the head.

"You're saying that my thought or question about something draws the answer?"

"Correct. Thoughts have frequencies that resonate to their own kind. You send out a question, the question being of a particular frequency, and the corresponding answer emerges, attracted by the vibration. In a sense, the question creates the answer."

Kelly looked sidelong skeptically. "Why, then, is mankind in such a quandary? Almost everyone I know is confused, dissatisfied, and searching for something. Most of them never seem to find it. They struggle their entire lives, dying lonely and unfulfilled."

Sadness filled his eyes. "That's true, and it is part of the reason we have come. Man's thoughts lack discipline. Unaware of the power of belief, you do not guard your minds from assault. You take in everything until the frequencies combine into a hopeless jumble. Then the confusion attracts more confusion. Man has reached the apex of a great spiral. With the current level of technology, information is overwhelming. Unless man turns inward and learns to discipline his psyche, society will fall again, as it did in the last age, in Atlantis.

"You can already see the effects on your young people. Their minds have no defenses. They take in everything such as the violence from your media. Because like attracts like, the savage thoughts draw violence to them, and they react in kind. It is a vicious cycle that can only be changed by disciplining their minds, altering their thinking."

Kelly closed her eyes, considering what he'd said. The turning point. Many were saying it, but she'd chalked it up to millennium fever. Perhaps the soothsayers were accurate this time. The pace of technology was increasing exponentially; she for one couldn't keep up. The computer she bought last month was already obsolete, although it had been light-years ahead of the previous model. It went without saying that violence among the youth was out of control—three of her friends had given up teaching for that very reason.

"You don't have these problems in your world?"

"Not to this extent. We are not perfect, not gods. We have disagreements; however, our lives are remarkably peaceful in comparison to existence on this plane."

"You don't have wars?"

"Not on our world, though we have been involved in peacekeeping efforts elsewhere."

"You've sent troops to other planets?"

"It is not our way to interfere in other's affairs; yet we have lent aid when requested. We do not have troops; we send advisors. Remember, thoughts are things. Guns and weapons as you know them have little power against concentrated thought."

"Do you have families?"

"Oh, yes. We have parents and siblings, just as you do, although our living arrangements are—what is the word?— communal. Disease has been virtually eliminated, so our life span is close to a thousand years."

"Do you live in houses?"

"We live in complexes beneath the ground. We would not think of destroying trees, flowers, and oceans for buildings. It would disrupt the flow of energy."

When he mentioned oceans, Kelly remembered Cara's comments about Sumerian legends of amphibious gods from the sky. "Are you amphibians?"

He laughed. "You have been reading ancient history. In the last epoch, before the transition, we were solid like you, and yes, we were amphibians. We lived in the oceans on our home world. You see, our gravity was much higher than yours, and the oceans provided buoyancy which reduced the stress on our bodies. We could walk on land, but it was very tiring. When we made the leap to the next level and evolved to our present, less substantial form, gravity was no longer a consideration, so we don't need to return to the sea."

"Your ancestors *were* the gods described by Sumerian legends?"

"Yes and no. The Sumerians were among the survivors from the collapse of Atlantis. The stories brought from Atlantis are far more ancient than the Sumerians' brief tenure in the Middle East. Our scientists in Atlantis returned to the sea periodically, for, although this planet's gravity is much less than our own, the pressures of walking on land were still great."

"Are dolphins your descendants?"

A strange look crossed Reese's face and he avoided her eyes. "All living things are connected."

He seemed flustered, which was hard to believe, since he had been the epitome of control so far. "You didn't answer my question."

Reese turned back toward her, still looking uncomfortable. "They, like you, are our descendants."

He was holding something back. "What else?"

"There are certain things I may not divulge. You will learn of them in time."

Kelly peered into his eyes. "Some people say dolphins are alien caretakers of this planet. Is that true?"

Reese leaned forward, resting his elbows on his knees, and stared at the sea. "There are many caretakers of which you are unaware. Some are ancient, having been here from the beginning. Others arrive at important junctures ...." He glanced at her meaningfully. "Many you do not see."

His last statement made her uncomfortable. Multi-dimensions, other planes of existence; she was having a hard time accepting it all. The thought of being under continuous scrutiny was creepy.

As the afternoon sun dropped in the sky, couples sipping cocktails spilled out of the cottages and condos to wait for the sunset. Kelly and Reese headed further up the beach to find another secluded spot. It wasn't until they were almost to the point, in front of the condos where she'd last seen Jake, that they found an empty seat.

"What exactly am I supposed to remember?" Kelly asked.

"You have an important part to play in upcoming events."

"And that is?"

"I don't know. You chose the mission in concert with the universal plan. While I have a sketchy notion of your function, you're the only one who knows the specifics."

She scowled. "Great. You're here to help me remember something, but you don't know what it is. I'm the only one who knows because I picked it myself, yet I don't remember .... You have to admit it all sounds like a bunch of mumbo jumbo."

"It does at that." Reese laughed.

Chapter 12

HAIR Project, Alaska
June 9, 11:00 A.M. ADT

The black spruce forest looked like all the others in central Alaska. Yet this one concealed a thirty-three acre gravel pad dotted with two hundred concrete towers, each supporting double pairs of crossed dipole antennas. A barbed wire fence ringed the compound, a primitive but effective means of keeping large mammals, like humans, a safe distance from low angle beams capable of raising internal body temperature and exploding flares or munitions stored in automobile trunks. Although surrounding air space was restricted, sophisticated radar—including S and X bands—shut the system down in the event a plane strayed into the area. The aircraft detection system was a mandatory component of the installation since its four megawatt transmissions would scramble aircraft communication, flight control, and navigation systems.

Colonel Stanley Houston had flown in from Colorado to oversee preparations for the experiment. By synchronizing transmissions from installations in Europe and Peru, he hoped to dissolve the storms, thereby shutting the door on the interdimensional intruders. Of course, no one at HAIR or the other facilities knew the real purpose for the exercise. The scientists thought they were trying to control destructive weather patterns. That was fine; in fact, the test results might actually yield useful information for that purpose.

He sat at a conference table in a sparsely furnished corrugated steel building in the middle of the complex. The project's director, Bob Coates, had stepped out to take a call. Houston was glad for the break, Coates was starting to grate on his nerves. A geeky, scientific type, Coates had pontificated and bragged for the better part of an hour. Houston nodded and smiled and tried to look interested. He was to some degree, but didn't give a damn about the installation's five megawatts of diesel generators, or the rectangular grid of thermopiles, or elevated ground screen used to shield site workers from stray signals. He just wanted the scientists to seal the holes in the ionosphere. If Coates could do that, he'd have Houston's undying gratitude. If not, well hell, nothing would matter.

The latest infiltrators were a scary lot. While the military couldn't control the saucers, they could at least track them. Nine times out of ten they could identify the people contacted and take steps to silence or discredit them. The new intruders zipped in and out so fast they could avoid detection. Lord knows what their technology was. Consensus said they came from another dimension. Were they peaceniks like the tall, fair-skinned aliens or impotent scientists like the short sleazeballs with the big eyes? If the military could capture one, they might get some answers.

Coates reappeared. "Sorry for the interruption. We're ready to go; I just need the coordinates."

"We want to focus on the Gulf of Mexico. The weather down there has been particularly unstable in the wake of that hurricane. Small tornadoes are still popping up." Houston put on reading glasses and checked a slip of paper. "Target the area around Fort Myers—81W52, 26N38."

Coates scribbled the coordinates on a pad of paper. "How do we time the transmissions?"

"Can you arrange around-the-clock standby for, say, the next two days?"

"That's a lot to ask of the other facilities."

Houston flashed his diplomatic smile. "I thought our best chance for success was to transmit while a storm was forming. Did I misunderstand?"

Coates clenched his jaw and stared.

"I can get real time readings from our satellites. If you guys hustle, we can zap the storm centers as they begin to swirl. I realize it's an inconvenience, but we could find out, once and for all, if the theory works. Don't you agree?"

Coates closed his eyes and sighed—the look of a man sorting through the list of favors he would have to call in.

▼▲▼

Sanibel, Florida
June 9, 6:00 P.M. EDT

"I made it, babe." Neal took a swig of beer and leaned back in the chair. He'd picked up frozen lasagna and a six pack from a convenience mart around the corner from Tillie's apartment.

"I was worried about you," Allison said, sounding tired herself. "How did it go?"

"Steve's afraid to say much, though something's definitely going on down here. He saw an AWACS the other day, and a Blackhawk helicopter flew over just before one of the storms. While Steve stopped short of saying the Air Force was behind the weather problems, he admitted they could disrupt communications. What's happening there?"

"Same stuff. Today we almost lost a 500kv line in eastern Florida and a nuclear plant in Georgia tripped off. An incident with one of the 765s in Virginia, too. It's lucky we're not in the middle of a heat wave. If the transmission lines were fully loaded, the whole East Coast could black out."

"Is there a pattern to the incidents?"

"Pockets of problems. Fort Myers/Sanibel has been one of the most active sites. We've also had recurring disturbances in the Florida panhandle, southern Georgia, and now Virginia."

"Any possibility it's related to Hurricane Ervin?"

"We thought that at first. The initial anomalies coincided with the hurricane, the storm spawned an unusual number of tornadoes. But Ervin's blown out and the faults persist. It's not equipment. The problem's atmospheric, though we don't know how. Scientists from the Electric Power Research Association are flying in tomorrow. They're going to set up monitors on major transmission lines. A crew is coming down your way."

"I don't suppose you've heard anything about auroras over storms or hovering fireballs?"

"No. You think this is related to that Alaska project, the ionosphere thing?"

"It's awfully suspicious. Other than your friend at Fort Myers, has anyone else made a connection to government experiments?"

"I mentioned it in the staff meeting—"

"Al!"

"I had to—it's my job. Government Relations is going to check it out."

"Sheridan, the former congressman?"

"Of course."

"He'll call everyone in Washington. I'll be scooped for sure."

"If secret military experiments *are* causing these problems, he won't find out anything."

"Yeah, they'll go underground which will make my job a whole lot harder," Neal countered, sounding perturbed.

"I don't care. If the military is involved, you could be in danger."

"You've seen too many movies, Al. I'm a civilian. They wouldn't bother me."

"Right—and city councilors always excuse themselves from votes where they have a conflict," she said sarcastically.

"We're talking federal government. They have higher standards and a bunch of laws to protect private citizens' rights."

"Just be careful. I've got a rain check for hot, hard sex."
Neal's groin twitched. He was suddenly wide awake.

▼▲▼

South Seas Plantation, Captiva, Florida
June 9, 6:00 P.M. EDT

No matter how much Kelly prodded and probed, Reese
would not reveal her mission. Frustrated, she decided to try
another tack. "If you can't tell me what the mission is, won't
you at least explain why I chose it?"

"Fair enough. Let's go back to the beginning. Your spirit
or essence, as we prefer to call it, has taken many Sirian
incarnations, and you were among the emissaries sent to
Atlantis before it's fall."

"Uh oh."

Reese nodded. "You were among the first group sent to this
planet. Your curiosity got the best of you in that embodiment."

"I was one of the fallen Starpeople?"

"Correct. Once you passed on, left that body, you realized
the error and set out to make amends. That's why you took
another Atlantean life: to try to awaken the population to their
true selves and higher purpose. Unfortunately, the descent
into matter had gone too far and your mission failed. The
ego's twisted logic had taken hold, and the people would not
listen. You drowned in a tidal wave in the early days of the
final upheavals."

Funny—she'd always had a fear of water, even hated to
get her face wet in the shower. Cara had speculated that she'd
drowned in a former life, but Kelly never believed it.

"You said ego had taken hold. A strong ego is a good thing,
isn't it?" Kelly asked.

"Your experts say that, but I use the term in a broader
context. We see ego as a limit to your awareness. Your true
self has no bounds, yet you view your consciousness as
confined to the tiny space of your body."

Boundless awareness. If someone had offered it to her last week, Kelly might have jumped at the chance. Now? She wasn't so sure.

She looked out to sea where a speedboat with a parasail in tow bounced across the waves. A woman in a pink swimsuit dangled like a puppet from the rainbow-stripped canopy. Kelly studied the woman and tried to imagine how she felt. Bobbing on wind drafts, the lady floated above the earth, temporarily liberated from the laws of gravity.

We're a lot alike, Kelly thought. Reese had loosened the bonds of time and space and now she was adrift. Unencumbered freedom, the very thing she'd longed for all her life scared her silly now. Free to soar also meant free to fall. The boat slowed, and the woman drifted lower. Down, down until her toes skimmed the water. Then the boat lunged forward, propelling the lady up with a shriek. Was it the sound of terror or of glee?

Reese put his arm around Kelly's shoulder and pulled her close. Stroking her arm like a parent comforting a child, he continued, "It's not necessary that you understand everything at once. My only goal is to ignite the spark of your Sirian self. If you remember that, the details of your purpose will unfold in time."

"You said that this is a critical period—why?"

"All vibratory levels are connected. It's not as simple as this plane or that plane being distinct places. We're all multi-dimensional beings. Your consciousness resides here in the physical, but you also exist at several higher planes. Those are the realms you contact in meditation or dreams. Similarly, my people, as all races, live on multiple levels. But there is overlap between our domains which creates an unbroken fabric of consciousness. That connection, that continuous flow of creative thought, is the life force of the universe. It must be maintained at all costs. Consequently, each race can only progress as fast as the slowest.

"Our scientists realized this eons ago, that Earth's progress determined our own. So we have sent emissaries throughout the ages—both through physical embodiments and visitors—to help this planet. Your world finally has attained the same level as before the fall—that's why you and other Starpeople have taken incarnations. It is time for Earthers to choose again. To choose the higher self instead of the ego so that we may all ascend to new heights."

"Are there many visitors like you and Joe?"

Reese shook his head. "Not enough." Kelly shrank back at his response. He chuckled and squeezed her arm. "This isn't an invasion, although it is a wide-reaching, coordinated effort. I contacted you because of your Sirian heritage. Other races play similar roles."

"You mean other aliens? Like in flying saucers?"

"Correct. The Pleidians are particularly active at the present time, and they still travel in ships. However, our allies bear no resemblance to the Neboki. Our ancient transgressions against the people of this planet have caused much of the suffering and pain through history. Our coalition seeks to right the wrongs of long ago. The only goal is to guide the people back toward their rightful path."

"Have you done this before? Awakened other people?"

"Many times. You see, it's difficult for us to tune down to your level and retain memory and perspective. Joe and I are part of a group specially trained for this purpose. But as your planet progresses and its frequency increases, more of us will be able to enter."

"Why do you lose your memory?"

"We don't lose all of it, except the important part—the connection to the higher self—is obscured at lower dimensions. Since our job is to uplift your world, that connection is crucial. Loss of the higher link was the cause of the fall in the first place."

Kelly paused as two teenaged males approached, one carrying a blaring boom box. Both had shaven heads and the taller youth had a ring in his nose. She frowned at the nose ring and looked for Reese's reaction. He merely arched one brow. "What can I possibly do to raise the consciousness of people like that?" she asked.

"Just be."

"Be how?"

"Be yourself. Once you remember, you don't have to do anything. All beings are connected. One raised vibration uplifts all others, at least for a while. However, unless the entity withdraws or gets support, his vibratory rate will be pulled down by the mass consciousness. That's why I can only stay in your plane for a limited time. But when sufficient numbers awaken and establish contact, they can sustain the higher frequencies. This critical mass will feed back on itself and catapult humanity to a higher octave of existence."

"There are enough Starpeople here, now, to create this critical mass?"

"Correct. Once Starpeople awaken, truth will flow to them and they will understand the universe and their place in the grand scheme. Because minds are joined, their remembering will ripple through the mass consciousness. When enough of them recall the truth, science, medicine, philosophy, . . . everything will make an instantaneous leap to a higher dimension."

Kelly laced her fingers behind her head, thinking about what Reese had said. The sun hung just above the horizon, shafts of orange and rose light dancing across the waves. She breathed out and let the muscles in her neck relax. Another puff and her shoulders went slack.

The spark of her Sirian self? Then the lump, the black spot, the THING at the back of her mind began to stir.

Chapter 13

Men are disturbed not by things that happen,
but by their opinion of the things that happen.
                                              Epictetus

South Seas Plantation, Captiva, Florida
June 9, 8:03 P.M. EDT

Kelly checked her watch and saw it was a few minutes past eight. She was late. Cara answered on the third ring.

"Reese *is* an alien," Kelly said calmly, surprised by her own composure.

"What happened?" Cara demanded.

"He showed me his natural state—he's ethereal. And there's another one named Joe. He popped in from a waterspout."

"The guy materialized in front of everyone?"

"It was raining hard so no one else was around."

"Where are they now?"

"Joe only stayed long enough to prove the point. Reese and I talked for a couple of hours. He told me so much, I wish you'd been there. He had to leave because the pressure in this plane is too much; they can only stay for short periods."

"Reese vaporized? Got in a spaceship? What?"

"He went into the cypress lagoon, told me not to follow. I assume he whipped up another waterspout."

"You're amazingly calm, are you all right? You're not missing time, are you?"

"I'm fine." It was remarkable, especially considering how she'd fretted and cried most of the previous day. Once Kelly'd gotten over the shock of Reese's ghostly essence and Joe's fantastic entrance, she'd enjoyed the afternoon. For some unexplainable reason, Reese made her feel warm, peaceful, ... even loved.

"Don't keep me in suspense, what did he say?"

"I can't go into everything; it's consistent with Betty's experience."

"Uh, Betty ... she's missing," Cara said quietly.

"Missing?" Kelly shouted, her heart racing.

"None of her friends know where she is. But, she was extremely upset about being followed and could simply be hiding out."

"Has she been gone long?"

"All day. Apparently I was the last person to see her."

"You're being careful, aren't you?"

"Don't worry about me, I have eyes in the back of my head. Betty's probably fine—just out on a hot date. After all, this is Las Vegas. High rollers with money to burn—they fly to Europe for breakfast. Don't be concerned. So, what else did Reese say?"

Kelly looked around nervously, then recounted her conversation with Reese. "I've taken this life to compensate for my past mistakes."

"What are you supposed to do?" Cara asked.

"I don't know, but there are a lot of Starpeople down here. Since minds are joined, the mass consciousness increases as Starpeople awaken which, in turn, raises the vibrations and enables more Sirians to enter this plane."

"Mass landings?"

"He didn't say that."

"I wasn't talking about an invasion, simply that more aliens would arrive. People around here think ETs will be considered a fact, even commonplace, by the next decade," Cara said. "Did he say anything else about the awakening? Will there be earthquakes or tidal waves?"

"No, he merely said we'd transcend to another dimension."

"I hope I get to go," Cara said wistfully.

"Come on, you're the highest person I know. Of course you'll be a part of it—you are now by helping me. I wouldn't be doing this if I didn't have your support and encouragement."

"Yeah, well, remember your friends when you blast into orbit."

"Don't worry, I'll come by to pick you up."

"I'll be waiting."

"Be careful in the meantime."

▼▲▼

South Seas Plantation, Captiva, Florida
June 9, 8:21 P.M. EDT

Frank peered through a palm at the tall, leggy woman talking on the pay phone. She was the same woman he'd seen earlier in the day, hanging on the arm of an older man. He'd thought the two were mismatched.

Collins had been waiting anxiously when Frank returned from the refuge. A telephone call from a foreign operative had been traced to a guest at the resort. Fortunately, Collins had an old friend who managed the hotel. Retired military, the manager understood that national security took precedence over virtually anything, especially bureaucratic details like court orders, and obligingly provided the resort's file on K. A. Saunders.

Saunders wasn't a suspect, Collins had said. Although the major had been vague—lying through his teeth, if you asked Frank—the foreign agent was linked to subversive activities on the West Coast, and Saunders was their only lead. Frank was supposed to stake out the condo while Jake monitored the calls. Their assignment was to find the foreign operative, not harass the civilian.

Frank had followed Kelly to the restaurant. Fortunately he was able to get a table within earshot and overheard the waiter give directions to a pay phone next door. Frank had used his cellular phone to alert Jake, hoping he could intercept the call. It was almost eight-thirty, and she'd been talking for twenty minutes.

▼▲▼

South Seas Plantation, Captiva, Florida
June 9, 8:22 P.M. EDT

Collins hung up the phone and shoved a slip of paper in front of Jake: the telephone number for the pay phone at the marina. If Jake had been thinking ahead he'd have gotten the numbers for all the public telephones hours ago. Now they'd wasted more than ten minutes. Could he make the connection before K. A. Saunders finished the call? Jake punched in the number and waited.

"... I wouldn't be doing this if I didn't have your support and encouragement."

He had it. Jake twisted a dial to clear up static, then stopped, startled. The voice was familiar.

"Yeah, well, remember your friends when you blast into orbit."

"Don't worry, I'll come by to pick you up."

"I'll be waiting."

"Be careful in the meantime."

The line went dead. *Blast into orbit?* Aliens. Oh no, it was Kelly.

▼▲▼

South Seas Plantation, Captiva, Florida
June 9, 10:35 P.M. EDT

"You know her?" Frank asked Jake incredulously.

Frank had tailed Kelly back to the apartment and waited about an hour until the lights went off. He didn't think she knew he was following, so didn't expect her to try anything cute, like sneak out in the middle of the night. To be on the safe side, he'd planted a remote sensor on her door to alert him if she left. Frank had also taken the opportunity to bug the Mercedes that was parked under her house before returning to his condo. When he got there, the special investigation team assembled in the living room for a briefing.

"I met her on the beach, and we had dinner last night," Jake said.

Collins' face turned red. "You were screwing around on assignment!"

Jake folded his arms with disgust. "We weren't screwing around. You hadn't gotten here. I went to the beach for some sun, she was there and we struck up a conversation. I ran into her at Chadwick's last night. She was alone, I was alone, so we ate together. That's it. Period."

"You've compromised the project," Collins barked.

"Maybe not," Frank interjected, "the lady's not a suspect, right?"

Collins shook his head grudgingly.

"Then there's no problem. If Kelly is the accomplice for a foreign agent, her relationship with Jake may come in handy. What do you know about her, Jake?"

"Not much. She's an economist, does research for big corporations. Lives here in Florida, around Orlando, I think. Single. She has some flaky friends. One is a New Age type who lives in Las Vegas." Jake closed his eyes and massaged his forehead. "Cara," he finally said. "Her friend's name is Cara."

Frank noticed that Collins got a funny look when Jake mentioned Cara's name. "Is there something special about Las Vegas?" he asked.

Collins said Frank was imagining things and went to the kitchen for a soda. Frank didn't buy it for a second, but knew he wouldn't get Collins to reveal more. "Did you notice anything unusual about her?" Frank asked Jake.

"Yeah, now that you mention it. I saw Kelly on the beach this morning, she seemed troubled. She has a quirky friend who believes she's a reincarnated space person."

Collins returned from the kitchen, laughing derisively. "The bitch is a nut case."

Jake set his jaw. "She said her friend met a guy who claimed to be an extraterrestrial—from the Sirius star cluster, I think. Kelly wanted to know what I thought."

"What did you say?" Collins snickered.

"I told Kelly it was a hoax, and her friend should be careful."

"Do you think she was talking about herself? Used the friend thing as a cover?" Sally asked.

"In retrospect, yeah."

"She looks about thirty. Is she that naive?" Frank continued.

"She's just a New Age type. A lot of people believe in UFOs and psychic phenomena. That paranormal TV show is in the top ten every week. A fair-sized crowd is obviously watching and they're not all loony."

"Probably your favorite show." Collins sneered. Jake glared.

"I like the show," Sally said, giving Collins a taunting smirk. Then, to Jake, "Would Kelly believe a story like that? I might believe in UFOs, but I'd be skeptical if you suddenly piped up and told me you were from Mars."

"Kelly's not a fool—she'd want proof."

"Proof? Like what, a spaceship?" Collins asked.

Frank snorted. Reincarnated space people? This was too damned much. Jerky Johnson, his counterfeiter, was an idiot but these people made J. J. look sane. For all her intelligence, Sally watched those lame-brained paranormal shows. Jake either had a thing for Kelly—understandable, she was a good looking woman—or he was a paranormal sympathizer himself. Collins was just a jerk, military through and through.

"By the way, I saw her this afternoon when we were leaving the resort," Frank said offhandedly, figuring he'd give Collins a good tweak. "She was with an older man. Light hair, slight build."

"Yeah, Kelly and the man were sitting on the bench outside this window when we got home from the refuge," Jake added, picking up on Frank's cue.

Collins went to the window and peered out. "A foreign agent outside this condo?" Collins bounded up the stairs to the secured transmitter.

▼▲▼

HAIR Project, Alaska
June 9, 9:00 P.M. ADT

There was a four hour time difference between Alaska and the East Coast. General Brandt's call came in at 9:00 P.M. Alaska time, which meant someone had gotten him up in the middle of the night.

Brandt didn't sound happy. "There's a foreign operative on the ground in Florida, down by Fort Myers. Know anything about it?"

Houston pushed aside the report he'd been reading and rubbed his eyes. He wasn't surprised. The storms weren't popping up for nothing. Brandt knew that. "I hadn't heard, but it's consistent with the pattern. Do we have a sighting?"

"Human appearance. Short, slight build, light hair."

That was the usual description of the interdimensional intruders. "Contact?"

"The unidentified's talking to a woman, Kelly Saunders."

Houston wrote down her name. "Who has the details?"

"Agents on site. Major Travis Collins is the team leader, he made the report. Look, Stan, I want this stopped. Everyone's getting nervous."

Everyone's getting nervous? Houston had been anxious for a long time and had warned Brandt months ago. Now a bunch of rich fools were nervous and things were suddenly critical. Houston wished the aliens would swoosh in and zap a few of them—the world would be a better place.

"I want to capture one of the intruders. We need to know what they're up to," Houston said.

"That's fine, but we've got to put an end to it at once. The electric companies are starting to ask questions about the disruptions on the East Coast. It won't take them long to figure out that something stinks, and if they start talking to the guys in the Midwest, we'll have a royal mess."

The thought made Houston ill. So far no one had said much about the fireballs and lights popping up in the heartland. If anyone put two and two together, linking the fireballs and tornadoes, damage control would be damned near impossible. "I'll talk to Collins. We've got Blackhawks down there with electronic countermeasures and a modified AWACS. They might be able to destabilize the electromagnetics. If that doesn't work, we're ready to go here. The other facilities are on standby. Any word from the Russians? Their participation would sure help."

"We found a little money to prime the pump, and they're thinking about it."

"Anything you can do, sir. We don't have many more tricks in our bag."

Brandt cursed. "Dammit, I'll call them now. I'm wide awake."

Whether Brandt agreed or not, they needed to communicate with the aliens. Houston knew they were entering through the funnel clouds with most appearances in pairs spaced two-to-four hours apart. Simple, he thought. The intruders zipped into this dimension through the first storm and went back in the second. They apparently couldn't stay on the surface too long, probably an incompatibility with the atmosphere or something. So if Houston could blanket the area where a vortex appeared with electromagnetic static, he might prevent the second funnel from firming up and trap the alien on this plane. The satellites could pinpoint the storms. Aircraft could flood the region with electronic gibberish. If the planes didn't have enough power, then he'd unleash HAIR.

Houston called his aide at home and got him out of bed. "Have MacDill launch the aircraft after the first appearance of a funnel. We have to disrupt the second storm of each pair. Blackhawks first, AWACS as back-up. Also, track down Major Travis Collins. He heads a team somewhere around Fort Myers. Tell him to do whatever it takes to apprehend the foreign operative. And, no witnesses, no leaks. Got it?"

Chapter 14

When one realizes one is asleep,
at that moment one is already half-awake.
P.D. Ouspensky & G.I. Gurdjieff

South Seas Plantation, Captiva, Florida
June 10, 3:00 A.M. EDT

It was the same dream she'd had over and over since child-hood. Kelly saw herself sitting in a classroom. The desk was similar to the ones in college, only made of a warm, transparent material. The room was huge with massive columns supporting a vaulted roof. An affable-looking guy with reddish blond hair and a gap between his front teeth sat next to her. An ancient man paced at the front of the room, lecturing in deep, resonant tones.

"No one knows anything, and yet they know everything," the teacher boomed. "Your goal is to expand awareness: to put a crack in the concrete definiteness with which Earth beings regard their perceptions.

"Is there another way to see? Yes, and it will usher in further development. The point is that thoughts are real and create reality as you know it. The universe is transformed by a change in thought or belief. This is not fearful, but exciting. To release a mind is the ultimate accomplishment. Freedom allows the mind's natural abilities to manifest.

"The ego restricts the inherent power of thought. Its limits impose form on the formless. Yet the form will change instantly as the confining thoughts are relinquished. You can change your world by changing your beliefs to good ones, thus forcing a beneficent structure on thought."

Kelly saw herself nod and somehow knew it made perfect sense. Her carrot-haired neighbor agreed, too. A holographic map of the Earth appeared next to the instructor, glowing gridlines crisscrossing its surface.

Her classmate leaned closer. "That's our mission. We must enliven the grid so the others may come." Kelly watched her head bob up and down.

A loud thump sounded, and Kelly bolted upright in bed, wide awake. Two eyes stared at her from the window. The gap-toothed redhead, she thought. They had to fix the grid.

She squinted and the window gradually came into focus. The eyes staring back were small, black, and close together. It wasn't her friend. She clutched the blanket to her chest. The eyes moved— A raccoon lunged from the window to the porch railing, landing with a thud.

Kelly sank into the pillow panting. *She could remember the dream!*

Kelly ran into Reese as soon as she stepped out of the condo. Six o'clock, the sun was barely up. She'd planned to get a newspaper and go to the beach to read it; but, Reese had other ideas. "Come," he said, leading her onto a trolley. He didn't speak again until they'd settled on a bench overlooking the marina.

"Something's troubling you," he observed.

Kelly looked out across the dock. So much had happened in three days. Where should she start? "From childhood I've had a recurring dream and until last night, could never remember much about it. This time I saw a system of gridlines covering the Earth. My mission is to energize them."

Reese patted her knee. "Your memory is returning."

"Ever since I met you I've felt a lump, or … something in my mind. It was scary, almost painful. This morning it doesn't hurt so much."

"The pain will grow less and less as you allow yourself to remember."

"The teacher in my dream said a changed thought could change the world."

"That is true."

"I've always supported that position—it's a common premise of the self-help movement. Yet I don't think I ever understood it or truly believed it. The teacher said good thoughts would *force* benefic forms on the world."

Reese nodded. "That is no different from the dismal framework you and your people project now. Good thoughts are as much of an illusion as the depressing ones, though less painful. True thought has no limits. It is perfectly fluid, yet stable in its pliancy. And that completely fluid/stable state is peace. There is no need to resist or change anything because it is perfect.

"Judgments are the limits you impose on thought. Withdraw the judgment and thought flows freely, expanding everywhere through all time."

"Judgments? You mean that things are good or bad, right or wrong?"

Reese shook his head. "It's broader than that. Every opinion you hold or label you put on anything limits reality. All thought systems—Christianity, Judaism, communism, capitalism, astrology, whatever—mark off boundaries and thus give rise to form. In actuality, thought or love needs no containment.

"You adopt limits because you are afraid of everything. You shrink from everything believing it to be nothing, nothing in the sense of form. You think you would be lost in such a formless state. It is only your specialness, your unique identity, which is threatened, and for most people that is the most terrifying fate of all."

"Can you blame us?" she asked sarcastically. "A body is all that we know. Is it so hard to understand why people might cling to it?"

A heron stalked over, stopping next to Reese. He reached out and the bird stared quizzically. Looking from Kelly to Reese, the heron inched closer, finally rubbing its head against Reese's outstretched hand.

Reese looked up at Kelly, grinning. "See? Trust."

"Trust? He's looking for food. That old guy is awfully tame; he's undoubtedly been around tourists for a long time."

"Correct, but at some point he took a risk. He put his fear behind him long enough to take food from the first human."

"That trust might bite him in the butt one day. He'll innocently approach a hunter, then what? Bam. Right between the eyes."

Reese shrugged. "The bird is shot, what difference does it make?"

"Difference?" Her face twisted in horror. "He's dead."

"Is he?"

"You're changing the subject. Look, I know that higher power, otherworldly, New Age stuff. I would have agreed with you last week. Today? The bird would be dead. That's it. I'd like to think there's more to it, but—"

Kelly walked to the end of the dock and leaned against a piling. Nothing made sense. She'd been handed the dream of a lifetime: confirmation of life beyond Earth, existence beyond death. She'd found the purpose she'd always sought, and yet she resisted it all. Why? She wasn't sure.

"Where is your identity? It is everywhere and nowhere," Reese answered the question himself. "How can I help you remember this? What would make you accept the truth?"

"How about a flash of enlightenment? It seems to work for the mystics and gurus."

"Enlightenment is here now, as it has always been. Open your mind—"

"I don't know how." Kelly spat the words and was immediately sorry. She was acting like a child. This man was trying to help her, she believed that. He deserved gratitude not anger. "Reese—," she started to apologize, then realized he was looking at something else. She followed his gaze and squinted, finally making out a helicopter approaching from the north. Painted a flat black, the aircraft flew low, the rumble growing louder as it drew nearer.

Reese took her arm and did an about-face. The helicopter passed directly overhead. "My time is limited."

"It's only a helicopter."

He waved off her remark. "I must go soon." He led her through the marina to a narrow strip of beach at Redfish Pass. "As I was saying, your fear of nothingness and loss binds you to forms you hate but are afraid to relinquish. Little by little you need to release the constraints you impose on the world. Replace them with other limits, perhaps; that is acceptable as long as the boundaries expand. If you do this consistently, you can loosen the fear and increase your willingness to accept more. When the boundaries are finally so broad you don't see them, then they can be relinquished with no loss or pain of any kind."

"What do I do?"

"The first step is to examine the limiting beliefs you impose on yourself. Expand each boundary, one by one. Determine to replace those thoughts with expansive, joyous ideas. The world of form will begin to change and as it does, you will be anxious to transform more of your thinking. So, what are your limits? Why does my message cause such fear?"

She hung her head and sighed. "You said it before; I'm afraid to lose my identity, my specialness. If I accept what you say, it's almost like dying. You say the truth entails no loss, but I don't feel that."

Reese stroked her cheek tenderly. "The notion of bodies is preposterous. A body—flesh—is but a thought defining or cutting off one little piece of space for yourself. In truth, all of space—everything—belongs to you. Why would you want to separate off one tiny portion for yourself?

"For once you separate off that space, you have to defend it to keep it special and that defense creates a wall in the fabric of consciousness, a barrier to its flow. Cut off from the nourishment of the whole—the true source—everyone feels deprived and hungry. In your defense, *they* perceive attack. Thus *they* are justified in defending/attacking back. That is the sick cycle, the vicious circle, in which Earth has become trapped. To rescue the planet from that meaningless dynamic is the reason you and the other Starpeople have returned."

He'd hit home again. Attack, defend, attack, defend; Kelly knew the cycle well. As a consultant for corporate litigation, that tactic was her bread and butter. Yet it had always troubled her. The victories were empty, and there was no fun in the game. Now she understood why. Guilt flooded through her. She'd been part of the very problem she'd come to correct. She thought of the comic strip Pogo. "'We have met the enemy and he is us,'" she murmured.

Reese picked up the pace. "Errors are mistakes, not sins, and mistakes can be corrected. The answers to all of your questions are available now. At the moment the ancient Starpeople began their descent, so did our leaders take steps to bring them back home. From that time forward, a message has been beamed at this planet. It plays continuously in a frequency band slightly higher than your own and proclaims the truth; the truth about yourself, this planet, the universe, everything. You can access that message if you relax and listen."

"Is that what I feel in my mind? The lump?"

"Correct. Everyone can access the transmission, but you and the other Starpeople have enhanced receptors. This trait was supposed to ensure your connection to the truth and the fulfillment of your purpose. However, you and your comrades were endowed with strong wills, too; so strong that some of you have suppressed the link to truth."

"The thing in my mind is a *will-encased receptor*?"

"That's one way of looking at it."

"It feels like a tumor."

Reese chuckled. "I'm not surprised. It has taken an amazing force of will to hold off the transmission, especially now, when we have increased the volume to the point that the average Earther can almost hear it."

Kelly grinned sheepishly. "Why have I gone to such lengths to hide from myself?"

"Misplaced empathy. In your desire to serve you have over-identified with the inhabitants of this plane. Yet, you have done them and yourself a disservice, for it is impossible to uplift from an equal footing. You must disengage enough to center on the truth before choosing a course of action. And the best plan from a universal standpoint would probably surprise you. True empathy is not to join someone in suffering, but to show them that their pain is merely an illusion."

Kelly waved emphatically. "That's where you lose me. Pain is everywhere. All a person has to do is turn on the television and they're inundated with wars, disease, murder, rape, … the list is endless. That pain is real."

"It is real, if you believe it's so."

She glared. "Don't say it: You create your own reality. Sure. And the bird isn't dead if you shoot him in the head? This is too much. I don't think I'm up to the task."

"Your mission is crucial to all of our futures."

She felt a stabbing pain at the back of her head. "Crap." She bit her lip and looked away.

▼▲▼

Charlotte, North Carolina
June 10, 6:00 A.M. EDT

Atlantergy's control room was a technological marvel. Glass-walled conference rooms lined the back of the operations center with computer consoles arranged in rows down the sloping floor. A gigantic electronic display of the East Coast's electric system covered one wall. Every electric plant, transmission line, and substation were continuously monitored by the glowing display. Like the control room for a NASA shuttle launch, the place conferred a feeling of excitement even when nothing was going on.

Allison had come to work at five-thirty. She'd tossed and turned most of the night, worried about Neal. If the government were truly behind the strange weather formations, he might be in danger. She hoped he'd think twice before doing anything rash.

She studied the numbers scrolling across the computer screen and tried to put Neal out of her mind. Her job would demand her full attention that day. The nuclear plant in Georgia was still out of service, two coal plants in the Midwest had gone down, and environmental restrictions had kicked in for the Northeast, meaning they couldn't run some oil-fired units. Short on generation at the very time they needed it the most. It was going to be hot, with record-breaking temperatures.

"Aren't you the dedicated employee," Massoud said as he leaned on the top of her terminal.

She grinned at the Jordanian engineer who'd recently been promoted to supervisor. "Couldn't sleep. Neal's away on assignment. I figured I might as well come in and get ready for the chase. They say the whole Southeast will top a hundred today."

Massoud pulled a chair over and straddled it. "I know. Pray we don't have a bunch of those strange storms. With everything running flat out, we won't have flexibility. If we can get through the day with only a brownout or two, I'll be happy."

"No new information on the anomalies?"

"The EPRA group is here." Massoud pointed toward one of the conference rooms. "They have lots of theories, but few facts."

"Any incidents last night?"

"Florida panhandle, one in Virginia, and Fort Myers again."

"Fort Myers?" she echoed, thinking of Neal.

"By an island off the coast. A small tornado was detected early this morning."

"Damage?"

"Didn't cause any electric problems, but it was sighted by a field crew. I'd say that's a bad omen—it isn't even hot yet."

Allison looked at the diagram of lights on the front wall. The transmission lines crisscrossed the outline of the southeastern states. They all glowed white, indicating operations within established parameters. In the event of severe voltage swings, the colors changed to yellow. Red meant that circuit breakers had severed the line or plant from the system. Luckily she didn't see much red. The nuclear plant in Georgia glowed crimson as did a handful of small plants in Ohio and Virginia; otherwise everything was white and yellow.

"Ever seen a cascading blackout?" Allison asked.

"I was around during the cold snap in the early nineties. The grid was on the verge of going, but we held it together. Florida had rolling blackouts. It would take a helluva shock to cascade today with all the new technology."

"But it could happen." Allison knew the loss of a big line could cause a voltage swing that trips a circuit breaker, which causes another circuit to crash, and so on until the outage ripples through the whole system.

"Sure," Massoud agreed slowly. "A disruption in our microwave communications could cause it, or a nuclear blast, or—"

"Stop," Allison said, waving her hands. "We've got enough problems without nuclear wars."

Massoud motioned toward the conference rooms. "You're right. They can't handle a few thunderstorms."

Chapter 15

South Seas Plantation, Captiva, Florida
June 10, 6:05 A.M. EDT

Frank was checking his gun and getting ready to leave when the remote sensor sounded. Kelly had left the apartment. He stuffed the small caliber weapon in the pocket of his windbreaker and grabbed a cellular phone. It was a little after six. Jake said he'd seen Kelly at eight the previous morning. Frank raced out the door and down a foliage-lined path. He figured she was going to the beach since she'd told Jake she meditated there every morning.

Frank jogged up the path and across the street to Kelly's unit. Lights were on inside, and the Mercedes hadn't been moved. Maybe she'd stepped out to get a newspaper. He looked around the backyard and sat down by the Jacuzzi. A few minutes later his phone started vibrating.

It was Collins. "Just got word. Apprehend the unidentified. Top priority."

"I may have lost the girl."

"What?"

"She left, or at least opened the front door, before I got here."

"Damn."

"Look, I can't hang around long without arousing suspicion. Like I said last night, we need to get into one of these units.

There aren't any lights in the one next door. Have you called your friend, the manager?"

"I'll take care of it."

"We need to find out if she's left."

"I'll send Jake with WIMP. If she's in there, he can hear her breathe."

Collins hung up. Frank stretched out in the chair and pretended to be asleep.

▼▲▼

Sanibel, Florida
June 10, 7:15 A.M. EDT

Neal ate a sausage and egg biscuit as he headed toward the Darling refuge. He'd decided to get an early start because the day was going to be a scorcher—upper nineties, hot even for Florida.

He figured he'd scout around the reserve, talk to Steve again, perhaps take him to lunch. Steve might be more forthcoming if Neal could get him off the property. Neal planned to do phone work at the condo during the afternoon when it was hottest. He'd check the hotels to see if he could locate Sally Carter, the scientist from Stanford University. He also needed background on the AWACS and Blackhawk helicopter. He thought he might find it on the Internet; otherwise, he had a few contacts at the Air Force.

Steve was pulling out of the visitors' center when Neal arrived. The ranger seemed to be in a hurry. Neal decided to follow, lagging back far enough to avoid the dust trail spewing from Steve's Jeep. There was no chance of losing him, since a narrow one-way road was the only route through the refuge. Steve pulled off a half mile later. Neal left his car at the intersection and followed the rest of the way on foot. The Jeep was parked next to a Fort Myers Electric truck. Steve was talking to a group of men outside a chain link fence which enclosed an electric box and several meters. Neal stood by the Jeep, listening.

"Rom Chavez," a tall Latin said, offering his hand to Steve. "Electric Power Research Association. We came in from California to check out the power problems. We're going to insert a special sensor."

Steve unlocked the gate and the men crowded into the enclosure. "The Feds were here yesterday, installed experimental equipment," he said.

Chavez examined a small device connected to the junction box. "An electromagnetic monitor," he said, obviously surprised. "That's what we're going to install. What agency put this in? Department of Energy? NOAA?"

Steve shrugged. "I can't say."

"Don't know or not talking?"

"A little of both. The park superintendent spoke to them, told me to keep it quiet."

"Where's the superintendent now?"

"At the dentist. He'll be in after lunch."

As they talked, one of Chavez' men examined the equipment, consulting a hand-held meter. "The sensor has a transmitter. Someone's getting these readings real time. We'll have to disconnect this unit for a couple of minutes to hook ours in."

Chavez frowned and turned toward a stocky man. "Your call, Bill."

"Technically, that junction box belongs to Fort Myers Electric. We should have been informed of any modifications."

Steve glared. "You're picking the fly shit out of the pepper."

Bill crossed his arms defensively. "That's our box, and we can hook in anything we want. This other sensor is unauthorized, maybe *it's* causing the problems."

"It was positioned yesterday afternoon, the outages have been going on longer than that," Steve said.

"Doesn't matter. We've got every right to insert our own monitors." Bill signaled the man with the meter. "Disconnect it."

Neal scribbled in his notebook. An electromagnetic monitor, installed by an unknown federal agency, transmitting data, and these guys were going to cut the cord. What a break. Neal couldn't wait to see who showed up next.

▼▲▼

South Seas Plantation, Captiva, Florida
June 10, 7:45 A.M. EDT

WIMP was parked in front of Kelly's unit, next to the Interval Management Office. As long as it didn't stay there too long, no one would be the wiser. After all, it could pass for a delivery truck or construction vehicle. Collins' contact promised to get them in the vacant unit next to Kelly's condo by afternoon.

Jake and Sally stayed behind to watch the unit while Frank searched the resort for Kelly. It had only taken Jake a few seconds to determine that Kelly was indeed gone. No sounds, no movement, nothing came from the condo. Even a person sleeping made some noise, and WIMP could pick it up.

"The sensor at the refuge just went dead," Sally said, hastily entering codes into her keyboard.

"Bump the frequency; maybe it's the transmitter," Jake suggested.

"I tried that—the thing is dead."

"The connection should have held unless someone messed with it."

"That area is a hot bed of activity, the data is crucial," Sally said.

"I can't leave. Do you know anything about wiring?"

"I've done simple stuff."

"You can fix a loose connection. Use the Caravan and take a cellular phone. I'll talk you through it."

Checking first to see that no one was around, Sally hopped down from the back of the truck. Then, in best tourist fashion, she sauntered across the street as if she didn't have a care in the world.

▼▲▼

Ding Darling Refuge, Sanibel, Florida
June 10, 9:00 A.M. EDT

Neal waited for the electric utility representatives to leave before approaching Steve. They never asked who Neal was and he never told them. The men had hooked in their equipment, reconnected the *unauthorized* device, then left. The whole process took less than forty minutes. Chavez was apologetic, obviously disturbed by the controversy. Bill, the electric employee, remained sullen and defensive to the end. Steve locked the gate and walked toward Neal looking grim.

"Nice guy," Neal said.

"I wanted to tell that nerd off, but couldn't. My wife works for the utility."

"Allison runs into her share of them, too."

Steve got into his Jeep. Neal couldn't let him get away. "I don't suppose you can tell me anything about the other meter?"

"Sorry. There was another waterspout after you left yesterday. Did you see it?" Neal shook his head. "A shame— it was a big one. That unauthorized monitor was installed shortly before the funnel appeared. Queer coincidence, don't you think?"

It made sense if government experiments were behind the weather anomalies. Install a monitor, test the system. "Did you see any aircraft?" Neal probed.

"Nope." Steve put the Jeep into gear; obviously, he was not going to talk.

"How about lunch?"

"Can't. My boss is out for the morning."

"Mind if I hang around in case someone shows up to check the sensors?"

Steve said "Suit yourself" and drove away.

Neal walked back to his car, figuring he'd move it to the access road. That way he could keep an eye on the throughway and enclosure at the same time.

An automobile approached and Neal flattened himself against the side of his Toyota. A blue Mitsubishi driven by a black man sped by. The same guy he'd seen at the observation tower the previous day. Coming to meet his weird friend? Neal wondered as he pulled his car around the corner and parked.

Waiting was the worst part of his job, and the temperature was already starting to climb. Neal typed his notes into the computer and wrote several leads for a story until the battery light on the laptop flickered, warning him to stop. Gawd, it was hot, he thought, as he laid the electronic notebook on the floor of the back seat. A hot breeze had started blowing, yet it did nothing to cool him. If anything, it made him sweat more.

Neal wished he'd brought along something to drink. There was a vending machine at the reception center, but he didn't dare leave. The G-men might arrive any minute, and this could be the break he needed. He checked his watch as a fat raindrop splashed on the windshield. The utility people had been gone for over forty-five minutes. Was anybody going to come?

A few minutes later, a white Dodge Caravan rounded the corner with Steve following in his Jeep. Neal grabbed a pad of paper and hurried to the fenced enclosure. He got there just as a woman got out of the van. He raced toward her, hand extended. "Neal Winters, pleased to meet you."

The woman was startled. "Uh, Sally Carter," she replied.

Now Neal was surprised. Flabbergasted. He'd just been reviewing his notes about her. Physics, Stanford University.

She was the scientist Dr. Rourke had mentioned, the one who'd told him about the flashes over thunderstorms in the Midwest. Her graduate assistant said Sally was working on a project for the Air Force. Air Force—Blackhawk helicopters, AWACS—it was all coming together.

Steve frowned at Neal as he unlocked the gate. Neal grinned apologetically and backed away.

"It should be working now," Steve said to Sally. "The utility had to pull the plug to install their own sensor. But, they hooked it back in."

Sally punched a number into her cellular phone. "Jake, I think the problem's been fixed. Check my console, would you?" She kept her eyes on Neal, who clasped his hands behind his back to hide the notebook. A big drop of rain hit him in the head.

"Good, I'll be back directly." Sally flipped the mouthpiece of the telephone shut.

Neal couldn't let her walk away, even if he had to tip his hand. "Dr. Carter, there have been a lot of electrical problems on the East Coast. A nuclear plant in Georgia was scrambled yesterday while a transmission line became unstable in Virginia. The electric system around here has had its share of problems, too, all accompanied by peculiar storms. Some scientists think that government experiments on the upper atmosphere are causing the problems. I believe you know one of them, Dr. Peter Rourke, San Francisco Institute of Technology."

Steve's eyes grew wide and Sally gaped. "Who are you with?" she demanded.

"The *Charlotte Sentinel*."

"No comment," she said tersely, turning toward the van.

The rain fell steadily and the wind picked up. Neal felt desperate. "I talked to your office at Stanford. I know you're working on a project for the Air Force."

"No comment."

The wind gusted and they had to struggle to keep their footing. Steve searched the sky. "Take cover," he yelled.

For a brief moment everyone froze. Steve had arrived in a Jeep with its top down, Neal's car was fifty yards away. Sally hesitated, looking from the men to the sky. "Into the van," she finally shouted. A sheet of rain hit the vehicle and a turbulent blast rocked the truck like a child's toy. Sally started the van.

"What are you doing?" Steve shouted.

She slapped the gear into reverse. "I want to see what's happening."

"It's a waterspout, I'm sure," Steve said.

Sally flipped on the headlights and turned down the main road. It was getting darker and darker as dense clouds churned overhead. The rain swirled, making it difficult to see. Bouncing through potholes and swaying in the wind, they drove toward the center of the storm, when Sally suddenly slammed on brakes.

Lightning flashed and a funnel touched down a hundred yards ahead. It kissed the ground once, twice, and a third time; hopping like a pogo stick across the clearing. A massive streak of jagged fire hit a tree nearby, splitting it in two. Then another thunderous boom and the tornado disappeared.

Sally was draped over the steering wheel, shaken. Neal had crawled between the bucket seats, straining to see. Only Steve was reasonably calm. "That's the way it usually happens," he said matter-of-factly.

"Amazing," Neal allowed as he wiggled out from between the seats.

"Look," Sally cried, pointing at red lights in the distance.

"Tail lights of a car," Steve said.

They had to go forward in order to get back to the enclosure; the road through the refuge was a one-way loop. Neal debated whether he should try to question Sally further. He probably owed his life to her; nonetheless, he had her cornered, and a chance like this might never come again.

"The Air Force created that storm, didn't they?"

Sally gripped the steering wheel and ignored him. Steve gave Neal a disgusted look.

"How did they do it? Was it the aircraft or the installation in Alaska—uh, HAIR?"

Sally set her jaw and pressed the accelerator. Barely slowing when she reached the highway, the van skidded onto the pavement. "No comment."

"Back off, Neal," Steve said sternly. "The lady doesn't want to talk, leave her alone."

"What's the big deal—unless she has something to hide?"

"Let it rest." Steve's tone said he meant business.

Neal started to reply but thought better of it. He needed Steve as a collaborating witness and couldn't afford to alienate him. Neal folded his arms with resignation. There was nothing he could do. He sat in pained silence for the rest of the trip— all the while cheering and lamenting the remarkable turn of events.

Chapter 16

To every thing there is a season,
and a time to every purpose under the heaven.
                                        Ecclesiastes 3:1

South Seas Plantation, Captiva, Florida
June 10, 10:00 A.M. EDT

The world?" Reese repeated. "Everything you see is an illusion. Mankind's thoughts impose the form.

"You are right, there *are* cycles of thought and the mass consciousness is changing. The disillusionment with authority and power structures is actually quite healthy since it encourages individuals to look within, where the answers truly lie."

He stooped to stroke one of his ever present avian companions. "The world is weary of being a victim and there is a movement to reclaim the power of the individual. This takes many forms such as democracy and doctrines which advocate reliance on self as opposed to experts and institutions. The swing toward self-reliance is somewhat isolating, but will not last very long. From this position of personal strength, people will come together willingly to cooperate. The difference is voluntary cooperation as opposed to authority imposed from without. Individual empowerment will lead to true equality. The next age will be the era of enlightened self-interest, however, before that can happen, the scarcity belief must be eliminated," he said.

"Scarcity is the cornerstone of my profession. I'm an economist. Do you know what that means?" Kelly asked.

"I believe so. Interesting coincidence, don't you think?"

"In what way?"

"You've come to uplift the planet; the scarcity myth is a major obstacle to this world's progress; and you're an economist. Convenient."

Kelly frowned. Every time she thought she was beginning to understand, Reese threw her a curve ball. "I think I'm here to energize a grid."

"Yes, the ley lines, though your mission may be broader than that."

"You think I'm supposed to do work on the scarcity problem, too?"

"It would make sense given your experience on this plane."

"What exactly is the dilemma?"

"The world is thought made manifest. However, thought is unlimited, so scarcity does not exist. Therefore, the belief in limits creates scarcity."

Her mental circuits were starting to overload again. "At one level I understand what you're saying, but I can tell you that most people on this planet, including myself, think that resources are limited. There is only so much coal, or oil, or … or food. That's scarcity. Everybody can't have everything, because there isn't enough to go around."

"There isn't?"

She buried her head in her hands, exasperated. She knew where he was going—*thought is unlimited*—yet there, at that moment, she couldn't fathom how to turn ideas into food or clothing. "You'd better explain it to me."

"Do you believe that matter, each element, is nothing more than a particular array of energy frequencies?"

They'd talked about that the other day. Physics, quantum mechanics, Einstein. "Sure."

"What if there were a limitless supply of energy? In theory, you would be able to create all the matter you wanted."

"First, you'd have to have the know-how and, besides, there isn't an unlimited energy source." Reese stared at her. A vision of the globe and the glowing energy grid popped into her mind. "The grid in my dream, the ley lines; is that what you're talking about?"

"Correct." A man with fishing gear approached, and Reese guided her back toward the marina, an entourage of birds trailing after them. "What would happen if there were unlimited quantities of everything?"

"We wouldn't have money—it's solely a gimmick invented to distribute goods. Without a need for rationing, there'd be no justification for currency. Social classes as we know them would disappear, because everyone would be economically equal. Greed would be eliminated since it arises from scarcity and the necessity for hoarding things . . . ." It was hard for Kelly to imagine a world without work and struggle.

Reese took up where she left off. "Until now mankind has functioned only slightly better than animals, primarily intent on survival. Survival guaranteed, men would be free to pursue activities that bring pleasure. Without scarcity, most would discover that true happiness comes from doing for others. Can you imagine the taste of food prepared by cooks who find pleasure in the process? Or the quality of workmanship in goods made by people who do it for joy and not coercion? You'll find out in the future."

A lovely vision. Kelly hoped she lived to see it. "The grid will provide an unlimited energy source?"

"It was the source of everything in ancient times. Energy, information, communication all traveled through the grid. The ley lines are your link to other realms and possibilities. It must be repaired before the next age can begin."

"What exactly is this grid? Is it a power field? Is there a big generator somewhere?"

"It is the web of thought, or belief, that created this world."

"A mind field?" Kelly quipped, grinning.

Reese didn't catch the humor. "All matter arises from energy directed by thought or intelligence. A belief precedes everything. The ley lines are this planet's psychic skeleton, the perfect thought that created this world. It is this planet's connection to us, truth, and higher realms.

"The grid no longer functions as a unified system. Some sections have been destroyed by man's technological assaults, other parts weakened by disuse and the discordant state of human affairs. The ley grid is the structure which keeps this world intact and in harmony with the universe. If the grid is not repaired soon, the planet will dematerialize. Signs of instability are already showing, much as they did in ancient times, in Atlantis. The warnings must be heeded or life on this planet will not continue."

"You mean the world will fly apart?"

"Correct."

She was taken aback by his response; it sounded so cold and distant. "All the people will be killed?" she demanded as they threaded along the marina's boardwalk, the retinue of birds in tow.

"No one or nothing ever dies; the living essence is indestructible. However, existence as you know it, in those bodies, will cease to be. This avenue for learning will be closed off forever."

"That's the critical juncture: mankind either moves on now or goes into oblivion?"

Reese regarded her tenderly. "That is the choice. The rest of the universe will wait no longer. Some of this planet's caretakers are already withdrawing, convinced that humans are incapable of change."

"Our caretakers?"

"Indigenous people—tribes—who never lost the ancient teachings. Such pockets of sanity have been scattered throughout the planet; their efforts have maintained the ley lines to this point. Yet mankind's assaults on them, each other, and the planet have become overwhelming. Many of the ancient, wise ones have decided to leave, believing the human experiment to be a failure."

Fear flooded through her, and she bit her lip to keep it from quivering. The end of the world, Armageddon, and she was supposed to keep it from happening. "How can we fix the energy grid?"

"It is your mission; you have the knowledge." Reese picked up the pace, the birds half-flying to keep up. He led her across the golf course and into a stand of trees next to a shuttered house. "It is time for me to go. My part is finished."

Her stomach wrenched. There was so much more she needed to know. "You can't leave—I don't know what to do," she said, struggling for self-control.

"You must take the next step yourself. Clear your mind. Listen. The answers will come. The message is there; it plays continuously."

"Will I ever see you again?"

"Certainly, if not here, there—on the other side."

Reese pulled away and stepped into the clearing behind the vacant house. Kelly watched from the trees, hugging her sides. Reese looked up into the sky, as he'd done on the beach the previous day. Puffy white clouds streamed together and started to swirl. Like sudsy water going down a drain, the vapor coalesced, growing thicker and darker until the outline of an angry funnel formed. Rain started to fall and Kelly was glad she was standing under the trees. Reese seemed oblivious to the downpour, arms folded across his chest, face raised to the heavens.

He breathed deeply and deliberately as if trying to suck the clouds into his lungs. A low rumble sounded in the distance.

Pu-lop, pu-lop, pu-lop—guttural whoops came from all directions, the ground reverberating from the percussion. Reese's eyes flew open. Two black helicopters emerged from the tree tops.

▼▲▼

South Seas Plantation, Captiva, Florida
June 10, 10:55 A.M. EDT

Frank had been up and down the beach twice. If Kelly and a foreigner were on the grounds, he sure couldn't find them. He'd checked out the restaurant, the golf course, water sports rentals, and the beach; the lady was nowhere to be found. And it was getting hot. Although he'd unzipped the windbreaker and shed his shirt, he was sweltering. With a gun in one pocket and cellular phone in the other, he had to keep on the jacket so he could get to the weapon quickly. He was heading across the golf course toward the marina when his telephone began to vibrate. It was Sally.

"Pressure's dropping, and we have an EM surge. See anything?"

He glanced at the sky. Storm clouds streamed in from the east. "A torrent's brewing at the bayou, over the seventh hole. I'll check it out."

"Whoa," Jake cut in. "Electronics—" The line went dead.

Frank ran past the clubhouse and into the street. He heard a low rumble—aircraft, a helicopter—then a loud bang. Sparks cascaded from a utility box next to the restaurant. Frank stopped dead; it was eerily quiet. Then he realized why. The air conditioners had all stopped, the resort was blacked out.

▼▲▼

South Seas Plantation, Captiva, Florida
June 10, 11:10 A.M. EDT

Kelly raced along the water's edge, heart pumping as if she were pursued by demons. Tearing through backyards, she jumped over flower beds and squeezed through hedges. Her condo was only a few hundred yards away. She'd left Reese at the vacant house, weak and disoriented. He'd stayed too long, and it was her fault. If she hadn't been thick-headed, he'd have left long ago, now they were after him. She had to get him out of the resort.

Reese said he needed to go to the park, the park on the other island, along the water. She couldn't imagine what he was talking about. One thing was certain: he couldn't stay there; the helicopters weren't spraying for mosquitoes. Kelly squeezed through a thick stand of oleanders and stumbled into the backyard of the condo complex. Her Mercedes was parked under the building. Thank God, she had the keys. The message light on her cellular phone blinked as she started the car. Kelly punched in the code to retrieve the message.

Cara's voice filled the car. "Betty's dead."

▼▲▼

South Seas Plantation, Captiva, Florida
June 10, 11:15 A.M. EDT

Jake saw the Mercedes from the corner of his eye as it turned onto the street. "Crap, where did she come from?" He tried to follow, but a trolley discharging passengers blocked his way. Jake strained to keep the car in sight as it rounded a corner and disappeared.

"Damn it," Collins cussed, pounding the dash. "Can't y'all do anything right? Can you clear communications, Sally?"

"Nothing. All we're getting is noise."

The trolley moved and Jake pulled in after it and inched down the road. People were everywhere—in the parking lots,

on the sidewalks, in the middle of the street. If Jake didn't
know better, he'd think they'd gone through a black hole and
emerged at Mardi Gras. Something had happened, but what?
He searched driveways and parking lots for the Mercedes as
they crept along.

Frank suddenly appeared when they reached the marina.

"What happened?" Collins asked.

"A transformer blew," Frank replied.

"Our electronics are dead, too. Scrambled."

"I think I know why," Frank said. "Two Blackhawks just
flew over, the EH model."

"Are you certain?"

"Had so many antennas they looked like sea urchins. What
are you doing here?"

"Kelly got away."

"Not again," Frank shouted.

"She must have sneaked through the backyard. Got in her
car, came this way."

"She didn't pass me."

"Then we've gone too far," Collins said.

Frank stood on the curb and peered down the road. He
caught a glimpse of Kelly's car pulling out of a driveway about
fifty yards away. She was headed for the front gate. "There
she goes."

"With all these people, we'll never get turned around,"
Collins said. "We've got to split up. Sally, you go back to the
condo and try to clear up communications. Frank, go with
her and get the van."

"Any idea where she would go?" Frank asked Jake.

"You said a transformer blew?" Sally said pensively.

"Yeah, I saw it happen."

"The refuge. They've gone to the refuge." Sally told them
about the reporter, the electrical problems, and the whirlwind.

▼▲▼

Charlotte, North Carolina
June 10, 11:30 A.M. EDT

The best and brightest from the engineering departments had emerged from the glass-walled conference room two hours earlier. Perplexed by the outages, they didn't have a clue what to do. Although the evidence was far from conclusive, most of the engineers thought the problem originated in the atmosphere. Somehow the weather affected the microwave network that fed the mammoth display which dominated Atlantergy's operations center. Remote sensors monitored every line, transformer, generator, and substation. Thousands of electronic eyes and ears were trained on the electric system, measuring the pressure and watching the pulse of the insulated arteries that nourished the body of industry and commerce.

As a part of the company's speakers' bureau, Allison had used the analogy of the circulatory system in her talks to elementary schools. Electrons for blood cells and voltage instead of blood pressure, it made sense to the kids. As she watched the monitors climb, the comparison seemed particularly apropos, except now the patient was sick.

With a few strokes on the keyboard, Allison brought up a weather map on the terminal. A real time link to the National Weather Service, she saw scattered patches of green along the South Carolina coast—isolated thunderstorms. Nothing to worry about, merely sea breeze showers. Another command gave her temperature and humidity readings for their service territory. Humidity was in the nineties and temperatures had risen five degrees in the last hour. Air conditioners were humming everywhere. She glanced at a digital gauge at the top of the system display. The demand for electricity had gone up by more than a thousand megawatts. The old record for electricity consumption would surely be broken that day.

Allison typed in the command for Florida. It wasn't part of the normal display because her company only served the

Panhandle. But the electric system was all tied together and a problem to the south could mean trouble for them—besides, Neal was there. Yellow and red dots blinked alongside Fort Myers.

"What do you have?" Massoud leaned over her shoulder.

"We're clear, but it's heating up in Florida. Violent weather on the Gulf Coast." She pointed at the colored splotches.

"Any news from Fort Myers Electric?" Massoud called over his shoulder.

"Minor outage on Captiva. Weather again."

"Show me the grid," Massoud instructed Allison. The background map changed to show the electric transmission system with the storms superimposed on top. Thin white lines snaked around the symbol for Fort Myers. "Two-thirties— probably nothing to worry about. Watch 'em." He moved to the next station.

She stared at the screen wondering about Neal. What was he doing?

▼▲▼

HAIR Project, Alaska
June 10, 7:50 A.M. ADT

Colonel Houston took a satisfied drag of a cigar and propped his feet on the ugly metal desk. His luck had finally taken a turn for the better. The Russians were going to cooperate, Coates was feeding them coordinates at that very minute. But the best news was that the Blackhawks had succeeded. They'd sealed the second funnel at Captiva; hit it hard, all frequencies, neutralizing the disturbance before the tornado had a chance to form. Houston had been worried, though. The interval between storms was longer than expected, six hours, the longest on record. The copters almost had to break off because of fuel. Of course, the AWACS could have taken over, it could be refueled in midair. But efficiency called for testing options in the order of cost and availability; that meant Blackhawk, AWACS, HAIR. No sense using a sledgehammer to squash a bug, the experts said.

Houston took another puff of the cigar and blew three swirling, misshapen smoke rings. Another vortex had appeared on Sanibel a couple of hours earlier. If the copters sealed the second of that pair as easily as the one on Captiva, he was home free. The aliens were stuck on *terra firma*, it was simply a matter of time before he got one.

Chapter 17

Learn to be silent.
Let your quiet mind listen and absorb.
                                        Pythagorus

Captiva, Florida
June 10, 11:45 A.M. EDT

The guard wasn't at his station when Kelly sped by; she wouldn't have stopped anyway. Reese slumped against the door, semiconscious and trembling. His body seemed to pulse and quiver, and she almost expected him to evaporate into thin air. It was all her fault. Why had she been so skeptical? He'd be long gone—off awakening another Starperson—someone more evolved, less pig-headed. Reese's face contorted grotesquely and he took a labored breath.

"Don't leave me, Reese."

"The park ..." he wheezed pathetically.

"What park?"

He closed his eyes and slumped forward. "Along the water. Listen. Trust yourself. Listen."

She could barely see through tears as she wound the car along the narrow road through Captiva. Betty was dead, and Reese was about to die. *Listen? Trust yourself?* She couldn't recall ever seeing a park, except perhaps at the elementary school. Surely, that couldn't be it.

The plop, plop of helicopters sounded overhead. The
bastards were after Reese. They'd torture him and dissect
him, like the government did in Roswell, New Mexico during
the 1940s. She hadn't believed the stories, ... but now? The
helicopters were real, military and clearly looking for something. She couldn't let them get Reese. She craned her neck
and watched them fly past, making a wide circle back toward
the resort.

▼▲▼

Ding Darling Refuge, Sanibel, Florida
June 10, 11:45 A.M. EDT

Neal was paying for a sandwich at the Island Quick Mart
when he heard the commotion. Not waiting for a bag, he scooped
up his lunch and ran into the parking lot. Two helicopters,
black and covered with antennas, flew over just above the
tree line. He threw his food in the car and tore off toward the
refuge. Steve was standing in the refuge's parking lot when
Neal arrived. He waved to the ranger.

"Power failure. Everything's out—even the telephones,"
Steve said.

"Has that happened before?"

"No. We've lost power many times; but never the phones."
Steve scrutinized the sky; clouds were starting to amass.

"I saw two funny-looking helicopters headed this way."

"Blackhawks. The lights went out immediately after they
passed."

"What is going on?"

"Damned if I know. But, the Air Force is up to something.
Ten bucks says a tornado is forming out by the observation
tower."

"I'm going to see." Neal raced across the parking lot, but
had to slam on brakes to avoid a Mercedes barreling down
the main road. A woman drove while the guy on the passenger
side appeared to be asleep. The gasping clamor of helicopters

sounded from the rear. Skimming the tree tops, the mean metal vultures were closing in fast. Unconsciously slowing at the sight of the aircraft, Neal stepped on it after they passed. He found the Mercedes parked next to the tower and saw an attractive brunette helping a man out of the car.

Neal parked down the street, grabbed his camera, and headed back to the parking area. For some reason Neal found the man vaguely familiar. "Need some help?" he called, approaching the woman.

"No, everything's fine."

"Your friend looks sick."

"He's an invalid. I brought him here for fresh air. He likes to feed the birds," the woman said.

Neal surveyed the churning clouds and heard the Blackhawks' rumble. "This isn't a good day for bird watching—a bad storm's brewing. If I were you, I'd get back in the car and go home."

Keeping a firm grip on the older man, she answered over her shoulder. "We won't be long—I hate to disappoint him. He's looked forward to this for days."

Feeding birds? Suddenly Neal recognized the man. It was the weirdo he'd seen the previous day at the observation tower. He'd been talking to a black guy, the same black Neal saw entering the park that morning. And, the man had seemed perfectly healthy yesterday. Was this some sort of trick? Was the old man setting up the lady for a perverted crime?

▼▲▼

HAIR Project, Alaska
June 10, 8:30 A.M. ADT

Houston chewed on the unlit cigar like a licorice stick. The boneheads in Florida had let the alien get away. How? How could experienced agents with sophisticated electronics lose someone when there was only one road in and out of the resort? Now the second vortex was forming over Sanibel. The Blackhawks had bombarded it with everything, but it wasn't working this time.

"Dispatch the AWACS," Houston growled at the young Air Force officer.

"It will disrupt electronics on the Blackhawks."

"Tell the idiots to get out of the way. And instruct Coates to get HAIR and the other facilities ready." The chewed end of the cigar came off in Houston's mouth and he continued to chomp the slimy mass. He spit the foul-tasting wad into a trash can and kicked the container against the wall. He had to have one. He had to have one of the new aliens. And by damned, he would get one.

▼▲▼

Charlotte, North Carolina
June 10, 12:30 PM EDT

People from all over the company stood at the back of Atlantergy's control center. The word had spread that an all-time peak would be set that day. A little past noon, the old peak demand for electricity had been exceeded by five percent. Most of the Southeast had already hit a hundred degrees and some forecasters were calling for temperatures as high as one hundred five degrees. All eyes watched the digital display ticking upward as more and more electrons coursed through the transmission system.

All eyes except Allison's, hers were glued to the display for Florida. The Sunshine State was sucking juice from Atlantergy as fast as they could pump it out. In and of itself, that was not a problem as long as their generating units could produce enough power to meet the needs of straining air conditioners. Even if they hit the limits of generation, they could still get the big industrial customers to shut down or maybe go to rolling brownouts: minor voltage fluctuations. A rational, controlled measure was available for virtually every generation situation.

The transmission system was the challenge. Every line was loaded to its limit. Lose a line—block the transmission path because of a tripped transformer—and all the little electrons would try to pile onto the other lines. Already at capacity, there wouldn't be enough room on the other lines, so another transformer would trip off, and another, and another and before you knew it, a blackout would cascade up the East Coast. Everything would stop, the transmission grid would collapse. Not because electricity wasn't being produced, but because there would be no way to move it around.

Green and red weather dots were still popping up around Fort Myers. Allison watched the colored spots and white transmission lines, worrying about Neal. The weather service had reported waterspouts and funnel clouds in the Fort Myers vicinity. Surely, Neal would be smart enough to stay clear. She closed her eyes and massaged her temples. Stay clear? Not Neal. If there was a story, he was in the middle of it. She opened her eyes and blinked at the screen. A white line had turned red.

"Fort Myers is on the line," a voice called. "They've lost Sanibel. Trying to cut it loose. Communications won't respond. Their system is starting to go."

One by one the lines on Allison's screen turned scarlet.

▼▲▼

HAIR Project, Alaska
June 10, 9:00 A.M. ADT

Houston leaned over the young officer's shoulder chewing the cigar so hard wells of brown spittle had formed in the corners of his mouth. The screen to his left was a real time satellite view of Sanibel. The display next to it magnified the sector around the Ding Darling Refuge where the storm was forming. The AWACS showed as a white dot in the upper corner of the screen.

"It's not working, is it?" Houston demanded, brown spit dribbling down his chin. He wiped it away with the back of his hand.

"It did initially, but the core is starting to reform." The officer pointed at a purple spot in the center of the display.

"Did the AWACS give it everything?"

"Yes sir, the full complement."

"Crap." Houston banged his fist on the console.

"General Brandt on the secured line, sir."

"Stall him," Houston spat the words along with froth.

"But, sir, he says the electric system in the Southeast is having problems. He needs to speak to you at once."

So damned what? Houston thought. Unless he could stop the alien intruders nothing would make any difference. Not the electric companies, or the Pentagon, or Brandt and his rich friends. It was over. All over. Life as they knew it would come to an end.

"Stall him, major," Houston barked. "Coates. Where's Coates?"

"Yo," HAIR's director answered from a nearby station.

"Is everyone ready to go?"

"On your mark."

Houston checked his watch. "Energize at 1:45 P.M. EDT."

▼▲▼

Ding Darling Refuge, Sanibel, Florida
June 10, 1:00 P.M. EDT

Kelly hugged Reese around the waist, trying to keep him on his feet. The red-headed guy was watching. Reese's condition had worsened: his body, always so hot, now felt absolutely frigid and his flesh was quivering. She had to do something, but what?

Listen, he'd said. Listen? She'd tried and gotten nothing. All she could think about was Reese dying and being dissected. *Help me, God. Help me*, she cried out silently in her mind. It started to rain. *Show me what to do*, she begged. An egret landed at Reese's feet, then a heron and a duck appeared. The heron pecked her leg and headed for a stand of bushes. The duck nudged from behind.

Was this a sign? Was she supposed to take Reese into the woods? The bushes rustled and she squinted in the direction of the noise. The wet foliage parted ... and she saw a face, it looked like Reese. Joe! Relief flooded through her. Squeezing Reese to her side, Kelly maneuvered him toward the bushes. A violent gust whipped through, parting the branches. Joe reached through the opening and pulled Reese in.

Neal was astonished. The old man had a twin!

Then, he heard a vehicle approaching and saw dust rise above the trees at the curve in the road. What was going on? Neal sprinted toward the brush to hide and watch.

WIMP sped around the corner, stopping behind Kelly's car. Jake and Collins piled out, handguns drawn. At the sight of the guns, Neal forgot the twins and dove into a thicket of sea grapes. Hardly daring to breathe, he watched the men search the Mercedes and, finding nothing, fan out in opposite directions. Crouching low with gun in hand, Collins headed toward the brush. Neal hunkered down and cocked his camera.

The wind gusted, and a bolt of lightning struck in the center of the lake. Rain flew wildly, streaming from every direction as whitecaps formed in the normally placid pond. Then the foliage parted, and the twins emerged, one supporting the other. Eyes fixed on Collins, they made their way toward the water.

"Halt," Collins shouted.

The aliens ignored the order and waded into the lake.

"You're surrounded. Don't move," Jake called, dropping to one knee.

The men seemed to comply, stopping waist deep in the murky lagoon. One drooped as if ill, the other stared at the sky. Jake and Collins crept toward them, weapons ready.

"Surrender—you won't get out alive," Collins warned.

The limp, sickly man turned toward Collins and smiled. Not a smug, mocking grin, but the expression an adult might give a naughty toddler. The man was clearly not intimidated by Collins and his threats.

Collins motioned to Jake and they plunged into the pond; but neither made it more than two steps. A toothy jaw jutted from beneath the muddy surface and snapped down hard. The startled men jumped back, scrambling to shore as fast as they could.

Collins was the first to recover from the encounter with the alligator. "Give it up you fools—I'll shoot."

Kelly leaped from the bushes into the line of fire. "Don't hurt them," she cried.

Collins set his jaw defiantly. "Move aside, lady," he said, waving his gun. "Shoot them, Jake."

Gun trained on the aliens, Jake scowled with bewilderment.

"Shoot!" Collins bellowed.

"Are you crazy? They're not going anywhere," Jake shouted.

"Yes, they are."

"How?" Jake was baffled.

"Leave them alone," Kelly pleaded.

"Move it, bitch." Collins took aim at Kelly.

Then a gust of wind whipped around the lake, buffeting Collins. The officer planted his feet and gripped the gun with both hands.

"Get down, Kelly." Jake rushed from the side, tackling her as Collins squeezed the trigger. A shot rang out, though it was too late. A waterspout descended, hurling the gun from Collins' hand.

It was over an instant later. The twins were gone, the gator was gone, and the lake was calm again.

That's when everything flipped into slow motion.

Neal saw the man called Collins retrieve his weapon and aim at Jake and Kelly. He heard Jake yell, "Collins, have you lost your mind?" and saw Kelly scramble for the woods. Neal followed.

Then Neal saw the white Caravan round the corner, the same van Sally had driven earlier in the day.

He saw Collins and Jake shoot at each other, Jake's bullet going wide and Collins' slug hitting Jake squarely in the forehead. And then a new guy, a stranger, got out of the Caravan and shot Collins. Collins screamed hideously and fell flat on his face.

Neal reached Kelly and grabbed her hand. They tore through the woods like bats fleeing hell.

▼▲▼

Charlotte, North Carolina
June 10, 1:42 P.M. EDT

Allison couldn't believe her eyes. Line after line in Florida went from white to red. The system was blacking out, cascading, doing what the experts said couldn't happen. Atlantergy had severed all the external ties to protect its territory. Florida might go, however, its area would be safe. Superior engineering, better planning, the executive vice president said. They would do what the other utilities couldn't—hold it together.

Massoud crouched beside Allison, clearly worried. "Sheridan wants to see you in the conference room." Her supervisor inclined his head toward the rear of the control center.

"Why does government relations want to see me?"

"There's another guy with him. They want to know why you think military experiments are tied into this mess."

Allison stared straight ahead, feeling like she'd been punched in the stomach. She'd have to tell them what she knew and Neal would be furious. "It was merely conjecture," Allison murmured.

"Tell them that."

She sat motionless, trying to summon the courage to get up. Meanwhile, the lines in Florida blinked out.

It started at Fort Myers, then spread north to Tampa and southeast to Miami. By 1:30 P.M. Orlando was out. At 1:40 P.M. Jacksonville collapsed. And it should have stopped there, at the interface to Atlantergy's system. 1:41 P.M., 1:42 P.M., ... no lines fell, the company's plan seemed to be working.

▼▲▼

HAIR Project, Alaska
June 10, 9:45 A.M. ADT

Coates was wearing a communications headset and pacing back and forth. Houston stood discretely at the back of the room, watching the monitor suspended from the ceiling.

"On my mark," HAIR's director said into the small mouthpiece that curved around his face. He watched the seconds tick away on the digital clock. −59:57, −59:58, . . . "Energize," Coates yelled into the slim microphone.

An electric hum filled the air as the giant transmitters came to life, pumping over a billion watts into the upper atmosphere. Pulsing, throbbing power danced through the thin layer of protection that was the blue planet's defense against the ravages of space. At that very moment weaker, but potent, beams were roused in Europe, Peru, and Russia; they would all converge over the Gulf Coast of Florida.

That much power had never been focused together before. It might be overkill, but Houston didn't care. They had to seal the rift and capture one of the interdimensional aliens. Coates and the other scientists were confident the beams would squash the vortex. Unfortunately, they weren't certain what else it might do.

▼▲▼

Ding Darling Refuge, Sanibel, Florida
June 10, 1:43 P.M. EDT

Kelly raced through the underbrush on the heels of the strawberry-haired man. She didn't even know his name. Yet, he seemed familiar—like the man in her *classroom* dream. An old Toyota Celica was parked on the road and her companion motioned her in.

Kelly yanked the door open at the precise moment the sky ignited. The clouds started to glow, each a brilliant spectral hue. And where there weren't any clouds, fingers of color formed undulating curtains of light that stretched into the heavens.

The flash jolted her senses, and her mind seemed to explode. In that instant she knew everything. Life, death, peace, war—everything made sense. And then a voice—a message—sounded in her head. *You are not alone, we are always with you. The answers you seek are here. Life is not about thinking or doing. It is being. And being requires no effort. Trust your brother—*

She jumped into the car and slammed the door. The message from the stars, the voice of the universe was playing in her head. *There is nothing to fear. We are always with you ....* Kelly felt better, more alive, than she'd ever felt before.

Her companion didn't speak until they turned out of the refuge onto the main road. "We made it," Neal said, smiling.

That's when she noticed the gap between his two front teeth.

Part Two

The Quickening

Chapter 18

Flagler Beach, Florida
June 9, 2:30 P.M. EDT

The stranger's skin was the color of fine milk chocolate and his eyes as black as coals. Forehead high and intelligent, his lined face was fringed by graying black hair streaked auburn from too much sun. As the Saturday volunteer for the GeoSphere, Timothy Burchens rarely got visitors, most seeming to prefer the camaraderie of the Friday evening services or Sunday meditations, which made the mahogany foreigner stand out all the more. Although the man had a faint British accent, he was surely not Canadian or even South African. He was different. Short, squat, some might say petite; yet, he exuded an intensity, a single-minded focus or determination that was unnerving, much like a cat eyeing prey.

The Earth Energy Institute drew all kinds, situated as it was at the junction of ley lines or the natural power conduits encircling the planet. Most visitors came as a lark, curious to experience the energy, the same power emanating from the Great Pyramid. Yet, a small loyal core understood. Sensibilities finely tuned, they could feel the subtle energies and, indeed, utilize them for healing. A faithful troupe of seventy-to-eighty-year-olds who looked and acted sixty was the mainstay of the Institute.

"Welcome to the GeoSphere," Timothy said, launching into his usual spiel. "This geodesic dome was built over one of the highest energy points on the planet. Many believe the energy here is as strong as the vibrations at the pyramids in Egypt, Stonehenge, or Macchu Picchu. The apexes of two giant energy funnels—one coming down from the sky, the other rising from the center of the earth—converge at this spot. The building's shape helps focus the frequencies, and our specially constructed vortex chairs concentrate the vibrations further. In addition, the crystal room is a favorite of regulars. Many have had extraordinary experiences and prophetic insights while meditating there. By the way, I'm Timothy."

The visitor inclined his head solemnly.

"Are you familiar with the energy grid surrounding the Earth?"

The black man nodded.

"You've been to other power points like Sedona or Egypt?"

The stranger pushed past him to the floral upholstered vortex chairs and carefully inspected the geometric form hanging over the seat. Pulling the cord that suspended the apparatus, he moved the spring-loaded mechanism up and down several times.

Timothy shifted nervously. "You position the point of the cone about a foot above your head. That seems to focus the energy best."

The black man sat down, lowering the angled form.

"Do you feel the energy?" Timothy asked.

The man started to sing in an incomprehensible language. His deep voice resonated from the triangular-faceted ceiling, bouncing around like the bass in a rock concert. Timothy backed away. He could feel the vibrations, and it was like nothing he'd experienced before, which was saying a lot, because meditations in the crystal room routinely became intense.

Timothy understood the power of chanting or toning, as some called it. The sounds set up vibrations in the atmosphere. Emit the proper tones in the right sequence, and one could produce vortexes capable of dissolving the earth or poking holes into other dimensions. The ancients supposedly understood the technique, which explained how American Indians produced rain by dancing in a circle or how soldiers blowing horns and marching around Jericho brought the walls down.

Is that what this guy was doing? "I didn't catch your name," Timothy said.

The singing stopped, and the man cocked his head. "Oooma."

At first Timothy wasn't sure if the word was a reply or part of the song. But the man *had* paused, Timothy reasoned, so he accepted it as a name. "Oooma," Timothy repeated, pointing at the stranger. The man smiled and launched into a new round of incoherent lyrics.

"Do you live around here?" Timothy ventured at a break in the recital.

Oooma spread his hands and smiled. "Far. Very far."

"England?"

"The Real Country. Below."

"Mexico? South America?" Timothy probed, suspecting he'd get a negative response. The man definitely didn't have a Spanish accent.

"Wallaby."

"Wallaby. Below. You mean Australia?"

Oooma nodded.

An Aborigine. Timothy had heard about them; ancient, weird, strange powers. Confronted by enemies, they could disappear into thin air or make themselves appear as a multitude. They spent their lives migrating around Australia—walkabout, he thought it was called—living off the land, choosing their route by psychic inspiration. In fact, Timothy seemed to remember that the Aborigines sang their routes. Songlines, there had been a book about it. Each tribe chanted or sang their way across the continent. The songs named the features, describing the route. According to the Aborigines' creation myth, the act of naming things brought them into being. Before being labeled, everything was just part of a great cosmic void. It was the naming that gave it substance.

Like Genesis, Timothy thought. And God said, "Let there be light," and there was light. "Let there be a firmament in the midst of the waters ...." And it was so.

What did Oooma's chanting mean? Was he naming the place, weaving it into a song and giving it substance? The Aborigine sang a few more unintelligible stanzas before stopping abruptly. "The future age draws near," he said. "It is time for the songs to unite, time for the great chorus."

"Okay." Gad, Timothy hoped Oooma didn't expect him to sing.

"The emissaries are coming."

"The emissaries?"

"The one with fiery hair and his tall sister. She must sing the song; he must silence the chaos."

Timothy had met dozens of New Age types at Institute functions. Some were authentic seekers striving to discern and follow the dictates of higher knowledge. Others were wishful thinkers, hoping to acquire truth through osmosis, by going to the right places and rubbing elbows with the *evolved few*. Then, there were the out-and-out fakes; a handful of whom teetered between reality and a psychotic wonderland while the rest were true con artists, shamelessly preying on wealthy dilettantes. But emissaries? Emissaries for whom or what? "I don't know who you're talking about."

"They will come. The songs must be sung. It is time for the arteries to pulse with life again."

"Arteries? You mean the ley lines?"

Oooma gave him a blank stare.

"Songlines?"

Oooma pushed past Timothy toward the crystal meditation room. "The planet bleeds. It is time to mend the wounds." He entered the chamber and shut the door in Timothy's face.

Timothy waited outside the room. Oooma was right—the energy grid was broken and it had to be repaired, and quickly. Key links between power centers had been severed causing instability in the Earth's spin. Although scientists made light of it, the Earth's rotation had speeded up and slowed down numerous times over the last few years and conventional wisdom had no good explanation.

But the Earth Energy Institute and its counterparts around the world understood. Mother Earth, Gaia, was out of balance. The energetic casing which kept the world intact had been corrupted. The stabilizing links between matter and energy, this plane and other realms had all but been destroyed. And of the ones still functioning, like the GeoSphere, Sedona and Giza in Egypt, very little energy flowed between the nodes. Like flesh starved for nutrients by clotted arteries, the Earth was withering away. That was the true purpose of the Institute—to focus the energy and re-energize the world grid thereby healing Gaia as well its inhabitants.

Timothy shifted impatiently. Oooma had been in the room for a long time. Perhaps the Aborigine had fainted, overwhelmed by the high frequencies. The Institute forbade loners in the chamber for that very reason. Timothy pressed his ear to the door. Surely Oooma was fine, just deep in trance. But what if he wasn't? Should Timothy peek in, possibly wrecking a transcendent experience and incurring the wrath of the formidable visitor? Timothy nudged the spring-hinged door and peered through the slivered opening. Seeing nothing, he pushed again, then flung the door wide.

The room was empty. Oooma had vanished.

Chapter 19

Sanibel, Florida
June 10, 3:30 P.M. EDT

Neal took another swig of beer and tried to slow his racing heart. The third one in a little more than an hour, he should've felt something, but didn't. He glanced at Kelly where he'd stretched her out on the sofa as best he could.

She was completely out of it, shock he supposed. She was spattered with blood—blood from the guy named Jake who'd taken a bullet in the middle of the forehead. Neal closed his eyes and tried to force the horrible image from his mind. He'd seen Jake's head snap and the back of his skull blow off. It happened so quickly. One second alive, breathing, trying to shield Kelly, and the next, hamburger. Then the shooter, Collins, had gotten it himself. Neal could still hear Collins' scream, hear the dull thump of his body hitting the ground.

What had Neal witnessed? Two men shot, two men vanishing in a whirlwind; the scene played like an episode from the *Twilight Zone*. Neal figured the guys with the guns were government agents because the white Caravan looked like the one he'd seen Sally Carter driving earlier in the day, and Neal knew she was working for the Air Force. Had the military come up with a new weapon that vaporized people? Is that what happened to the old men in the lake? How did Kelly fit into the scheme and why did the agents kill each other?

Neal sipped his beer and picked up the phone for the umpteenth time. Finally a dial tone. The telephone had been dead since they'd arrived at Aunt Tillie's apartment. Desperate to talk to Allison, he punched in Atlantergy's number. Her phone rang a half dozen times before a male voice answered. It was Massoud, Allison's supervisor.

"Massoud, it's Neal. Allison around?"

"Uh, no, she left early." Massoud's voice was strained.

"What's wrong? Has anything happened to Allison?"

Massoud mumbled something about her having a headache. Neal knew that was a lie. "Everything all right?" Neal demanded.

"Sure thing."

What kind of answer was that? "You're afraid to talk?"

"Okay."

Something had happened, and Massoud couldn't talk about it. "I'll call you at home."

"I'll be sure to give her the message."

Neal slammed down the receiver. Allison, not Allison. What had he gotten her involved in? Feeling frantic, he called their apartment and let it ring at least fifty times, then dialed Ben's number at the television station.

"Bud-Ro," Ben said at the sound of Neal's voice. "You should have been here—the sky lit up like the Fourth of July. Power's still off and they say the whole East Coast went out."

Ben's statement made Neal feel worse. Allison was definitely in trouble; nothing in the world would have kept her away from work during a crisis. She'd have crawled from her deathbed for a blackout. "Same here. I need your help, Ben. Allison may be in trouble."

"What?"

"I've stumbled into a wasp's nest. I witnessed two murders this afternoon and now Allison's missing. Her boss knows something, but won't talk. I've got a nearly comatose lady here who's involved in the shootings—I think she was an intended victim, and I helped her escape."

Ben's voice was calm. "Go to the authorities."

"I can't. It was the authorities who were killing each other! There's more, but I don't want to talk about it over the phone. I don't dare talk to the police until I find out what this woman knows. You've got to find Allison—I'm afraid for her life."

"How does this relate to Allison?"

"I've been researching the power outages. I thought the government was responsible and she brought it up at a staff meeting."

"Geez, what are you going to do?"

"I have to get out of here; a park ranger knows where I'm staying. If the Feds are involved, they'll find me." Neal swallowed hard, pushing down a wave of panic. "I don't know where to go."

"Get off the beaten path. You need to find a place that no one would ever connect you to."

"Where? I don't have much money, and my credit cards are maxed-out. Besides, I'll bet I can't check into a hotel in the middle of this outage."

"Florida, ..." Ben mused. "Remember the story I did about the psychic visiting Charlotte? The one who predicted the Hornet's star player would quit to become a minister and the mayor would resign amid a sex scandal. She did a reading for me. She said I was her son in a former life. Catherone Steel, remember?"

"Vaguely."

"A real character, not afraid of anything, thrives on intrigue. She lives in Cassadaga, south of Daytona Beach. Go there; she'll put you up."

"Barge in on an old lady?"

"No one would find you there. I'll call her. She liked me, and even said we would have dealings again. Maybe the old girl knew what she was talking about after all."

Neal downed the last of the beer. "Okay, I don't have other options. But you've got to find Allison. Does your computer have a battery back-up?"

"Of course."

"Turn it on. I'm going to e-mail a story for safekeeping."

Neal checked on Kelly. Finding her breathing normally with no outward signs of distress, he raced downstairs for his computer. Neal sent Ben the article, attempted to reach Allison several more times, then packed the Toyota with his belongings. Everything set, he tried to rouse Kelly. She twitched and stirred then her eyes fluttered open.

"Can you stand up?" Neal asked, putting his arm around her waist. "We need to get out of here."

She grinned at him, glassy-eyed. "Okay-y."

"We're going to walk downstairs to my car. I'll help you." A good four inches taller, she was a real handful. Holding both of her arms, he guided her through the front door, then leaned her against the outside wall while he set the dead bolt.

Kelly watched him hazily. "Reese got away."

"Yeah." Neal took her arm and led her down the hall.

Kelly blinked and stared at him, her face only inches from his own. "You have a gap between your front tee-e-eth," she said in a thick-tongued voice.

Neal humored her with a grin, but kept walking.

▼▲▼

Cassadaga, Florida
June 11, 1:46 A.M. EDT

Catherone Steel's trailer was nestled in a stand of scrub oaks at the eastern-most edge of an overgrown lot. In truth, the weathered blue 1978 pre-manufactured home sat on the neighbor's property. Conveniently not noticing the orange boundary markers at the corners of the yard, Catherone put the mobile home amidst the stand of trees because she liked the vibes. There was no one to complain, since the farmhouse next door had stood vacant for years.

A stocky woman in her mid-sixties, Catherone was slumped forward, snoring, in a threadbare rocker when the door bell rang. She jumped, startled by the sound, and realized the electricity had been restored. The bell chimed twice more as she eased herself out of the chair and smoothed down her hair. Leaving the safety chain on, Catherone cracked the door and peered through the opening. She saw a red-haired man supporting a tall, brunette woman.

"Mrs. Steel, I'm Neal Winters, Ben Miller's friend. Did he call you?"

"Ya-as," she said, releasing the chain. "Come on in."

Neal walked—half-dragged—Kelly into the cramped living room and eased her onto the couch. Kelly was no better, murmuring throughout the six hour trip about the voice of the universe and her mission to repair an energy field. At times she'd seem to be snapping out of it, looking around, commenting on his hair and teeth, yet each improvement was temporary. It was as if she'd dropped LSD and were having a fantastic trip.

"And who is this?" Catherone looked Kelly up and down.

"Her name is Kelly. It's a long story."

"What's wrong with her?" Catherone placed her hands on Kelly's head.

"The aurora—did you see it?"

"Of course."

"It did something to her. She's been drifting in and out of consciousness ever since."

Still holding Kelly's head, Catherone closed her eyes and took a deep breath. Straightening her shoulders, she raised her face to the ceiling, took another breath, then released Kelly and backed away. "Let her be. She'll come around. Help me put her to bed in the guest room."

Neal guided Kelly down the trailer's narrow hall to a bedroom with one window and a single twin bed. Observing the blood spattered over Kelly's clothes, Catherone retrieved a gown from her bedroom and shooed Neal away.

Happy to let Catherone take charge, Neal returned to the living area and sank into the once-rust-colored rocker, allowing himself to relax at long last. The tiny room was warm and cozy. Scented candles in mason jars burned on a coffee table in the center of the room while a miniature waterfall gurgled on a table in front of the side window. In the far corner a four foot blonde angel stood like a sentry. Undoubtedly a remnant of Christmas, the angel held an electric candle which she raised and lowered rhythmically as her head rotated with a swishing sound. For the first time that day Neal felt like laughing and struggled to control a wave of hysteria. Everything was surreal—Catherone, the angel, the aurora, the guys disappearing, the murders ....

"Can I get you something to drink?" Catherone asked.

Neal regarded his hostess. Although slightly stooped, Catherone cut an imposing figure. Short gray hair and pixie bangs fringed a full face of porcelain skin. She wore a long, flowing lavender blouse over black stretch pants and though her upper body was substantial, her legs looked childlike in the tight-fitting slacks. "Water's fine," Neal replied.

"Water? You've come a long way. How about a scotch?"

Neal grinned. This granny was pretty hip. He should have expected as much, Ben had been so taken by her. "That would taste real good."

Catherone returned with two ice tea glasses filled to the brim with liquor. She nudged his shoulder with a glass. "That's my chair."

"Sorry." Neal took the drink and shifted to the faded sofa. "You talked to Ben?"

"Ya-as, he called about nine o'clock. Telephones have been out. He said you were his best friend. You needed a safe

place to go because you'd crossed the path of some criminals."
She took a sip of her scotch and gave him a questioning look.

Neal gulped his, the virtually straight alcohol burning his
throat; yet he didn't care. He was so tense he felt he might
explode.

"That's not exactly true, is it?" Catherone asked.

Neal hastily tried to devise a plausible response that
wouldn't tip his hand, then stopped cold. Who was he kidding?
The lady was psychic and was trusting enough to give him
refuge in the middle of the night. This was not the time or
place for games. So Neal took another gulp of his drink and
told her everything.

They talked for two hours, the storytelling stopping long
enough for Catherone to replenish the drinks several times.
She listened intently, making few comments and showing little
emotion as Neal recounted his tale, although Neal thought
he saw a pained look on her face every time he mentioned
Allison. Catherone asserted that the killers—the men shooting
each other—were government agents and the one left standing
would avenge the death of the first. The middle one, Collins,
had a black heart and there was another evil one far away, a
heart of stone Catherone surmised—she saw him surrounded
by rocks, granite.

By four o'clock Neal was pleasantly plastered and having
spilled his guts—revealing absolutely everything he knew
about anything—he asked Catherone about her background.

Catherone said she was a Scorpio, originally from Kentucky.
At seventeen she met the man of her dreams, Hank, whom
she married at eighteen. They moved to his hometown, a
northern suburb of Cincinnati. She became pregnant almost
immediately and had a child, Hank, Jr. who presently owned
a Harley-Davidson dealership in Indiana. Hank, Jr. didn't
get down to see her much, although he came once for Bike
Week at Daytona Beach.

"La-a, really shook up the town when he and his buddies
rode in on their *motorsickels*. I thought the old people would

have a hissy fit," Catherone said, laughing. "Good for 'em, keeps their blood pressure high."

A long haul truck driver, Hank, Sr. was on the road most of the time. While he was away, Catherone entertained herself by studying astrology. Hank had three sisters who made a point of *checking* on her, which was a polite phrase for spying, whenever he was out of town. Because of Catherone's interest in the occult, the rigid old biddies thought she was a witch, and though they didn't like Catherone, tread lightly for fear she might put a hex on them. She did nothing to dispel their misgivings, and actually encouraged their suspicions since it kept the meddling sisters at bay. Once she'd even gotten a bunch of chicken feet from the butcher—those were the days of real meat shops—and scattered them around the house before one of the sisters' routine, *happen-to-be-in-the-neighborhood* visits.

"Best thing I ever did, sorry I didn't think of it sooner. Priscilla, the youngest, got so scared she never set foot in our house again. Hazel, the oldest, was a shrewd old crab, the most like me of the bunch. Hazel ignored the shriveled, severed feet—looked past it all, as if nothing were wrong. I gained respect for her that day. She was a bitch, don't get me wrong—a spying, spiteful bitch—but she died a painful death: cancer. I was sorry."

"What brought you to Florida?" Neal asked, concentrating hard to get the words through his numb lips.

"Big Hank died. Killed ten years ago in an auto accident. He ran over a car full of lawyers, if you can believe it. Bless his heart, he was too young to go, but did a good deed on the way out."

Neal was stewed to the gills. "To Hank," he said, raising his glass.

"To Hank," she said reverently. "He was a good man."

"How did you end up in Cassadaga?" Neal continued.

"This is the psychic capital of the world."

"It is-s-s?"

"After Big Hank's funeral, I sold everything and high-tailed it here. Hell, people in Cincinnati thought I was a witch anyway, figured I might as well be among kindred spirits."

"Everyone in Cassadaga is a witch?"

"No, psychics and mediums. That witch stuff is old school."

Neal sank into the sofa and tried to look nonchalant. The best he could achieve was drunk, trying to look nonchalant. "What's a medium?"

"A medium is a go-between. You know there is no death, right?"

Neal gave her a blank stare.

"I mean the body is nothing but a temporary container for your consciousness. You come down here—to Earth—to learn some lessons or do good deeds and you take a body to accomplish it. You shed it when you're finished, dropping it like a butterfly leaves a cocoon. Although the body dies, your soul lives on. It's immortal and retains the memories of what you've learned from your past lives.

"Now, some of the ones who've passed on want to help the people down here. They're spirit guides—guides who are spirits. Unfortunately, most people can't hear their guides directly, though everyone has them. Yet there are sensitive people who can. They are mediums. They can hear your spirit guide and tell you what was said. Translators, basically translators."

Neal had had one hell of a day. Old men had vanished before his eyes, he'd seen a couple of murders, he'd picked up a gooned-out lady obsessed with his front teeth, and now, after a couple—he'd lost count—of straight scotches he'd learned he had invisible helpers from other lives. A Capricorn who could withstand much, Catherone said, even his stolid circuits were starting to overload. Neal reclined on the couch.

"You're a good soul, I figure," Catherone chattered on. "Ben was my son in a past life, did he tell you that?"

"Yes."

"Ben loves you like a brother. Told me so. 'Course I knew it before he said a word. That's why I let you come. Anyway, Ben said he was sending a check to cover your expenses. He's a good boy, was in that other life."

"What was that life?" Neal mumbled.

"In Atlantis."

Neal was so drunk he could barely keep his eyes open. "Atlantis—you believe that crap?"

"Crap?" Catherone drew back haughtily. "I'll have you know *that* was our past life with Ben and the woman."

"What woman?"

"Kelly." Catherone shot him a searing look, but it was wasted. Neal had nodded off to sleep.

▼▲▼

Light Display Blacks Out East Coast

Associated Press   **June 11**

SANIBEL, FL—At 1:46 P.M. EDT the electric power grid for the East Coast died. It didn't sputter, ripple and cascade, it just blinked out all at once. But as buildings went dark, the sky lit up. History will record it as the most amazing display of the aurora borealis ever witnessed.

Visible all the way into South America, scientists are at a loss to explain the unlikely phenomena....

Chapter 20

Cheyenne Mountain, Colorado
June 11, 6:30 A.M. MDT

Colonel Stanley Houston chomped on a Danish pastry, shaking his head. He did not like the news his aide, Captain Persman, was relaying.

"General Brandt wants you to call ASAP. He's in a rage about the East Coast blackout. Wire services have picked up the story, and there's considerable speculation about the cause of the aurora. No one's connected it to HAIR or the other projects so far, but Brandt figures it's merely a matter of time. He thinks the Russians will leak the story—they're in such bad financial shape, they'd sell their soul for a dollar, and plenty of tabloids will be waving money."

Houston choked down the last bit of the bun and wiped his mouth. In all likelihood the general's assessment of the Russians was correct. Houston needed to think about damage control. There would be a congressional investigation for sure; however, Brandt had friends and could handle the politicians. The weather angle was clearly the way to go. Write it off as a once-in-a-lifetime confluence of atmospheric conditions. He'd get Stack's intelligence department to start planting the story at once.

Controlling public opinion would be doable, though difficult. The actual problem was that they hadn't stopped the aliens. If anything, incidents had increased while the region was blacked-out. The new guys entered at will, and Houston didn't have any idea what they were up to. Until now he'd concentrated on capturing an intruder and eliminating the witnesses. With HAIR's failure, a change in strategy was in order. If he couldn't get an intruder, he'd have to settle for the contactees.

"What's the situation in Fort Myers?" Houston asked.

"Our man Collins and an FBI agent were killed."

"By the unidentifieds?"

"By a Secret Service agent."

Houston stared at the Navaho rug hanging on the wall in front of his desk and tried to stay calm. Collins was supposed to eliminate the other two, not get killed himself. What the hell happened? "How about the girl seen with the unidentified?"

"She got away."

Great, the general will love that one. "Who's down there now?"

"A team has been dispatched from MacDill to mop up. The Service is sending their own man to investigate the shooting."

We have to put a stop to that, Houston thought. The inter-agency task force had been Brandt's idea—keep everyone in the dark by spreading the assignments among different agencies. It wasn't going to work anymore, they had a sighting and witnesses they couldn't control. One hundred percent military from here on—Houston would insist on it.

"Have Sammy take charge of the squad in Fort Myers. Tell him about the girl and the Secret Service agent."

"Specific instructions?"

"He knows what to do," Houston said crisply. "Any other good news?"

"In addition to the hurricanes, there's been a lot of strange activity in the Atlantic. What with the aurora and all, the media has pounced on it, speculating the events are related."

"What kind of strange activity?"

"Geomagnetic fluctuations—some pretty big. High seas, sudden storms."

"Crap like that is normal for the area."

"The magnetic variation is higher than usual. In fact, the Space Environmental Center released a statement warning off commercial aircraft."

"When did this happen?" Houston asked.

"Couple of hours ago."

What did that mean? Were the aliens responsible? But, that mystery would have to wait; first things first. "See when I can meet with Stack and call the general. I might as well spread the good news around."

Twenty hours ago Houston thought he had the problem licked; now the whole thing had blown up in his face. Although he'd get chewed out, Houston was glad he wasn't in the general's shoes, because Brandt would have to inform the big guys, the Cadre.

A hundred of the world's richest people, the members of the Cadre were the powers behind the scenes of world governments. Harkening back to the glory days of the British Empire, the loose-knit group controlled world events through gifts, campaign contributions, and when money stopped talking, violence. No longer dominated by white Anglo-males, the elite fraternity had their dirty fingers stuck in the bowels of every major government, meaning there was little they couldn't do if they set their minds to it. Of course a consensus was rare, since more often than not they competed with each other. Occasionally, they did agree on common goals—essentially anything that threatened to erode their markets or limit their control.

Free energy, for instance, was a definite no-no. Every device that promised a cheap, unlimited power source was quickly scoffed up and relegated to a vault somewhere. The Cadre wanted to sell energy and didn't care if it destroyed the environment. Pollution was actually a boon, for not only would they get to sell the equipment and fuel to generate the power, they'd get to clean up the mess afterward. Always hedging bets, the members of the Cadre typically won in any situation.

Aside from market dominance, the other thing they agreed on was the need to maintain their influence. It was the prospect of losing control that made the Cadre so afraid of the aliens. They could deal with the short, gray intruders who were motivated by self-interest—the two groups spoke the same language. And as long as the *visitors* kept a low profile, the Cadre wouldn't interfere and actually had cut deals for some of their technology.

No, it was the idealistic extraterrestrials that drove them wild. How could you reason with entities who weren't motivated by power or profits and didn't get a rush from manipulating others' lives? While the peaceniks in the flying saucers had been visiting for a long time, the Cadre had used their influence to discredit witnesses and squash media coverage— thus the UFOs were not viewed as a major problem. But the new aliens were popping up everywhere, doing who knew what, and most importantly, were absolutely out of control. That was a problem—everyone agreed.

The light on Houston's phone flashed. "Good morning, general."

"I don't see anything good about it. Everyone in the world is snooping into that friggin' electric outage. It's just a matter of time before the whole story gets out. Congress is asking questions, and I'm certain you can guess what our *friends* are saying."

"Sure. I've given it a lot of thought, and I'm convinced the weather angle is our best bet. Even the scientists at HAIR believe it was the reason for the exercise. We pass the aurora off as a fluke. The Air Force has enough scientists under contract to get dozens of collaborating statements. The experts won't have to lie, merely say our explanation is plausible. The crucial point is to reassure everyone it will never happen again."

"What was the cause, the aliens or the broadcast?"

"There's a good chance the broadcasts did it."

"Terrific. We blacked out the whole East Coast and don't have a single thing to show for it. Can you imagine how much money was lost yesterday?"

"I wouldn't hazard a guess." Why did it always come down to money? Houston wondered. National security? Mankind's future? Moolah was all Brandt cared about. How much was the general getting on the take? And how many other high ranking officials were on the payroll?

"Have you seen the news wire?"

Houston typed a command into his computer bringing up the Associated Press. "No sir, I flew in a couple of hours ago."

"Crime went through the roof during the blackout."

"Doesn't surprise me—looters always take advantage of situations like that."

"It wasn't just looting. Murders, assaults, and suicides. Naturally, with that aurora, a lot of people thought it was Armageddon or World War III. You weren't here to see it, but it took my breath."

"I'm sure," Houston replied evenly, trying to downplay the incident as much as possible.

"My point is that the kooks are coming out of the wood-work. There are several wire stories claiming the episode was a government mind control experiment."

"Damn." Houston suddenly felt depressed. He thought he'd put that problem to bed months ago. If the press started up on mind control, it was only a stone's throw to electro-magnetic fields. That would be disastrous—the Cadre would pee in their collective expensive pants.

"I'll talk to Stack as soon as we hang up. We'll have our experts lined up and stories planted in a couple of hours."

"Don't forget the Internet. Have spoilers hit the chat rooms. I'll bet cyberspace is buzzing."

▼▲▼

South Seas Plantation, Captiva, Florida
June 11, 11:00 A.M. EDT

"For chrissakes, you shot him in the back." Frank's boss, Carl, glared angrily.

Frank folded his arms across his chest. "What would you have done? I saw him blow Jake's brains out then take aim at the woman. Collins went berserk. I just reacted. I tried to wing him, but he lunged."

Carl turned his back on Frank and strode to the window. "You're suspended indefinitely, pending a full investigation."

"Suspend me? That's crap." Frank inserted himself between Carl and the window. "Something stinks here, and you know it."

"Back off, Frank. You're suspended with pay."

"That's supposed to appease me? I smell a frame. My partner was nailed by an Air Force officer, and I'm supposed to say *I'm* sorry? No way." He smacked the glass belligerently. "I'm not taking the blame for this one. Collins was paranoid or a fruitcake or both. I refuse to be the fall guy."

Carl turned away from Frank again. "I'm not saying you're responsible."

Frank stayed in Carl's face. "No? Under normal circumstances I'd get a desk job during the probe."

"Don't press your luck, I'm giving you pay."

"Come on, this job's been squirrely from day one. Who ever heard of an interagency task force?"

"Sure, for drugs, smuggling—"

"But weather? Espionage? That's what's supposedly going on here. Have you ever heard of the CIA letting anyone on their turf?"

"Drop it. That's just the way it is. Period."

"Drop it? Jake's dead and what happened to Sally? Why did the Air Force hustle her away so fast?"

"She's under contract to them; they have their own debriefing procedures."

"I'll bet." Frank sighed. "This isn't like you, Carl. We've worked together twenty years—who's putting pressure on you?"

"No one. This is standard procedure."

"I doubt Sally will ever be heard from again."

"That's not our concern."

"Goddamn."

"The Service is out of it, effective now."

"You expect me to forget what's happened?"

Carl set his jaw. "You will if you know what's good for you. Put your stuff in the car. We're going back to Richmond."

"Walk away—just like that?"

"Darn right. Move it."

Frank clenched his fist and took a step toward Carl. Frank wanted to deck him so bad he could taste it. Jake was dead and Sally'd probably turn up in a ditch somewhere. Yet Carl expected him to pretend nothing had happened.

"Don't even think about it," Carl warned, stepping forward himself.

"The blood's on you too," Frank barked as he snatched his suitcase and stalked out of the condo.

Neither man spoke all the way back to Richmond.

Chapter 21

Cassadaga, Florida
June 11, 9:30 A.M. EDT

Neal woke up, irritated by a ringing telephone. Disoriented, he looked around, then remembered Catherone and realized he'd slept on her sofa. His shoes had been removed, but otherwise he was fully dressed. A green blanket wrapped around his legs, holding him hostage.

On about the tenth ring, Catherone appeared from the end of the hall in a pink nightcoat. She was pushing on her teeth as she picked up the receiver. "Good morning," she said, finger still in her mouth adjusting the uppers.

Neal extricated himself from the blanket and sat up. His mind felt swollen and slow—how many drinks did he have? Nonetheless, his first thought was of Allison. Maybe the caller was Ben.

"Ya-as, dawlin', they arrived late last night," Catherone said. "Do you want to speak to him?" She waved the old-fashioned black receiver at Neal.

Neal took the phone and sat down at a Formica table. "Did you find her?" he demanded.

"No, but I think she's okay. I contacted her boss. He's scared and made me meet him at an interstate rest stop after work. Massoud said the company's government relations man and a stranger came to see Allison yesterday afternoon."

"Sheridan," Neal guessed. "He's a former congressman."

"They wanted to know why Allison thought government experiments were behind the power failures."

"I was afraid of that." Neal hit the table with his fist.

"They talked to her for a long time. Then Allison got her purse and said she had a headache, was going home. Massoud didn't believe it because Sheridan's companion waited by the door and followed her out."

"They've got her," Neal said flatly. "I'm coming home."

"Don't. I think they're trying to frame you. You shouldn't come back until I get a better handle on the situation."

"Frame me? You mean about the government experiments?"

"It's broader. Massoud said Sheridan questioned him after Allison left. The guy intimated that you were dealing drugs. He asked if anyone knew about you and Allison snorting or popping pills."

"They're setting her up to be fired. She warned me; I wouldn't listen," Neal said angrily.

"Sheridan was anxious to know your whereabouts."

"Damn, they've taken her in for questioning. Man, I've got to come home."

"Let me do some snooping first. I have contacts with the city police and state troopers. I'll call them as soon as we hang up. Also, it's probably not wise for us to talk from Catherone's; we don't want to get her involved. Everyone knows we're friends and my calls might be traced. Use a pay telephone, and call me at the station, they can't possibly monitor all of those calls. Heck, we get hundreds."

Neal's head was pounding, and he felt nauseous. Catherone slid a cup of coffee in front of him. He looked up appreciatively, meeting her concerned gray eyes. She nodded as if to say that Neal should follow Ben's suggestions. "I'll play it your way. When should I call back?"

"Four o'clock. The place will be a zoo with everyone getting ready for the five o'clock show."

Neal started to choke up. "You've got to find her."

"I will."

Neal replaced the handset and stared at the coffee Catherone had put before him. "Are you really psychic, Catherone?"

"Ya-as."

"Where's my wife? Is she all right?"

Catherone sat down, took his hands, and closed her eyes. She seemed to be listening for something. "Allison's in a brightly-lit place with strange people. She's safe and ... happy, very happy—happier than she's ever been in this life."

Happy? Maybe she'd been drugged. God, was she dead? Neal had heard stories about people walking into the light and feeling peaceful. "Is she alive?" He could hardly get the question out, fearing what the answer may be.

Catherone tilted her head. "A very different place—I can't put my finger on it—but, ya-as, she's well."

A wave of relief swept through him and Neal's eyes filled with tears. He'd never forgive himself if anything happened to Allison.

Catherone made pancakes, and Neal ate a three-inch stack. Except for alcohol, he hadn't put anything in his stomach since the previous afternoon. Because of the blackout all the stores had been closed until he reached Orlando and then, having come that far, he'd kept going. It was amazing they'd made it at all—Neal figured he'd driven the last few miles on gasoline fumes.

After breakfast, Neal went to the car for a razor and clean clothes. He returned to find Kelly sitting at the kitchen table. Neal slid into the chair across from her. Kelly's eyes were wide but fairly focused. Catherone was holding her head as she'd done the previous night. Neal looked to Catherone expectantly.

"She's a little groggy. Would you like some coffee, honey?" Catherone asked Kelly.

Kelly nodded absently, her eyes fixed on Neal. "I know you," she said.

"I rescued you from the park yesterday," he replied.

"Before that. I knew you long ago."

"You're confusing me with someone else. I've never seen you in my life." He took a sip of coffee. "Do you remember what happened at the park?"

Kelly didn't answer. "Where am I?"

Neal and Catherone introduced themselves and gave her a quick summary of the last twenty hours. Kelly listened intently, trying to make sense of the fantastic story.

"Do you recall the Ding Darling Refuge?" Neal asked.

"I was there with Reese. Jake, . . ." Kelly started to cry. "He's dead, isn't he?"

"He was shot," Neal said reluctantly.

Catherone drew Kelly's head to her ample breast and stroked her back. "Betty's dead, too; there was a message on my car phone. Reese got away, didn't he?"

"The old men disappeared in a waterspout."

"Good." Kelly wiped her eyes.

"Who were those guys?"

Kelly pulled away from Catherone looking frightened and confused.

"Don't push too hard," Catherone warned. "She's had quite a shock. She'll talk in her own time."

"I want to tell you; I really do, but the knowledge is dangerous," Kelly said.

"Look, I'm already in trouble and my wife is missing."

Kelly buried her head in her hands. "Aliens," she murmured.

"Illegal aliens?" Neal asked.

"No, alien aliens—like from space."

Neal nearly fell out of the chair.

▼▲▼

Cassadaga, Florida
June 11, 12:30 P.M. EDT

Kelly felt better within a couple of hours thanks to Catherone's ministrations of flower remedies and therapeutic massage. The sadness over Jake and Betty remained, yet Kelly was able to push it to the back of her mind. And the voices— the message that had consumed her for the last twenty-four hours—had also subsided. It was there when she needed it, though not overwhelming. To both Catherone and Neal's surprise, Kelly was the picture of confidence and poise by midday, anxious to get on with her mission.

As they sat around the kitchen table drinking herbal tea, Kelly calmly told them about Atlantis, Reese, and Joe. She recounted the dream she'd had throughout her life, how it haunted her, was too vague to understand, and how everything had fallen into place after meeting Reese. Her mission was to repair the ley lines encircling the planet.

"And you're supposed to help me," Kelly said to Neal.

"Get serious."

"You're the man in my dream, the one I sat next to in the classroom. You said, 'We must enliven the grid, so the others may come.'"

"It's not me, Kelly. Your imagination is working overtime."

Catherone reached across the table and patted his arm. "It *is* you."

"How do you know?"

Eyebrow arched superciliously, Catherone looked down her nose. "I know—you'll get proof shortly. And I'll tell you this: your wife's welfare depends on the success of Kelly's mission."

Neal's eyes darted from Kelly to Catherone. "What does this have to do with Allison? You said she was okay."

"She has a stake in this venture."

"We're talking about aliens, for godssakes. Allison's not involved and neither am I."

Catherone narrowed her eyes and spoke deliberately. "It was no accident I met Ben, which is how you came to be here. It was no accident that you came to Florida and were at the park to rescue Kelly. If you think about it, Allison was responsible for your presence there. We all play our parts, although we don't necessarily understand the purpose behind our actions. We have known each other in previous lives and have come back together for a reason."

Neal moaned. "I've never heard of ley lines. What are they anyway?"

"The perfect thought which created this planet," Kelly said. "Everything, all matter, is nothing but thought-directed energy."

Neal got up and started to pace. "Thought? How do we fix this grid, sit around and meditate real hard?"

"Our course will manifest in due time." Kelly heard herself say the words and was surprised by their certainty. She *knew* they were true. It wasn't a rote mouthing of platitudes, there was conviction, true knowledge behind the pronouncement. Kelly marveled at the change. Only days before, she'd been a mass of doubts and insecurities. But now, with the voice— the universal chorus—playing in her head, she felt as if she had an invincible legion urging her forward. Every negative, insecure thought instantly met a positive correction, and there was a rhythm to the message, a soothing melody which bathed every cell of her body. If only Neal could hear it, he'd have no doubt.

"I, for one, am hungry," Catherone stated flatly. "Don't have much here—I wasn't expecting company."

"Let's go out," Neal volunteered quickly.

But a few details stood in Kelly's way. She'd left Captiva with nothing, abandoning her car, purse, keys, credit cards, everything. Although her home was less than forty miles away, she couldn't chance going there. Clothes, toiletries, bare necessities were an issue. Catherone had been able to wash most of the blood stains out of Kelly's shorts; however, the blouse was hopeless. Catherone lent Kelly a Hawaiian print shirt that hung on her like a tent.

Appraising Kelly's physique, Catherone said, "You're about the same size as Jeri down at the cafe. She's a nice girl. Let's go there for lunch. I'm sure she'd be willing to lend you some things."

They walked the three blocks to the Cassadaga Hotel and the Lost in Time Cafe. Typical of resorts from the turn of the century, the hotel was a stucco and wood structure encircled by a wide porch lined with white rocking chairs. Only a handful of people were there, mostly locals who knew Catherone. They took a table by a window overlooking the porch. An old telephone booth, complete with folding door, corner seat and rotary dial phone, was against the wall.

A tall blonde approached with menus. "Haven't seen you in a while," the woman said to Catherone as she passed out plastic encased sheets of paper. "Doing a lot of readings?"

"Quite a few. Everyone seems to be in crisis," Catherone responded. "Jeri, I'd like you to meet some friends. They're staying with me. Kelly Saunders, Neal Winters, this is Jeri Osborne."

"Nice to meet you. For an off-worlder, Catherone's one of my favorites," Jeri said.

"Off-worlder?" Neal asked, looking worried.

"Non-camp. You know, not part of the official Cassadaga Spiritualist Camp." Jeri turned to Catherone. "They're new to this, I take it."

"Ya-as, but coming along rapidly." Catherone smiled. "Aside from the great food, one of the reasons we came here was to talk to you."

"Terrific, let me get that other table first."

"Are you going to tell her why we're here?" Neal asked after Jeri left. "Shouldn't we keep this quiet? After all, there have already been a couple of murders, and my wife's missing."

Catherone scanned the room. "What do you think?" she asked Kelly.

A voice sounded in Kelly's head. *Trust your brother.* "I think we should take her into our confidence."

Neal rolled his eyes. "You don't know her—heck, she could be a government agent."

Kelly and Catherone said in unison, "She's not."

"Okay, what do I know?" Jeri arrived with water at that moment, and Neal took an anxious gulp.

"You need a favor, Catherone?" Jeri asked.

Catherone gestured at Kelly. "Ya'll are about the same size, wouldn't you say?"

"I'd say so."

"Kelly's run on hard times. I can't explain it here, but, she literally has nothing. The shirt on her back belongs to me. I thought you might be willing to lend her some things."

Jeri looked sad. "Absolutely. I have lots, much more than I need. Come over tonight. It's my turn to host the message service. It should be finished by nine, nine-thirty at the latest. Timothy is coming, too. You remember him, Catherone, from the GeoSphere? I'll get Kelly situated, and we'll catch up on old times. I have a lot to tell you. Timothy for one thing. Our relationship has, well, ... become significant."

Catherone poked Jeri's arm. "I told you so, didn't I?"

Jeri blushed. "You certainly called this one. I thought you were daft for pushing us together, but you were right about Timothy."

"Destiny," Catherone pronounced.

The group ordered lunch and made arrangements to meet Jeri at nine-thirty.

"What's a message service?" Neal asked.

Catherone sat back and puffed out her chest. "As I told you last night, the camp people are mediums. They channel messages from entities on the other side."

Neal was startled. "Aliens?"

"No, departed spirits—people who've passed over. You know, died. Ghosts," Catherone said, chuckling at his puzzled expression.

He grimaced, unabashed.

"Honey, I told you this *was not* and *will not* be our only lives. The body is transitory, though the spirit never dies. And, some of the spirits who've passed over want to help their loved ones down here. They send messages and signs, which mediums can hear and pass on."

"You're saying that dead people talk to the living in these message services?"

"Ya-as."

Neal thought of his father who'd died in an accident when Neal was fifteen. In a rebellious phase, Neal had said some hateful things in their last conversation. He'd sure like to tell his father how sorry he was, but would his father want to speak to him?

Neal turned to Kelly, "Have you ever been to one of these message services?"

"Sure, I don't live far from here. I came when a friend visited about a year ago. . . Cara—" Kelly paused, sadness clouding her eyes. "There's nothing scary about it."

"You believe dead people can talk from the grave?"

"It's not from the grave," Kelly protested. "Simply another realm of existence." She was startled by her own words. She'd gone to Cassadaga to humor Cara. While the message Kelly received turned out to be accurate, she'd written it off as coincidence. Now she was defending the process and knew at a deep level that it was true. "Why don't we go tonight," Kelly found herself saying.

Catherone agreed, and although Neal was skeptical, he finally assented.

The food came and after they ate, Catherone gave them a tour of the camp, stopping at the post office along the way. An express letter from Ben was waiting. It contained a check for one thousand dollars.

▼▲▼

Cassadaga, Florida
June 11, 3:30 P.M. EDT

The lunch and tour took longer than Neal expected. He was supposed to call Ben at four o'clock so he prepared to leave as soon as they arrived back at the trailer. He was surprised when Kelly got in the car with him.

"I have to call my friend, Cara. She's probably frantic."

They went straight to a Texaco station where they filled up with gas and bought a telephone credit card. Kelly tried to reach Cara first, but got the answering machine. She hung up without leaving a message.

Neal had better luck. "Ben."

"You okay?" Ben asked tensely.

"Fine, did you find Allison?"

Silence, then: "No, we found nothing. That's good, according to my contacts at the police—means the Feds have taken her into custody for questioning. They say she'll be safe. Short of espionage, the Feds don't hurt people."

"Don't hurt anyone? I know better, Ben. I've got to come home."

"I'll take care of this. Don't come back. Stories about your dealing drugs are circulating. My sources say you'll be picked up the minute you step into the state."

"You didn't tell them where I was, did you?"

"Give me some credit. I told them you'd witnessed a government-backed crime which made you a sitting duck. They understood. There's no love lost between the Feds and state. State guys are tired of being superseded and treated like retarded slime. They also know the Feds engage in shady activities from time-to-time which involve innocent civilians.

"There's nothing you could do here. Both city and state officers are looking for Allison. They're anxious to find her since they believe this is another botched federal operation. They'd love to embarrass the FBI for a change."

"I can't thank you enough," Neal said.

"Save it. When this is over we'll all sip mimosas, eat ham biscuits, and laugh. Did Catherone get the check?"

"Yes, I owe ya. We sure needed the money."

"What, exactly, are you involved in?"

Neal glanced at Kelly for reassurance. "This is so big it would blow the roof off the planet."

"Pulitzer?"

"Try survival," Neal said quietly.

Ben whistled. "That's pretty strong."

"It is strong. I've witnessed two murders, and Kelly knows of another. Be careful what you say and to whom."

"Chrissakes, I've got a few more dollars stashed away— let me know if you need it. All I ask is joint credit on the Pulitzer."

"Got it."

"I've got to go. Call me tomorrow, three o'clock, the phones will be jammed with the usual preparations for the news. You'll never be noticed."

▼▲▼

Cassadaga, Florida
June 11, 7:15 P.M. EDT

Kelly, Neal, and Catherone filed into the auditorium.

Jeri was seated at the door. "You're lucky, Reverend Land is reading tonight. She's incredible."

They took a seat on the second row. The service began at seven-thirty with a meditation, then Reverend Land, a rotund senior citizen took the microphone. She scanned the audience, ultimately settling on Neal.

"The man in the black tee shirt, may I come to you?"

Neal glanced at his shirt, wondering if she was referring to him.

"Yes, you. May I hear your voice?"

Neal said hello.

The Reverend took a deep breath, and her eyes became glassy. "You have been through much in the last week and are standing on the brink of a marvelous discovery. Much of your discomfort comes from your resistance to change. You are quite a skeptic, so much so, you don't see the forest for the trees. Spirit wants you to lighten up and try to be more trusting."

The Reverend paused and Neal figured she was finished. Maybe there was something to this stuff, he thought. The message wasn't earth shattering, but she had picked up on the chaos of the previous few days.

"There's a man here with me," Reverend Land boomed, jolting Neal. "He passed over very young, suddenly. Family, ... red hair, ... your father?"

Neal gasped, heart racing. *Dad?* Could it truly be his father? Tears welled in his eyes.

"He wants you to know that he's proud of you. You've turned out to be a fine man. You're having trouble now, and he wants you to know he's here, with you, to help. When you feel confused, quiet yourself, and listen. He is trying to give you advice." The Reverend stopped again as if listening to an unseen companion. "You're facing an important decision, the most critical of your life. You will receive confirmation of the proper path in unmistakable terms. Soon, very soon."

The medium shifted her focus and began reading for an elderly woman. Neal was oblivious to his surroundings, so stunned by the message from his father. A redhead? That could have been a lucky guess; after all, Neal's hair was strawberry blonde. But dying suddenly, too young? It had to be his father. Emotion welled up. He couldn't control it, alternating waves of sorrow and joy pulsing through him. "I need air," he whispered to Kelly and bolted for the door.

Neal raced out of the building and leaned against a tree, sobbing. "Dad," he whispered through tears. "If you're up there, help Allison."

The sobs turned to choked heaves as the full force of every painful memory descended in a rush. How long Neal stood there, he didn't know. Eventually the sobs came less frequently, and the tears dried up. Neal headed for the bathrooms at the rear of the building to wash his face.

"Neal." Someone called his name as he rounded the corner at the side of the auditorium. He spun toward the sound and caught the outline of a shadowy figure beside the lake. His first thought was of his father. Neal barreled toward the figure and came face-to-face with Reese.

"What are you doing here?" Neal asked, backing away when he realized who the figure was.

"I've come to confirm your part in Kelly's mission."

You'll get confirmation soon, the Reverend said minutes earlier. *You're facing an important decision, the most critical of your life*. The world had gone crazy—things were happening too fast. "Were you in the message service?"

"I'm aware of what transpired. My name is Reese."

"I figured as much. You're Kelly's alien, the Sirian?" Neal asked guardedly.

"Correct."

"You zipped in from a whirlwind?"

"In a manner of speaking."

"I'm supposed to help Kelly fix the grid?"

"Correct."

"So, how do we repair it?"

"You'll find out shortly."

Doesn't anyone give a straight answer? Neal thought. Riddles, that's all he had gotten for the last two days. *Wait*; *it'll manifest later*; *don't do that*—it was driving him crazy.

Reese continued as if he could read Neal's thoughts. "The pieces are coming together as Starpeople awaken. Soon we will reach the critical mass, the time for action."

"Starpeople. You mean me?"

"Correct."

Neal heard people talking and knew the meeting had broken up. Reese stepped backward into the pond. Then a wind gust descended almost knocking Neal off his feet.

"Wait," Neal cried, reaching out for Reese. "Don't go. Tell me what I'm supposed to do."

Reese opened his mouth as if to reply, but no words escaped—the whirlwind whisked him straight up, into the blackness of space.

▼▲▼

Cassadaga, Florida
June 11, 9:30 P.M. EDT

Timothy Burchens was waiting when they arrived at Jeri's apartment house. A clapboard structure with a screened front porch, the building was reminiscent of the 1920s when wealthy patrons escaped from frigid northern climes to spend a season in the peaceful surroundings of the Cassadaga Spiritualist Camp. Judging from the peeling paint, a few wealthy patrons were sorely needed to restore the aging compound. But with all the options made possible by modern air travel, patrons flew in for a reading or two, staying at posh hotels in Orlando or Daytona Beach, then flitted off to another exotic setting. They didn't hang around long enough to feel an authentic connection or the motivation to help preserve the quaint village.

Jeri led the group through the unlocked door to her apartment, making introductions as she flipped on lights and lit candles. The small living room was furnished with a tattered couch covered with an Indian print throw, a straight backed wooden chair and assorted cushions stacked in one corner.

Neal smiled to himself as Catherone made a beeline for the sofa, establishing position at one end. Timothy grabbed a pillow and sat cross-legged on the floor. Neal opted for the chair. He was feeling uneasy from the encounter with Reese, thus the hard seat fit his mood.

"How about some tea?" Jeri asked as she put a kettle of water on the stove. "Kelly, let's see what we can find for your wardrobe while it's heating." The two women retired to the back room.

"It's been a long time since I've seen you, Catherone," Timothy said.

"Ya-as, we were at the hotel, the night you met Jeri."

Timothy smiled broadly. "You introduced us, as I recall. You insisted that I join you. Do you remember that?"

"I knew you were supposed to meet. Jeri said you still work at the GeoSphere. How's Wally Christian?"

"Amazing, as usual. I don't know where the man gets the energy—well, actually, I do—but for eighty-four he's beyond belief. He works ten to twelve hours a day and never gets tired. He's building a new design, one that focuses energy even more efficiently. I'm telling you the vibes up there have increased exponentially."

"What kind of energy?" Neal asked.

"Geomagnetic. I work at the Earth Energy Institute in Flagler Beach. It's a geodesic dome built over a natural energy vortex."

Vortex—the word gave Neal a start. Catherone perked up also, as if two and two had miraculously combined to yield four. "That's fascinating." Neal called excitedly, "Kelly, you need to hear this."

She emerged from the bedroom with a cardboard box of clothes, shoes and assorted bottles and cans.

"What?" Kelly put the box by the front door and sat next to Catherone.

"Timothy works at a place that's an energy vortex."

Kelly's mouth flew open. "Where?"

Timothy responded, "About fifty minutes from here. It's one of the most powerful sites in the world—on the same level with the Great Pyramid. Major ley lines cross there."

"That's it," Kelly exclaimed, turning to Neal. "We've got to go there. That's where we must re-energize the grid. I know it."

Jeri came from the kitchen with a tray of steaming mugs. Timothy took one, then sipped his tea thoughtfully, looking from Kelly to Neal. "The man with the fiery hair and his tall sister," Timothy muttered to himself. "You're the emissaries."

Kelly and Neal exchanged baffled looks.

"An Aborigine came to the Institute two days ago. Oooma, a real piece of work. He said the emissaries would be coming: 'the one with fiery hair and his tall sister.'"

"That's y'all for sure," Catherone said.

"He also said, . . . how did he put it? . . . 'It's time for the arteries to come to life again.' I'm sure he meant the ley lines. The coincidence is too much."

"An Aborigine?" Neal asked, slipping into reporter mode. "Did he say anything else?"

"It was time for the songs to be sung, and *you're* supposed to silence the chaos."

"Aborigines travel through Australia, marking their routes with songs," Jeri added helpfully. "Walkabout is a spiritual journey which retraces their ancestors' steps—a way of reconnecting to their origins. They find the route by singing their clan's song. The lyrics make references to streams and hills, physical features that allow them to find their way. The songlines crisscross the country; in effect the continent is like a great symphony."

"A chorus, Oooma mentioned that too," Timothy said, wagging his finger for emphasis. "And when I asked him where he came from, he said Wallaby, must have meant the Wallaby clan."

"What the heck would singing songs have to do with the ley lines?" Neal asked. "And, what did he mean by silencing the chaos?"

Timothy stood and stretched. "Disruptions in the energy grid cause a certain amount of chaos—geomagnetic fluctuations—perhaps that's what he meant. And the songs—sounds, like chanting, can have powerful effects. Sounds are vibrations like everything else. In the right combination they can dissolve matter or move mountains."

"Move mountains?" Neal scowled.

"Harmonic resonance. High notes break crystal goblets. Surely you've heard about soldiers marching across bridges and because their rhythm jibes with the structure's natural frequency, the whole thing collapses. Sounds can do that, too."

"It's one thing to break things, but dissolve matter?" Neal asked doubtfully.

"You need to talk with Wallace Christian, founder of the Institute. He can explain it better than I can; it has to do with the fact that matter is swirling patterns of energy."

Kelly stared at Neal. "I think we should go to the Institute first thing tomorrow morning."

"I'll meet you there," Timothy said. "I wouldn't miss this for the world."

Chapter 22

Richmond, Virginia
June 11, 8:40 P.M. EDT

Frank sensed something was wrong the instant he stepped across the threshold of his condominium. Then, a blunt object caught the back of his head, and a foul smelling rag was clamped over his mouth and nose. He delivered a good lick to the assailant's midsection before the cloth's fumes annihilated his senses and turned his muscles to jelly.

He awoke in a musty room with a single bed, toilet, and sink. The only illumination slanted through a transom over the doorway; otherwise the cubicle was devoid of light, life, and had precious little air.

Frank rolled to his side trying to figure out what had happened. His brain throbbed like he'd been on a weekend drunk and the back of his skull felt as if he'd been hit by a brick . . . . Yes, he *had* been hit, immediately after entering the house. He sat up, too quickly, and moaned in pain. Where was he?

He wasn't sure how long he sat there before the door opened. Frank blinked at the bright light framing a tall figure. A second later the man pushed Frank backward onto the bed, ripped open his shirt and administered a hypodermic in his arm. Then another man entered, this one squat and husky. Frank caught the second man's profile and noticed a deep scar on the side of his neck.

"How long until it takes effect?" the short man asked with a thick accent.

Spanish? French? Frank couldn't tell; his head was beginning to spin.

"A minute or so," the tall man responded.

"You're certain he will not be able to lie?"

"Absolutely."

"This man is a trained agent—he's a lot tougher than the girl."

"Doesn't matter. The drug's been tested extensively—99% effective."

"He won't remember anything about the session? You're sure?"

"Certain. One in a million."

Frank gritted his teeth defiantly. The bastards had never tested a Sicilian. *He would remember. He would remember. He would* ....

▼▲▼

Cheyenne Mountain, Colorado
June 11, 11:00 MDT

Colonial Houston was fast asleep when the siren blew. He had two phones. One rang normally—that was the number he gave his sister and few friends, mostly golfing buddies. The other was a secured link to his office which blared like a fire alarm. His aides had strict instructions to use it solely for emergencies. After ten years, its screech still scared the hell out of him.

"What?" Houston said into the handset. It was Sammy.

"Sorry to wake you, I thought you'd like to know the outcome of our interrogations. They're both clean."

"No knowledge of the aliens?"

"Right."

"No suspicions?"

"None. Both bought the weather warfare story."

"You're sure? No chance they're lying?"

"Absolutely not—we used the new drug."

"Do you have plans to release them?"

"You know me better than that, Stan. Of course I have plans. We're going to take the secret service agent home and tuck him into bed. He'll wake up tomorrow with a headache and think he's had a whopper of a dream. We're doing the same thing with the Stanford physicist. If she remembers anything it'll only be scattered images. She's a smart cookie and valuable asset to the Air Force. Of the two, she's the one we'd want to save."

"You're confident neither will recall the examination?"

"The drug's been thoroughly tested."

"Release them both, then. What about the other girl, Kelly, and the reporter?"

Sammy cleared his throat. "No luck. We've staked out her apartment, but she hasn't shown up, and the reporter's missing, too. We interviewed the guy's wife and got the address of the place he was staying—an aunt or something on Sanibel. He made a hasty getaway, judging from the looks of the place. We suspect Kelly was with him. We've dusted the apartment for prints, and are waiting for the results now."

"Has the wife heard from him?"

"No."

"Keep after her, she must have an idea where he would go."

Sammy cleared his throat again. "That's going to be tough—she's disappeared."

"What?"

"She's gone, and so is her tail."

"How the hell—"

"We found her at work, that big electric utility in Charlotte. Hanson did a preliminary interview there, then had the company send her home so he wouldn't raise suspicions.

He was supposed to follow and take her into custody. Hanson reported in from his car phone, and that's the last we've heard."

"Goddammit. Any question about Hanson's loyalty?"

"How does one ever know?"

Houston threw the covers back and stood up, screaming into the telephone. "Dammit, your group looks like a bunch of fumbling idiots. The general will fry us both."

"I know—we'll find them. Don't worry."

"Dammit, Sammy, there's no room for screw-ups. Find Hanson, the wife, . . ." the veins in Houston's neck bulged, "...that Kelly, find every damned one of them. I will personally kick the butt of anyone who makes another mistake."

Chapter 23

Cassadaga, Florida
June 12, 7:30 A.M. EDT

Neal's mouth flew open when he saw the headline at the bottom of the front page.

Suicides Linked to Mind Control Experiments

NEW YORK (AP)—The rates of suicide and violent crime tripled on June 10 for the eight hour period beginning with the appearance of the East Coast aurora. Most experts attribute the rise to religious fanatics and the mentally disturbed who believed the fiery blazon was the harbinger of Armageddon. Yet a small group of scientists and government watchers think both phenomena were caused by military mind control research that is thinly veiled as attempts to control weather.

Reputable sources claim the government's weather experiments broadcast extremely low frequency (ELF) radio waves which not only caused the aurora but the rash of savagery, too.

Human brain waves as well as the Earth's magnetic field have a normal frequency of approximately ten hertz. Because of the electromagnetic nature of the brain, it is plausible that humans may be affected by electromagnetic stimulation. Studies show a correlation between psychiatric admissions and solar storms which affect the Earth's magnetic field. Likewise, it is well known that certain glands, particularly the pineal or "third eye", respond to light which in turn affects the body's production of hormones such as seratonin and melatonin. Hormone imbalances are widely recognized as factors in some types of violence....

Neal was astonished. The old doctor who'd cornered Ben at the TV station said the same thing, and Ben later discovered research to support it. Neal wondered if Ben ever did a story. If not, he'd been scooped by the Associated Press and was no doubt kicking himself.

The thought of Ben reminded him of Allison and Neal felt a flood of grief. Important stuff was happening—after last night he was certain—yet it was hard to stay focused on anything other than Allison's welfare. *God, protect her*. Neal felt so helpless, especially because he couldn't call Ben to check on things.

The screen door swung open hitting him on the rear as Kelly slid out and sat down. Not wanting to disturb anyone, Neal had walked to the hotel for a newspaper and perched on Catherone's front stoop to read.

"She's fine," Kelly said.

Neal looked away, knowing his eyes were rimmed with tears. "I hope so."

Kelly stared straight ahead, purposely not looking at his face. "The encounter with Reese changed me—rather, the encounter with Reese and the aurora did. If you'd met me a couple of weeks ago, you wouldn't believe I'm the same person. Now I have a confidence, *a knowing*.

"Reese said his people have been beaming a message at this planet. It plays continuously and explains the truth about the universe and our place in the grand scheme.

"Starpeople have enhanced receptors, but they also have strong wills. In my case, and maybe yours, our wills are so powerful we were able to block the message." She laughed. "Reese marveled that we could ignore the broadcast since they've turned up the volume so high the average person can almost hear it. My mother always said I was willful and stubborn. I guess she was right."

"My parents said the same thing, especially my father." Neal felt another pang of sadness.

Kelly continued, "The aurora did something. I can't explain it, but I *know* things, and I *know* your wife is all right."

Neal shook his head. "I want to believe, but won't until I see her with my own eyes. I've learned enough about this New Age stuff to realize that y'all don't believe in death. I'm afraid your 'Allison is all right' means she's blissfully dead."

"She's not dead."

"Is she being held by the government? The FBI, CIA, military—who?"

Kelly thought before answering. "Wherever she is, she's alive and happy."

"Catherone said that. What does it mean? Has she been drugged?"

"All I know is she's feeling no pain. I'll say it again— she's happy. I know this is hard for you, I'd be skeptical, too." Kelly paused to watch two squirrels sparring over a crust of bread from an overturned garbage can across the street. "Do we go to the vortex today?" She nudged Neal with her elbow.

He stood up, sending the squirrels scurrying. "Yep, I guess we should."

▼▲▼

Flagler Beach, Florida
June 12, 9:30 A.M. EDT

Wallace "Wally" Christian was soldering copper plates together when Timothy ushered Kelly and Neal into the basement of the GeoSphere. As the group entered, Wally extinguished a propane torch and pulled off goggles revealing a round face rimmed by sparse white hair.

"Don't tell me it's Saturday," Wally said with a twinkle in his eye. "Did I slip into a time warp and skid right through Wednesday, Thursday, and Friday?"

Neal thought of the *Rocky Horror Picture Show* at the mention of time warps and smiled as he took in the paper and metal geometric forms hanging from the ceiling and stacked in the corners of the room. Was this the mad scientist, Frank-N-Furter's lab? He glanced back at Wally. Naw, not Frank-N-Furter, more like the Wizard of Oz.

"I took the day off," Timothy replied. "I have some new friends I want you to meet. Remember the Aborigine who came by last Saturday?"

Wally listened as he inspected the convoluted copper shape he'd been assembling when the group entered. "Certainly."

"I believe these are the emissaries he's looking for."

Wally appraised the newcomers. "Please have a seat." He pointed to a table in the corner of the room. The octogenarian sat in front of a window overlooking a weed infested yard embellished by a spiral design of large stones and cinder blocks. At the center of the layout was a circle of smaller rocks. The circumvolution reminded Neal of American Indian artifacts and he made a mental note to ask about it later.

Timothy introduced everyone and outlined the reason Neal and Kelly were interested in the vortex. Afterward, Wally didn't say anything for several minutes. The silence made Neal uneasy, because for the first time he realized how far-fetched the story sounded. Coming from Timothy, the tale seemed fantastic, the stuff of science fiction. Doubt washed through him. Had he been carried along by Kelly's misguided enthusiasm?

"I knew something was about to happen," Wally said. "The currents have gotten stronger, and the separation between this plane and other dimensions has grown thinner. At times the other side comes through without any intervention.

"You know, this building is situated at the junction of two great vortices. The dimensions unite here." Wally motioned toward the geometric forms strewn around the room. "These structures are tools for focusing natural energies, but, we haven't needed them lately. And, I've received similar reports from our sister sites around the world."

Timothy looked surprised. "I hadn't heard about that."

"Most of it has happened since you were here on Saturday, when the Aborigine arrived. Native people have been showing up at energy points everywhere. Two Indians pitched a tent on a cliff at Sedona. Sarah Harding in Virginia Beach says a Tibetan monk arrived Monday and set up housekeeping on the steps of the Institute. Another Aborigine arrived at Stonehenge and shamans in Peru. It's as if a great magnet is drawing people to appointed places for the finale of a grand drama."

"What do you make of it?" Neal asked.

"I think your alien was right—the time has come to make the leap to a higher dimension," Wally responded.

"What do the Indians and Aborigines have to do with it?" Neal said.

"Their religions are tied to the earth. They are sensitive to the subtle currents and allow themselves to be drawn by them. Their attunement to the earth is obviously crucial to the impending leap."

Kelly spoke, "If Neal and I are the emissaries that Oooma mentioned—"

"I have no doubt about that," Wally stated emphatically.

"If it's true, I'm earmarked to sing a song. Neal is supposed to silence chaos. Does that mean anything to you?"

"I've given it a lot of thought and discussed it with Sarah. You see, each of our sites vibrates to a slightly different frequency, which is in harmony with a musical note. If all the notes were played together, or better still, in sequence, it would make a song. A common characteristic of all the natives who have turned up at the energy centers is a strong tradition of chanting or singing. Song—sounds—are an important component of their religious traditions. Sarah and I believe their chants are necessary to align the nodes and energize the grid."

"Whoa, you're going too fast for me," Neal sputtered.

"Are you familiar with the concept of ley lines?"

"Kelly and Timothy mentioned it. Doesn't it have something to do with dowsing? The guys who use forked sticks to find water?"

Wally chuckled. "You're on the right track. See, the planet is crisscrossed by currents of energy. Actually, it goes farther than that; the planet *is* energy."

Neal folded his arms defensively. "You mean, Einstein, $E=mc^2$."

"Not quite. Einstein was close, but missed an important nuance. It's more than matter being converted to energy; matter *is* energy. Swirling vortices of energy compose everything."

"Do physicists agree with that?"

"The ones on the cutting edge do."

"Where do you get your information?" Neal asked skeptically.

"I was born knowing certain things; other knowledge comes from my dreams. I test the theories here—this is my laboratory." Wally waved at the room. "But, there's no need to get into theoretical physics; we were talking about dowsing for water. Do you at least believe in that?"

Neal nodded.

"Good. The dowsing rod merely locates the currents, in particular, the energy associated with water. There are other currents too, some strong, some weak, at a whole range of frequencies. Where the currents or ley lines cross, you have an energy node with mirror image energy funnels: one coming down from the sky, so to speak, the other going down into the earth. These vortices are portals to other realms as well as anchors for the planet in this dimension. Regrettably many of the currents and energy nodes have been disrupted by development and technology. The energetic casing of the planet has become increasing unstable to the point we're starting to see real physical effects, like changes in the earth's rotation and sudden shifts in the poles. The grid must be balanced and restored to avert global catastrophe. I believe that's what you and Kelly are here to do."

"I don't know anything about chanting," Kelly protested. "I wouldn't know where to begin."

"Don't worry. I believe Oooma will return. Timothy, didn't Oooma say that he and the tall woman must sing the song together?"

"Yes."

"What about silencing the chaos? How do you interpret that?" Neal asked.

"That's harder," Wally conceded. "The grid has been disrupted by a number of factors. One is development. The landscape has been gouged by mining, construction, and war; all of which disturb energy flows. Another problem is the desecration of ancient energy sites. Many of the old monuments like obelisks, pyramids, and mounds were put there to dissipate or balance energy flows. As these artifacts are lost to development and age, the nodes become unstable again. Finally, there's technology: electricity, radio, television. Mankind, indeed all living things, are being bombarded by constant, unnatural concentrations of electromagnetic waves. With the weakened state of the Earth's grid, this electromagnetic gibberish counterbalances much of what remains."

Neal remembered the article on mind control and almost shouted. "Gibberish—chaos—that's it! Electromagnetic fields. Electric utilities. I know something about that, my wife works for Atlantergy," he blurted, then fell silent. He hadn't thought of Allison for over an hour. He rubbed a hand across his face. This was all theory. His wife was missing—that was a hard fact.

Wally regarded Neal with knowing eyes. "I believe you're right," he said in a voice barely above a whisper. "If the electricity were turned off, the Earth's grid would be easier to energize. Once restored it would probably be impervious to electric fields."

"The aurora and the blackout," Timothy interjected.

Wally's eyes grew wide with excitement. "Yes, the vortex's strength increased astronomically. That's when I witnessed the dimensions blending of their own accord. Although not as high now, field strength has remained above normal. That's it, I'm sure of it. Neal, you're supposed to turn off the electric system."

"Hold on—that's a tall order! If it were possible, which I'm not sure it is, and if I could do anything, which I'm not sure I can, my contacts are at Atlantergy which only serves the East Coast."

"Perfect," Wally said, waving his hands. "The weakest part of the Earth's grid is on the East Coast. Why haven't I make this connection before? The ley lines are weakest in the area with the highest level of development. Don't you see? The east coast of the United States is one of the most highly industrialized—meaning electrified—areas in the world, and the grid is weakest here. We're the weak link. Repair it, and the rest is a piece of cake." Wally started to pace. "That's it, that's it. Neal's the crucial link."

Timothy gave Neal a congratulatory slap on the back.

"Wait, guys, I can't do anything. I can't even go back to Charlotte without being arrested. My tie to the utility is through my wife, and she's disappeared." Neal started to choke up. Kelly jumped in, explaining that Neal was the target of a smear campaign, most likely because of the murders at the refuge.

Wally sat down and looked Neal in the eye. "I understand all that, but you *are* the emissary, the man with the fiery hair." Everyone looked at Neal's strawberry-colored mane. "There must be a way; you simply haven't thought of it yet. That is your role in this epic; that's your mission, your point for being here, and you must do it."

Neal knew Wally was right, but felt overwhelmed by doubt. Allison would know how to handle it. He couldn't do it without her and wasn't sure he even cared what happened to the world if she wasn't in it.

"I'll help," Kelly offered. "Think about all the stuff you've learned from Allison, the answer's there somewhere. You can do it. You have to do it—humanity's fate depends on you."

▼▲▼

Daytona Beach, Florida
June 12, 2:30 P.M. EDT

Kelly and Neal chose a pay phone close to the boardwalk. College students in skimpy swimsuits strutted their stuff on the walkway, while cars with teenagers hanging out the windows crept along the beach below. Kelly had lived in central Florida a long time but had never gotten used to cars driving on the beach. It was a long-standing Florida tradition, the Daytona Beach races getting their start on the hard-packed, sandy expanse at low tide.

After a tour of the GeoSphere, they lunched with Timothy and Wally at a seaside cafe. Wally Christian proved to be a fascinating subject and they could easily have spent the entire day talking about his theories and inventions. Since he and Timothy were joining them for dinner—at Catherone's insistence—they'd cut the visit short.

Anxious about the welfare of Cara and Allison, Kelly and Neal stopped in Daytona Beach to use the phone. Neal handed Kelly the telephone credit card he'd purchased earlier, giving her the honor of the first call.

Kelly pushed star-six-seven to block caller ID and dialed Cara's home number. There was no answer. Next she called Bruce Hooker, Cara's alien expert friend. She'd decided not to reveal her true identity in case the line was being monitored.

"Hi Bruce, I'm a friend of Cara's. We've never met, but she's mentioned you many times. I wondered if you know where I can find Cara? I've been trying to reach her."

Bruce started to stutter, clearly upset. "You haven't seen the newspaper?"

Kelly's heart raced. "I've been out of town."

"Cara's dead. They say it was a botched burglary."

Kelly was too stunned to speak. Neal took the phone from Kelly's hand and hung it up.

"Cara's been murdered," Kelly murmured, stumbling toward a nearby bench. Betty, Jake, now Cara. Everyone she'd discussed Reese and aliens with had turned up dead.

Neal wasted no time calling the television station. It seemed like an eternity before Ben picked up.

"Have you found Allison?"

"Not exactly," Ben said.

"Don't play games."

"The police found her car out by the old airstrip."

"Oh, God," Neal said, fighting to stay calm.

"Don't panic, there's no sign of a struggle or violence. My contacts say that's good. The CIA, FBI or whomever probably followed her out there and took her into custody. Remember, Massoud said one of the guys questioning Allison left immediately after she did the other day. I figure she tried to lose him but he eventually cornered her at the airstrip."

Neal smashed his fist against the telephone enclosure cutting his knuckles. "Ben, people are being killed!"

"My sources are confident she's in no immediate danger. Don't worry—they're looking for her. If anything, they're more determined to find her, seeing how the Feds kidnapped one of their citizens. Massoud and a bunch of her coworkers have raised money for a reward. He's really broken up about it, feels it was his fault, says he should have taken her home himself."

"I wish he had. Ben, I've got to come home."

"Absolutely not," Ben said forcefully. "A rumor is circulating that her disappearance is tied to your involvement with drug dealers."

"Who would say such a thing?"

"My source said the utility's government relations guy, Sheridan, has spouted the theory. Maybe he started it, maybe he's repeating something he heard, I don't know."

"There's been another murder," Neal said sharply. "I've got to be careful. Will you be there for a while? Can I call you back?"

"Sure, I'll wait."

Neal hung up the phone and sat on the bench beside Kelly, fearful the news about Cara might have pushed her back into a stupor. "Are you okay? We've got to go."

She nodded. "What's wrong?"

"Allison's car was found abandoned at an old airport. Ben thinks the Feds have taken her in for questioning."

"God," Kelly gasped. "The government is trying to silence everyone with any knowledge of the aliens. You know this won't end until we complete our mission."

Neal grabbed her arm. "Maybe. I need to find another telephone."

They drove south on I-95 to SR 44, the exit for Deland and New Smyrna Beach. They rode in silence, each absorbed in their own thoughts. Kelly thought of Cara; her zany quirks, quick wit, and all the fun they'd had. Her murder redoubled Kelly's resolve to complete her assignment, only then would Cara's death have meaning.

Neal stopped in front of a fruit stand with a telephone booth. "You're right, we've got to do something," he said. "Damned Sheridan. I'm going to bring down the electric system and expose those bastards if it's the last thing I do."

He slammed the door as he got out of the car. Kelly watched as Neal talked to Ben, relieved that they were finally in agreement about fulfilling their purpose. She saw Neal gesture emphatically, knuckles bloody from his assault on the first telephone. She couldn't imagine the pain he must be feeling, the agony of not knowing what had happened to his wife.

In a way Kelly envied Neal, because his pain showed the depth of his feelings. He'd said Allison was his best friend, the love of his life. Kelly didn't feel that about anyone. She was alone, completely alone, especially now that Cara was gone. Her eyes stung with tears as she thought of Cara, Betty, Jake, and even her parents who'd passed away years earlier.

Kelly had nothing to lose, there wasn't anyone the government could threaten, nothing that would keep her from finishing the job. *There are no accidents*, she thought grimly. Maybe that's the reason for Cara's death. If Kelly were in Neal's place, would she be as strong? Could she resist walking into the fires of hell itself if her soul mate were in danger? She wasn't sure. In Neal's shoes she'd likely throw logic and caution to the wind even if the act meant destruction for everyone else. Doubtless, that was the reason she'd never married. At some deep, subconscious level her spirit knew it would interfere with her primary goal—the upliftment of the planet itself. Small price to pay, she thought as Neal got back in the car.

"Ben will help us. He'll be in Savannah tomorrow night for a film premiere, and we're going to meet him there. I told him to bring Massoud. Without Allison, Massoud's our only hope of shutting down the electric system. Short of blowing up transmission towers, the only way to pull it off is from the inside. It may not be possible even then, electric utilities have redundancy in all of their systems."

"Something will manifest; other Starpeople will come forward," Kelly said, looking out the window at a bank of angry black clouds. The weather had remained sultry with storms developing in record numbers, reports of tornadoes and waterspouts had become commonplace. Each time Kelly heard of one, she thought of Reese and figured the Sirians were awakening someone else.

Neal said, "I hope the Sirians show up soon. Aside from pleading for Massoud's cooperation, I sure as hell don't know what to do."

Lightning split the eastern sky. Neal turned west toward Cassadaga. When they arrived back at the trailer Catherone was well along with dinner preparations. A crockpot of barbecued pork simmered as she put the finishing touches on a bowl of cole slaw. Kelly offered to help, but Catherone waved her off, insisting she wanted to do it herself.

"Wally likes barbecue," Catherone said. "It's an old recipe I'm making especially for him. He's coming, isn't he?"

Kelly and Neal exchanged surprised looks, both noticing Catherone's tone when she said *Wally* and the fact that she was making the dinner *especially for him.*

"Yes," Neal answered. "Wally's anxious to see you. He'll be here about five-thirty."

The corners of Catherone's mouth turned up as she mixed the slaw. Kelly and Neal poured iced tea and sat at the kitchen table, briefing Catherone on the day's events.

"You think natives must chant at the energy centers at the same time Neal disconnects the electric power?" Catherone asked. "How will you coordinate that?"

"We have no idea," Kelly said. "We're hoping the Aborigine will know or maybe another Starperson will show up with the answer.

"Wally was going to poll his colleagues at other energy centers for ideas. Timothy thinks we might be able to time it by solar activity or changes in the Earth's gravitational field. He promised to check some Web sites and bring the results tonight."

"It must be done soon, within the next few days," Catherone said emphatically.

"Why do you say that?" Neal asked.

She gave him a disgusted look. "I'm psychic, remember?"

"I wasn't questioning your abilities," Neal said quickly, "only wondered if you sense other details?"

She put the slaw in the refrigerator and sat down. "You'll get help from an unexpected quarter, and you must be careful, danger's lurking."

"Danger! Can you be more specific?"

"Influential people are working against you. Your mission is a threat to their position and they will do anything to stop you."

"Will Massoud cooperate?" Neal asked.

Catherone took a deep breath and thought. "Mmmm-m, I believe he will. He's very upset about the disappearance of your wife, blames himself. If he helps, it will be because of guilt."

"I don't care what his motives are, as long as he does it." Neal averted his eyes. "Can you sense anything about Allison?"

Catherone shook her head. "She's well and is in a strange place, I see violet and lots of light. Well, I've got to change before Wally gets here. Neal, I want you to go to the store and get some wine," she said, poking him on the arm. "Get the good stuff, you know, the white table wine in the box? The container is green and yellow, know the one?"

Neal forced back a smile. "I believe I know what you're talking about." It was approaching four-thirty, so he left to do her bidding without delay.

Catherone retired to the back bedroom, emerging exactly one hour later in radiant splendor. Her floral scent preceded her by a full minute, and she seemed to float into the living room, suspended by the flowing sleeves of a gold lamé blouse worn over purple leggings. Three large crystals hung from gold chains around her neck, and her eyes looked dark and seductive. Neal rose when she entered to show his appreciation. Kelly was transfixed by her eyes.

Catherone alighted on the edge of her chair like a magnificent bird perching on a willow branch, swishing the lamé and fluttering false lashes. "What do you think? Can Wally possibly resist me?"

"No way," Kelly said.

"Putty in your hands," Neal stated.

Catherone giggled like a school girl. "The old fool is late. Let's have a drink."

Neal was filling glasses from the wine box when Timothy, Wally, and Jeri arrived. Catherone greeted the guests with a great flourish and much swoshing. Wally presented her with a box of candy to which she batted her lashes demurely. Timothy carried an armful of papers while Jeri brought a cake.

The first part of the evening was consumed by pleasantries, the mating ritual between Catherone and Wally overshadowing everything else. At seven they ate, some at the kitchen table, others balancing plates on their laps. By eight they had finished the main course plus Jeri's cake and were ready to get down to business. Timothy spread his papers out on the kitchen table.

Neal picked up a colored map of Earth labeled *NOAA/TIROS Energetic Particles*. "What's this?" he asked, indicating a red blotch that covered most of South America.

"Background radiation for the Earth. The red area is the South Atlantic Anomaly. Earth's magnetic field is unusually weak there, allowing in more radiation from space."

"Aren't UFO sightings common in South America, especially Peru?"

"Hmph, I've never made that connection," Timothy said. "Perhaps the weak field allows aliens to enter more easily."

Wally pointed at the map. "Except for regions close to the poles where auroras are common, North America, particularly the United States, has high levels of radiation."

"Caused by a weak magnetic field?" Neal asked.

"No."

"You believe the electric system is responsible?"

"If not the sole cause, it's a major factor," Wally replied.

Timothy sorted through the papers and pulled a thin document to the surface. "We don't have time to go through all of these, so I'll leave them for you to study later. In a nutshell, two important trends are occurring. First, the Earth's magnetic field is weakening. At the current rate of decay, some scientists believe the poles will vanish completely within 2000 years. Considering that the magnetic field is the planet's protection from the radiation of space, especially the sun, its demise has important consequences. Secondly, while the magnetic field is diminishing, solar activity is increasing." Timothy waved a paper called the *Solar Cycle Project*. "Since the 1800s, sunspot activity—which releases radiation and—"

"Solar wind," Neal said, recalling his conversations with the professors about HAIR a mere five days earlier. If he'd known then what he knew now, Neal would have asked more questions and paid closer attention.

Timothy was surprised. "Yes. The next cycle is predicted to be the largest ever. Of course, cycles go up and down and we appear to be close to the bottom now. That may be the reason your alien friends are in such a hurry to get us into the next dimension."

Kelly agreed, "Reese said the planet would go into oblivion if we didn't progress soon."

"Assuming that's true, what is the proper time for disabling the electric system?" Neal asked. "If I'm able to do anything, I suspect we'll only have one chance."

"I'm getting to that." Timothy fished another document from the stack of computer reports. "This is a forecast from the Space Environment Center. Recent readings have been unusually erratic, but, both solar and geomagnetic activity are expected to be at the lowest level in recent history three days from now."

"Ya-s-s, of course," Catherone exclaimed. "The new moon, time for new beginnings. It's in Gemini, which means new starts with respect to the environment and communications."

Jeri said, "Leaping to a higher dimension would certainly qualify as a change in the environment—"

"And communications from other realms," Wally added.

"Three days. That's impossible," Neal protested.

"Don't think that way," Catherone warned.

"It must be done—it's our best chance," Wally said.

All eyes were trained on Neal. He got up and went outside.

Chapter 24

Richmond, Virginia
June 12, 10:30 A.M. EDT

Frank couldn't remember the last time he'd felt so bad. His head pounded and he thought he might vomit at any minute. If he lay still the nausea subsided, yet his head felt worse. Could he make it to the bathroom for ibuprofen? Could he keep them down if he got that far?

Frank stood up carefully, leaning on the headboard for support and was surprised to find himself wearing boxer shorts. He normally slept in the nude. I must have really been drunk, he thought, as he shuffled uncertainly to the bathroom. He found the pills in the medicine cabinet, tossed down three and splashed water in his face. Frank knew he had to get something in his stomach fast.

Not bothering to find a robe, he sidled downstairs, uncustomarily holding the handrail. His suitcase and a pile of newspapers were scattered next to the front door. In the kitchen, he found a sleeve of saltine crackers which he ripped open. He brushed aside empty bottles of Dewars and Wild Turkey and slumped into a chair at the glass cafe table. Wild Turkey? He kept whiskey in the house for parties, couldn't stand it himself—too sweet. Surely, he hadn't consumed it on top of scotch. The thought made his stomach knot. He must have mixed them to feel this bad, but why? He couldn't remember anything—his mind was a complete blank.

Feeling better as the pills took effect, Frank shuffled to the living room and stretched out on the leather sofa, munching crackers and trying to relax. A few minutes later, the phone rang. It was Frank's sometimes partner and friend Don Trimble.

"How are you holding up?" Don asked.

Frank was puzzled. "Why do you ask?"

"Well, the suspension and all. I'm really sorry."

"Suspension?" An image of Collins killing Jake flashed through his mind. Then Frank remembered meeting with Carl in Florida. It was hazy, ... seemed they'd had an argument.

"I've been assigned to the investigation, but I wanted you to hear it from me."

"Oh."

"Don't worry, Frank. I'm sure you had good reasons, and we'll find them. Thought you'd like to know that we might have a witness."

Slowly, his memory was coming back. Frank said, "The girl, Kelly Saunders?"

"She's disappeared; abandoned her car, purse and hasn't been back to her condominium. It's under surveillance. Lucky for you, there was another person at the park, a reporter for the *Charlotte Sentinel*, Neal Winters. He'd been interviewing one of the park rangers. I'm flying to Charlotte this afternoon to talk to him."

Friend or not, Frank knew better than to tell Don everything. "I'm glad you're on the case, that way I'll get a fair shake. I'm being framed. The assignment was peculiar from day one. Collins, the Air Force geek, shot my FBI partner in the head. It was pure chance I was there to see it. I had to do something—he was taking aim at the girl, Kelly, when I pulled the trigger. If I hadn't been there at that exact moment, it would have been written off as Jake going insane or Kelly wielding the weapon. A frame-up, no question about it."

"You know I'm bound by procedure not to say much. We'll get your statement tomorrow. We've worked together for a long time, and off the record, I agree. The scenario stinks. I'll get to the bottom of it. In the meantime, you lie low. After you've made your statement, go fishing or something. I'll take care of the rest."

Frank felt better in spite of his physical complaints. "Thanks, Don."

"You'd do the same for me."

"Yeah, I would," Frank said and meant it.

Maybe Carl wasn't out to get him after all; he *had* assigned Don to investigate the shooting. If there was anyone in the world Frank trusted, it was Don. They'd saved each other's lives several times and each owed the other a lot.

A possible witness was good news. The reporter might collaborate his story, putting an early end to the inquiry.

Frank laid back, munching another cracker. Memories of his conversation with Carl came flooding back, and then he thought of Sally. He needed to hear that she was all right.

Frank called information to get her telephone number. It was still early on the West Coast and her office line was answered by a graduate student who obligingly provided her home number. Frank suspected he was being paranoid, but called anyway, intent on tying up at least one loose end. Sally didn't answer until the seventh or eighth ring.

"Hello." Her voice sounded weak and distant.

"It's Frank Scortino."

"Who?"

"Frank, from Captiva."

"Captiva?" She sounded dopey, drugged.

"Did I wake you up?"

"Yes, I've been asleep."

"You remember me and Jake don't you? South Seas Plantation?"

There was a long pause. "Sure, Jake, Frank. I'm sorry, I don't feel well."

"What's wrong?"

"I have a terrible headache."

Frank pulled back, surprised by her response. "When did you get home?"

Another long pause. "I don't know."

"Did you fly straight from Captiva?"

"I don't remember." Her voice quivered.

"Did anyone ask questions about our project?"

She sounded like she was crying. "I don't know, I can't recall. My head hurts so bad."

"Sally, go take some aspirin. I'll call you back later. Is that okay?"

"Sure."

Frank hung up the phone and relaxed into the leather couch. Sally couldn't remember where she'd been, what she'd done, and had a bad headache. *Amazing coincidence.*

▼▲▼

Richmond, Virginia
June 12, 10:00 P.M. EDT

Frank was lounging in bed watching a Perry Mason rerun when the telephone rang. Although he felt considerably better, he still wasn't one hundred percent. He didn't get dressed until three in the afternoon and then only ventured as far the local market. He'd talked to Sally about five and gently probed about the events of the previous two days. To his dismay, she couldn't remember anything that happened after she'd learned of Jake and Collins' deaths. Frank told her it was understandable, considering the shock of the news. But, he knew better—he couldn't remember anything, either.

Frank picked up the handset.

"Sorry to bother you so late, I just got in from Charlotte."
It was Don Trimble.

"How was the trip?"

"Disquieting."

Disquieting? Don didn't talk like that. "How so?"

"I shouldn't tell you this, but ... the witness was a dead end."

"He didn't see anything, huh?"

"No, both he and his wife are missing. Her car was found abandoned at an old airport. No one's seen him for days. Rumor has it he was into drugs, and this is a drug-deal-gone-bad."

The government had no imagination whatsoever, Frank thought sourly. A drug deal was the cover for every screw-up any federal agency made. "What do you think?"

"Same as you, I think it stinks. Remember Jim Smith? He's stationed in Charlotte now. I asked him to snoop around, I'm not giving up on the reporter. The real reason I'm calling is to arrange a time for your statement, the sooner the better. I need it before proceeding further."

Frank told Don he'd be there at eight o'clock. Then he replaced the handset and pulled the phone book out from under the answering machine. US Airways flew nonstop to Charlotte and with any luck he could be there tomorrow for lunch.

Chapter 25

Charlotte, North Carolina
June 13, 12:46 P.M. EDT

Charlotte/Douglas International Airport was one of Frank's favorites. Named for the city's former mayor, the facility opened the area to the world and ushered in a period of unprecedented growth. Sometimes called *little Atlanta* by outsiders who did not realize the insult, Charlotte's genteel elite viewed Margaret Mitchell's hometown as a good place for shopping or weekend flits, but little else.

Frank guided the Ford Taurus out of the rental car parking lot and made a left on Billy Graham Parkway. He drove a short distance, then took another left on Wilkinson Boulevard. Jim Smith had agreed to join him at the Ranch House for lunch. Frank's morning meeting had been short and sweet. He gave his statement, glanced through mail stacked on his desk, and was on the way to Richmond International by ten o'clock. He'd hoped to see Carl, but didn't. Picking a fight with the boss was a stupid thing to do, especially when he faced expulsion from the Service or, worse, being charged with murder. He'd been out of line, Frank saw that now and was sorry he hadn't had a chance to apologize.

He had called Jim from the Richmond airport. Frank was surprised Jim took the call. After all, Jim was involved in the investigation and bound by department policy to keep his distance. However, the two had been good friends years before when Jim was stationed in Richmond. They'd played on a softball team together and had gone to a few Richmond Braves games. Even so, Frank knew Jim was sticking his neck out by meeting him for lunch.

Jim was sitting in a corner booth when Frank arrived. They traded pleasantries and brought each other up-to-date on their jobs, lives, loves, and travels. After about twenty minutes a harried waitress appeared to take their order.

"Can we talk about the investigation?" Frank asked after she left.

Brow furrowed, Jim steepled his fingers. "I had a feeling you weren't in town to shoot the bull."

"I gave my statement this morning. I was forced to shoot the Air Force officer, who had already killed the FBI agent and was taking aim at a civilian. I think I'm being set-up as the fall guy for something bigger. Awfully convenient the witnesses are missing, don't you think?"

"I agree, but what are you planning to do? If I answer your questions, what then?"

"I'm not going to do anything stupid, Jim, but I can't sit around doing nothing while my career is ruined and my retirement shot to hell. If I find anything, I'll bring it to you. View me as an extra pair of legs."

Jim leaned forward. "What do you want to know?"

"Don told me the reporter and his wife are missing. I also know that rumors of a drug-deal-gone-bad are circulating. That sounds like a Class A government cover-up. Either they've been taken into custody for questioning, or the couple has gone into hiding, and the rumor's being circulated to discredit them in the event they talk later. Have you located friends, family, or anyone they might call in a jam?"

"I've found his mother as well as her parents and sister; they don't know anything. The reporter's best friend, a Ben Miller, works for the ABC television affiliate. I spoke to him this morning, and he claims he hasn't heard a word from Neal."

"Claims? You don't believe him?"

"My gut says he's lying."

"A good place to start," Frank said.

The sandwiches came, and the conversation shifted to less controversial topics. Frank didn't push, knowing Jim had taken a giant leap onto thin departmental ice. An agency zealot could easily bring Jim up on charges. Perhaps that's why he wolfed down his sandwich and left scarcely ten minutes later. Frank couldn't blame him, Jim was close to retirement, too.

Frank paid the check and got the television station's address from the phone book. There was no time for finessing. He arrived at the station at two-thirty, flashed his card to the receptionist and was immediately ushered to a cubicle in the newsroom where a young man worked at a computer terminal.

"Ben, you have a visitor," the receptionist whispered, then slinked away.

Frank offered his hand, "Frank Scortino, Secret Service. Do you have a minute? I'm looking into the disappearance of Neal and Allison Winters."

Ben was startled, but recovered quickly. He pulled a chair from the station next door. "Have a seat."

Frank checked to see who was within earshot. Although most of the cubicles were occupied, the ones adjacent to Ben were thankfully empty.

"I understand you and Winters are close friends."

"We went to college together. Neal's a fraternity brother," Ben said matter-of-factly.

"Have you heard from either of them?"

"Like I told the other agent, I have no idea where they could be."

"Did either of them use drugs?" Frank watched Ben's mouth. The lips, not the eyes, were the true gauge of a person's emotions.

Ben's lips twisted angrily. "Absolutely not. They're normal, hard-working people. Hell, they rarely drink, much less use drugs."

The guy was smooth. Frank decided to put him on the defensive. "Do you use drugs?"

Ben's face reddened. "No. What is this?"

"Maybe your friends were users, but kept it quiet since you don't use yourself," Frank suggested, satisfied he had Ben's attention.

"I would have known—we're best friends. They're positively not into drugs."

"Can you think of any place they might have gone?" Frank thought he detected a change in Ben's demeanor. His jaw seemed to tense.

"No."

"Neal was working on a story down in Florida. Did you know about that?" Frank thought Ben was definitely agitated now.

"He mentioned it to me, but I don't know anything about it."

"Did he say anything about government experiments causing the strange weather we've experienced lately?"

Ben cleared his throat. "Yeah, he said something in passing. I don't recall the details."

"Do you know if he ever got back from Florida?"

"I told you, I haven't seen or talked to him."

The phone rang, and Ben looked frightened. He answered, momentarily turning his back on Frank, who took the opportunity to slip a card into the pocket of the blazer that hung from the side of the work station.

Ben dispatched the caller quickly. "Sorry for the interruption."

"No problem, I'm finished anyway." Frank handed Ben another business card. Ben glanced at it, fingering the raised insignia. Frank smiled, knowing that Ben had just activated the homing device implanted in the embossed design. "Keep my card with you and give me a call the minute you hear from them."

"Why is the Secret Service interested in Neal and Allison? Don't you guys primarily handle federal officials?"

"The drug connection, money laundering, you know." Frank couldn't believe he was using the drug excuse. Ben seemed satisfied, and Frank marveled that the tired, old pretense had worked again.

Frank flipped on the homing beacon's wallet-sized receiver before leaving the building. He retrieved his car from the public garage and parked down the block. Frank's intuition said he wouldn't have to wait long. Ben definitely knew something, and Frank expected him to try to warn Neal as soon as possible. As expected, Ben left the building a short time later and emerged from the parking garage in a sporty red Toyota. Slapping his Taurus into gear, Frank followed Ben to a large office complex on the outskirts of the city—the Atlantergy Operations Annex. A Middle Eastern-looking man got into the car with Ben.

They took I-77 south to Columbia where they picked up I-26 to I-95 south. A little over five hours later, Ben pulled in front of the Hyatt Regency in Savannah, Georgia. A doorman took their luggage and ushered the men into the crowded hotel as a valet drove away in the car. Frank waited a couple of minutes before following.

"Sir, you can't leave your car there," a valet said curtly.

Frank flashed his identification.

The valet's demeanor softened immediately. "Sorry. Here for the premiere? Washington bigwigs coming? The president?"

"Can't say," Frank said in his best Secret Service voice as he pressed a ten dollar bill into the young man's palm. "Keep an eye on it, will you? I don't want it towed."

"Yes, sir," the valet called as Frank made his way into the bustling lobby.

People in formal attire milled around the room, sipping drinks and chatting in small groups. He scanned the area, located Ben and his companion at the registration desk, then stepped behind a potted plant to watch. A stunning woman standing beside the front desk caught his eye. At least six-foot-two, the lady had straight black hair that brushed her shoulders and skin so white it glowed. Attired in a filmy green gown cinched at the waist by a silvery sash, she exuded confidence, poise and innocence all at the same time. A short, older man faced her, his back to Frank. A starlet with a studio executive, Frank surmised.

He forced his mind back to his task as Ben and his buddy headed for the elevators at the far end of the cavernous room. Frank rushed after them, intent on discovering the elevator's destination. Standing to one side, Frank could see that the two men were alone in the elevator. Good, he thought, there'd be no doubt about their floor. Whereabouts narrowed down, Frank would have no trouble picking up the tracking signal.

The stainless steel doors started to close, but a husky man slipped between them. My luck, Frank thought; now he would have to scan multiple floors. The elevator stopped on the fifth floor and stayed there until summoned back to the lobby a few minutes later. The hoist was empty when it returned.

Figuring the two men would come down for dinner, Frank snatched a discarded newspaper and found a seat with a view of the elevators. Scanning the room, he caught sight of the exotic woman in green and, to his surprise, she was staring in his direction. He swung around to see what she was looking at, and finding nothing, sunk behind the newspaper. When Frank peered out again, she'd taken a seat a few yards away. The woman seemed vaguely familiar, and he found himself sneaking a glimpse of her every few minutes.

About twenty minutes later, Frank heard voices coming from the escalator to the parking garage. He turned toward the sound, but straightened quickly. Kelly and a red-headed man had entered the lobby.

▼▲▼

Kelly and Neal arrived in Savannah later than expected, they'd hit several severe storms along the way. They got to the Hyatt about nine. Since Ben and Massoud had not arrived, they took a walk through the historic district. A large crowd was milling around the registration desk when they returned, so Neal used the house phone to locate Ben.

"Come on up," Ben said. "Room 505."

Kelly and Neal took the elevator, never noticing the man watching them from behind a newspaper. As soon the doors to their lift closed, Frank followed.

Upstairs Neal made introductions and explained the situation to Ben and Massoud, who was dumbstruck.

"I know this is hard to believe," Neal said, "but it's absolutely true. In fact, it's the reason Allison's been taken hostage. Think about it. I thought the HAIR project was responsible for the strange weather and electric outages. So what? Thousands of people suspect the government of plots and secret shenanigans, yet they aren't kidnapped for questioning. It would take a lot more than that, like extraterrestrials, to drive the authorities to abduct civilians."

"Even if I believe your story," Massoud said, "I can't sabotage the transmission system. They'd lock me up and throw away the key."

"Is it possible?"

"The cleanest way would be to shut down the communications network which monitors the lines and substations. But I don't think anyone could do it because the company's operations are controlled by tandem mainframes. You'd have to shut down the system at both computers simultaneously. It can't be done, or at least I'm not capable of doing it."

"Who could?"

"I dunno, perhaps one of the computer jocks."

"Allison's safety depends on our turning off that system." Neal was ashamed he'd stooped to playing on Massoud's emotions, but he didn't have time to argue. The plan had to be executed in two days. Wally and Timothy already were coordinating efforts with the other energy spots. Calling it a ceremony for planetary healing, they'd asked each center to devote the day to chanting and prayer. Naturally they weren't telling anyone about the planned blackout of the East Coast.

Massoud slumped forward, head in his hands. "I should have taken Allison home myself. I *knew* she was upset. I *knew* something weird was going on. It's my fault she's missing."

"Don't blame yourself. I'm as guilty as you are," Neal said ruefully.

"Let's take a break. We're all tired and I'll bet you're hungry," Kelly said, looking to Ben for help.

Ben nodded. "I am starving. Let's go for a bite to eat. Things will look different on a full stomach."

They all agreed and prepared to leave.

▼▲▼

Savannah, Georgia
June 13, 11:00 P.M. EDT

Frank had a clear view of room 505 from the vending area across from the elevators. Following Kelly and the redhead upstairs, he'd had no problem pinpointing the room. While the lobby was packed, most of the guests were apparently engaged in the gala for *Mint Julep*, a much-hyped movie making its debut the next day. He hadn't seen anyone on the fifth floor until a door opened at the far end of the hall and the stately, green-clad goddess from the lobby appeared, ice bucket in hand. Frank was stunned.

"Waiting for someone?" she asked.

Transfixed by her almond-shaped, violet eyes, Frank stared like a hormonal adolescent. "The bellman. The drink machine's jammed," he mumbled.

She went about filling her bucket with ice when the door to Ben's room opened and Frank heard voices. The group was leaving, and he couldn't let Ben see him. Frank ducked around the corner and bumped into the tall beauty. At that exact moment a husky man jogged by.

"Stop him," the towering Venus cried. "He's going to kill those people."

Frank hesitated, but sprung through the door, gun in hand. The man dropped to one knee in a shooting posture. Kelly, Neal and the others froze at the sight of the man's gun.

As the squat stranger sighted Kelly, light flashed from a scar on his neck. Memories flooded back and Frank recalled the foreigner who'd drugged and interrogated him. Adrenaline surged. "Get back," he yelled. Frank leapt forward, smashing the back of the man's head.

"How do you like it?" Frank muttered through clenched teeth, giving the assassin a hard blow to the gut. He pushed the man's head back, pressing his forearm across the assailant's neck. "Who do you work for?" The stocky man didn't respond. "Who sent you?" Frank held his fist back, poised to deliver another blow, when Venus' escort from the lobby appeared with handcuffs.

"I'll take care of him."

Frank scowled. "Who the hell are you?"

"Hotel security. I saw the whole thing. Lucky you happened by." He jerked the manacled man to his feet and pushed him toward the elevator.

"Yeah," Frank mumbled, feeling dazed. He glanced up and caught Neal's eyes which flashed with recognition. So much for his clandestine operation. "Get back in the room," Frank ordered gruffly. The group obeyed.

Then a soft hand touched Frank's shoulder. It was Venus, and she was smiling.

Part Three

Critical Mass

Chapter 26

Savannah, Georgia
June 14, 12:15 A.M. EDT

Venus' real name was Pira, and she came from a distant star system.

Frank stood by the door of Ben's hotel room listening without comment. Kelly, Neal, Ben and Massoud sat around the room like children at story hour, eagerly hanging on every word the bewitching lady uttered. She'd come to aid the upliftment, Pira said. Her people had been visiting the planet for a long time, seeking out and awakening reincarnated souls from her world. She claimed to have a ship *parked* outside of town.

Ben and Massoud seemed genuinely stunned while Kelly and Neal showed mild surprise—in on the scam Frank figured. At one point Kelly and Pira started conversing about the Syrians. Frank thought, *ah-ha*, a motive for the charade was finally coming to light. However, it soon became clear that they were talking about beings from the Sirius star system and not inhabitants of the Middle East. Kelly'd asserted that her companion from Captiva had come from Sirius.

"The man in the hall is one of us," Pira told Frank.

"The hotel's security officer?"

She smiled, exposing even teeth so white they sparkled. "Adam is a member of this city's police department. He came here at my request."

Frank leaned against the doorjamb, arms folded defensively. "How did you know, in advance, that an agent would attempt to assassinate these people?"

"We have been monitoring the activities of certain operatives."

Frank clucked derisively. "Your space brothers?"

She smiled sweetly in the face of Frank's gibe. "Our kinsmen as well as their detractors."

"Which was he?"

"You tell me," Pira countered. "You've met him before, in a small room, a dark room with light above the door. You vowed you would remember ... , seems you did."

Frank straightened, unconsciously patting the gun tucked into his belt. He did recall the man with the scar, could almost smell the dank cell where he'd been held captive. It was hazy and vague, but she was right. But ... how did Pira know unless she was in cahoots with them? "I don't know anything about the agent. Have you been following me?" As soon as Frank asked the question he knew the answer was no. She'd been at the hotel when he arrived; there was no way she could have known he'd be following Ben.

"We have ways of detecting things," Pira replied innocently.

Kelly and Neal seized the lull to relate their plans for re-energizing the ley lines. Pira's head bobbed approvingly as they described the migration of natives to the energy centers, the chanting strategy for planetary healing, and the necessity of silencing the chaos, which Neal interpreted to mean blacking out the East Coast.

"Does that make sense to you?" Neal asked. Pira nodded. "Can you help us?"

"Electric systems go out when UFOs fly by. Why don't you black it out with your ship?" Frank said sarcastically. She fixed her liquid-violet eyes on him. A tingling current shot down his spine, settling in his groin. She was the most magnetic woman he'd ever encountered, but he couldn't let that affect his judgment. Frank stuffed his hands in his pockets, trying to appear unfazed.

"We may help, but cannot do it for you. The final steps must be taken by this planet's inhabitants."

Convenient response, Frank thought. He'd seen a couple of the space programs, the ones with lizard people, aliens with brains on the outside of their heads, and other childish rot. The good guys had a noninterference rule—the prime directive he thought it was called. In this case Frank suspected noninterference meant *I can't do it.* "Ah, come on, give them a hand. After all, they're your kinsmen."

Pira strode to his side and draped her arm around his shoulder. He tensed. She kissed him on the cheek. "*They're* not my kin, *you are*," she purred.

Frank pulled away, sliding down the wall until the doorknob caught the small of his back. "Save it, lady. I'm not a starry-eyed kid."

"Of course not," she whispered, drawing closer. "You're a lot like Adam."

Frank felt her breath on his cheek and a twitch in his abdomen. Her presence was overwhelming. Pira smelled like a flower, so sweet it made him drool while her half-closed eyes begged him to take her in his arms. For a fleeting moment he imagined pulling her toward him, pressing those exquisite breasts against his chest. He shuddered and stepped away, conscious of four pairs of eyes staring in his direction. He had to keep his distance to maintain objectivity. He cleared his throat.

"You people are nuts. Believe anything you want, that's fine with me. My sole reason for being here is to get a statement about Captiva," he said pointing at Neal and Kelly. "I'm under investigation for shooting Collins. I need you to collaborate my story, to tell them I had no choice except to shoot the crazy jerk."

Neal shook his head, jaw set with determination. "Can't do it, not until I turn off the electric grid and find my wife. Want a statement from me? You'd better help. Faster my business is finished, faster you'll get your statement."

Kelly grinned at Neal with admiration. "Same here. I'll go back with you and explain everything as soon as our mission is complete."

Frank knew he could force them to go at gun point; however they might retaliate by having him convicted. Or, he could use the drug allegations to coerce Neal, but he didn't have anything on Kelly. In any event, there was the problem of what to do with Ben, Massoud, and Pira. They had him.

"You won't finish this ridiculous mission because you'll never shut off the electricity." Frank knew enough about utility operations—built-in redundancy—to be confident they couldn't pull it off.

Neal asked, "Pira, how much aid can you give? If we come up with a plan, can you help execute it?"

"That is allowed if it is a strategy of your own making."

Neal turned to Massoud. "How could we pull it off?"

"If I knew, I wouldn't tell you. I don't believe any of this."

"Would a spaceship convince you?" Neal glanced at Pira, who nodded.

"Well ... uh ... I'm not—"

"I'll go ... for Allison," Neal declared. "It's the only way we'll see her again."

"Don't play with me," Massoud protested. "She could be dead for all we know."

"She's not," Kelly and Pira said in unison.

"How do you know?"

"She's with us," Pira said softly.

▼▲▼

Savannah, Georgia
June 14, 3:00 A.M. EDT

Frank refused to let Kelly and Neal out of his sight. He sat between them in the back seat of the Savannah police car with Pira in the front seat and Adam, her *contact*, driving. Ben and Massoud followed in Neal's car. The mood was somber as they drove west on I-16, then south on I-95 toward Fort Stewart. In spite of his earlier bravado, Neal was nervous, alternately fidgeting and biting a hangnail. Kelly appeared resolute. Sitting with his feet on the hump in the middle of the floor board, Frank was cramped and disgusted. This escapade ranked among the silliest things he'd ever done. If his career weren't in jeopardy, he'd have washed his hands of the whole bunch, advising them to run, not walk, to the nearest mental institution. Unfortunately, his career was on the line, so he had to go along with the farce for a little while longer.

He just couldn't figure Adam, though. The guy was a sergeant on the Savannah police force and seemed normal, or as normal as any inner city cop can be who has to deal with thugs, drug addicts and crazies on a daily basis. Maybe the poor guy was under Pira's spell—voodoo was big in this part of the country. The woman had something special, Frank had to admit. While logic and training told him Pira was a fraud, the rest of his being was mesmerized. Perhaps it *was* black magic; he'd never had such a strong reaction to anyone before.

Frank tapped Adam's shoulder. "Hey, Adam. Known Pira long?"

Adam stiffened, eyes darting at Frank in the rearview mirror.

Frank held up his hands and leaned back. "Take it easy, friend, just curious."

Pira winked at Adam. "About six months," Adam finally said.

"How'd you meet?"

"I have a fish camp on the Altamaha. She showed up one day, and we started talking."

"Dressed like that?" Frank motioned toward Pira and her silky sheath.

Adam grinned mischievously into the mirror. "She had on shorts. Short shorts."

Frank felt a tinge of jealousy. Why the grin? What was the nature of their relationship? "She just sat down and told you she was from outer space?"

"For a long time we merely talked, ya know, about fishing, the sorry state of world affairs, that kinda thing. Every time I went fishing she'd appear. After a while our discussions got serious. Philosophical. A couple of months later she took me to her ship and told me who she was."

"You believe it?"

"You will, too." Adam signaled a right turn and guided the car down an exit, eye on the rearview mirror and Ben's car. They drove down a two-lane country road lined by tall pines. Adam turned several times, taking them deeper and deeper into the woods, eventually steering onto a narrow dirt road. They bounced along the rutted lane for the better part of a mile when it dead ended. Adam cut the headlights; Ben pulled behind and did the same.

The night was clear, the moon a mere sliver in the western sky. The air was warm and damp, scented with the musty odor of decaying pine needles. Frank got out of the car and turned slowly to get his bearings. He instinctively patted the side where his gun should have been, then remembered he'd given it to Adam. Pira had said it wasn't necessary, but Adam insisted, so Frank went along. After all, his goal was to keep an eye on Kelly and Neal; if it required surrendering his weapon, so be it. Anyway, the group seemed harmless enough and Adam, though potentially dangerous, was under Pira's control, and obviously she wanted Frank to be there.

Frank stood aside as the group crowded Pira expectantly. What kind of hoax was the tall beauty going to employ? Lights suspended from the trees, perhaps? Or maybe she had a mockup of a flying saucer, round with a dome on top and strobe lights, no doubt. If she were truly creative, the contraption would be suspended by ropes so it would appear to hover.

This is going to be good, Frank thought as he followed the little troupe into the woods. They weaved, single file through towering pines for about a hundred yards to a clearing with a small lake. Pira was waiting at the forest's edge when Frank emerged and flung her arm around his back.

"You're such a skeptic," she whispered in his ear. He felt her breath on his neck and heat rushed through his body. She led him to the edge of the lake, the others spread out on either side. Then she fingered a small pendant hanging from her neck. The lake lit up. A V-shaped craft hovered above the pond. Looking like an enormous boomerang, the ship was a good three stories high at its center, tapering to about ten feet on either side. Soft blue lights lined its underside, shining on the water below. "Pretty, isn't it?" she asked as a yellow-illumined portal opened at the apex of the craft.

Frank was too amazed to speak. This was no joke, or if it was, the trick was on a Disneyland-scale. It was huge. How could anyone fabricate such a thing? Or ... was it an optical illusion, a hologram? A lightweight transparent bubble positioned above the water with projectors around the perimeter of the lake. There were probably power lines nearby which supplied the juice. But why? Frank asked himself. Who would shell out that much money? The scam would be astronomically expensive.

Frank was trying to make sense of the spectacle when a violet ray shot from the ship's opening to the shore. Two figures appeared in the doorway—one tall like Pira, the other average height—and proceeded to walk down the light beam. The tall one led the way in a white and orange jumpsuit. A woman, she looked much like Pira except her hair was shorter and she had a chunkier physique. The second, also female, had long brown hair and wore a kimono several sizes too large.

"Allison!" Neal raced to the shorter woman, picking her up and spinning around. "I was afraid you were dead." At the sight of Allison, Massoud slumped to the ground and began praying to Allah. Kelly kneeled to comfort Massoud; Ben was frozen in place.

"What do you think?" Pira whispered to Frank.

"Holy—," was the only thing he could manage.

The tall woman greeted Adam, hugging him like an old friend. They conversed for several minutes, then approached Frank and Pira. Pira introduced Teinutta, who clutched Frank in a bear hug. Frank grinned stupidly, too surprised to do more than mumble.

Adam laughed. "Said you'd believe, didn't I?"

Dammit, he did believe. Frank thought of his conversation with Jake and Sally at Captiva, how he'd thought them silly for watching paranormal television shows. Now he was in a plot straight out of science fiction: a spaceship, aliens, and Pira was pushing him toward the purple ramp. He gulped down a wave of terror and allowed himself to be herded into the vessel.

Bright yellow light, emitted by a glowing domed ceiling, flooded the room they entered. An apparent storage area, barrel-shaped containers lined the outer perimeter, while the inner wall was filled with drawers and cubbyholes. Teinutta motioned toward plastic-looking benches arranged in a semi-circle against the side wall.

The group sat down; Allison and Neal snuggling happily, Kelly and Ben looking serious while Massoud showed signs of shock. Pira waved her palm over a glossy wall panel, and a table rose from the floor. She, Teinutta, and Adam sat on the far side of the platform facing the group.

Frank felt like the accused at an inquisition, the triumvirate standing between him and the door, him and freedom. His muscles tensed. Pira flashed a reassuring smile.

"I am Teinutta, from the star system you call Lalande," the taller alien stated slowly in English with a slightly slurred accent. "Do not worry, we have come to help you."

"Believe her," Allison broke in, "they saved me from being kidnapped."

"Allah," Massoud muttered, looking ill.

"The government?" Neal asked.

Allison nodded. "Sheridan's crony."

"Why?"

"Because of Neal's knowledge of the government project, HAIR, and its connection to the tornadoes."

"But I was wrong—the project didn't produce them," Neal said. "The storms were caused by other aliens, the Sirians."

Allison gave Pira and Teinutta a questioning look. "That is correct," Pira said. "The radio waves were intended to trap the Sirians."

Frank's mind raced. Things were starting to make sense.

"Your government has started to eliminate our compatriots. That's why we intervened to save Allison."

"In Las Vegas?" Kelly asked, looking stricken.

Las Vegas? Frank recalled Jake's reference to Kelly's friend there. "What about it?" he asked.

"Betty and Cara, my friends, were murdered."

Cara, Frank remembered the name. Collins had tipped off the assassins! If Frank ever had regrets about nailing Collins, they were gone. Frank said, "Compatriots?"

Pira replied. "Countrymen, like you and Adam."

"I'm not your countryman. I'm American. My parents were Francis and Maria Scortino. I was born in New York. I have brothers and sisters and a birth certificate."

"Yes." Pira's lips spread into a sultry smile.

"So, it's impossible."

Kelly started to protest, but Adam spoke first. "I know it's a hard to buy, pal, but you used to live on their planet."

"Have you been smoking crack?"

"Reincarnation, ace. Like you, I didn't believe it at first."

Frank glanced toward the door. The portal was approximately twenty feet away. If he lunged, taking them by surprise, he could be out of the ship before they knew what happened. Yet, at the very moment he had the thought, the door to the portal snapped shut. He glared at the trio who were now holding him captive.

Kelly patted his hand. "I didn't believe it until Reese showed me his natural state."

"I saw Reese disappear in a funnel cloud," Neal added.

The whole damned bunch had lost their minds, Frank told himself. Nuts, all nuts, and he wasn't buying any of it. He folded his arms across his chest and glowered at Adam.

"Haven't you ever had a memory or inkling of having lived at another time, in another place?" Kelly asked.

Frank wasn't going to dignify the question with a response. Of course not . . . then he thought of the dark-haired enchantress of his dreams. He saw them running through a meadow, her teasing him, playfully taunting. The colors of the countryside were indescribably vivid; the air had the scent of vanilla. He was happy, oh so happy, . . . yet that was it, Frank always woke up before he reached her. A tingling surge of energy shot up his spine. *Magod, the woman looked like Pira!*

"I've come to take you home," she said.

Frank pulled away from her, his brow furrowed with disbelief. *How could it be true?* And, what about Adam? How did he fit in?

Adam understood. "She was my sister," he said. Frank sank back, surprised by his feeling of relief.

"Neal asked for our help," Pira said to Teinutta. "I explained that we cannot do it for them, though we may lend aid. The final step must be taken by the inhabitants of this planet."

"The final step?"

Kelly told the group about Atlantis, the descent of the scientists, and the crossroads mankind had reached. "We move forward now, or our planet will disintegrate."

"Disintegrate?" Massoud entered the conversation, having finally recovered from the shock of finding Allison and the alien vessel.

"The ley lines, the energetic casing which keeps the planet intact has been corrupted to the point that the world will fly apart unless drastic action is taken," Kelly replied. Neal jumped in, explaining to Allison about the Aborigine, chanting and the necessity to deactivate the electric transmission system.

"You'd have to simultaneously bypass the logic in both control room computers," Allison said.

"It can't be done," Massoud complained.

"Yes, if we installed receivers and transmitted the instructions to both computers at the same time," Allison countered.

"Install receivers on both computers? Come on! They're in separate rooms with different security systems. It's impossible," Massoud objected.

Neal looked to Pira and Teinutta. "You could do it, couldn't you?"

"We may only assist."

"Why?" Frank asked.

Teinutta responded, "Because we cannot interfere with your free will. The pitiful state of this planet was caused by mankind's hatred and fearful thoughts, thus the correction must come from the minds that created the thought-forms. When humans accept the fact that they are more than flesh and blood, that their true essence is immortal and part of everything in the universe, Light will flood their minds. If they then direct the Light to the planet, the mass conscious-ness will be healed.

"This is the *End Time* prophesied by your sages. Yet humans have missed the point of the prophecies. Knowledge of the future was given so that man could take steps to avert the disaster, not cringe in fear, adding to the negative atmosphere which hastens the planet's descent."

Her comments hit Frank like a punch in the gut. At a deep level, he knew it was true.

"If we planted the devices, could you activate them from your ship," Neal asked.

"That is permissible, but you must position them your-selves. This is *your* responsibility."

Kelly looked to the others. "This is it, guys, the turning point. Starpeople came in for this very purpose and are being drawn to the right places at the right time. It's no accident we're here together. Whether you know it or not, one of you has the knowledge to get past the security systems."

Neal, Ben, Massoud, and Allison looked at each other.

"I don't know the alarm codes," Massoud protested.

"If I show up, the company cops will descend like locusts," Allison observed.

Neal said, "I couldn't get past the front door."

"Ditto," Ben agreed.

"I can do it," a hushed voice spoke.

"What?"

Frank leaned forward, shaking his head. "I can get past the security system." He looked to Pira. "Can you manufacture electronic devices to my specifications?"

She smiled, and a hot wave shot up his spine. "If you help me."

Frank thought she'd never ask.

▼▲▼

Rural Georgia, Near Savannah
June 14, 5:30 A.M. EDT

He'd been lying in the pine needles watching for over an hour. Eaten up by *no-see-'ems* and mosquitoes, Sammy wasn't sure how much more he could endure. He'd seen his assistant captured by the Savannah police, then bided his time and followed the group out into the woods.

They'd intercepted the phone call back in Charlotte between Ben and Massoud about meeting Neal in Savannah. They'd tried tapping the television station's phones, but it got too many calls. Sheridan at the electric utility had been more than accommodating when they'd asked for Massoud's direct number. From there it was easy; they'd barely gotten the bug in place when Ben placed the call.

While Damore shadowed Kelly and Neal around Savannah, he'd placed a homing device on their Toyota. A fortunate precaution, because the next thing he knew Damore was being led off in handcuffs. Luckily, Ben had followed the policeman in Neal's car, otherwise Sammy would never have found them in the woods. Lord knew he didn't want to inform Colonial Houston about another mistake. One operative missing, another in the Savannah jail—Houston and the general were livid.

Sammy slapped a mosquito away from his cheek. He figured he'd wait another five minutes, then go back to the van and track Neal's car from there. Sammy had parked the vehicle on a logging road close to the dead-end, so there was no way the group could get past him without being seen.

He smacked his thigh as another predator took a bite of his flesh. Blasted bugs, he thought, I've had enough. At that moment the door to the ship opened. Kelly, Ben and the Savannah policeman walked out.

Chapter 27

Cassadaga, Florida
June 14, 12:30 P.M. EDT

Catherone couldn't stand waiting or losing control. As a Scorpio, she was mystically inclined, secretive, and sexy as hell; yet, control was the defining characteristic of the sign and she had four planets there. The phrase *knowledge is power* was undoubtedly coined by a kindred November native who craved information on everyone and everything for the manipulative edge such intelligence gave. And nothing would earn a scorpion sting faster than the feeling of being duped, left out, or surprised. Not having heard from Kelly and Neal for over twenty-four hours, Catherone was cranky when Hank, Jr. and two friends pulled up on Harley Sportsters.

"Mumma," the heavyset man called as he knocked on the screen door. "Mumma, it's Hank, yo baby boy." He grinned at his buddies who were leaning on their bikes.

"What are you doing here?" Catherone asked, swinging the door wide.

Hank's face fell. "Uh, a bike show in Daytona. Is this a bad time?"

"No, come on in." Catherone forced a smile and motioned to Hank's friends. "You caught me in the middle of something." She gave him a hug and pecked his cheek. The men ambled in, clanging as they walked, a long chain hanging from the belt loop on each man's jeans to the wallet in his back pocket. Catherone rolled her eyes at the swaying chains—little boys with long phallic symbols. But, Hank Jr. had come by it honestly; Big Hank had been the same way, macho truck driver and all.

The men tried to make small talk as Catherone served sweet tea. She loved Hank, was happy to see him, wanted to talk, but not now. The Aborigine had returned to the GeoSphere, and Wally Christian had called several times looking for Kelly. Jeri phoned twice to report that her spirit guide believed Kelly and Neal were in danger. While Hank knew of his mother's occult leanings, she didn't want to get into a discussion about Kelly, Neal, and aliens in front of him and his friends. Catherone heard a car door slam; she needed to get rid of Hank, fast.

"Baby boy, you have to go."

"What, Mumma? We just got here."

"It's a bad time, dawlin'. A lady's staying with me—" Catherone had to think fast. Why couldn't he stay around Kelly and Neal? Contagious disease? That wouldn't work; Hank knew she had no patience with sick people. Running from the law? Naw, that'd freak him out. Abused. Although the big guy looked like a thug, he was a pussycat at heart. "—she's an abused wife. Her brother helped her run away. She's hiding out from her husband," Catherone fibbed.

Hank glanced at his buddies. "We afraid of a wifebeater?" They balled their fists and mumbled, "No way." "Bring on the scum."

"She's been traumatized real bad, tortured. Afraid of all men except her brother. I fear the sight of you strapping fellas might send her over the edge, and I've just gotten her calmed down."

Hank shrugged and stood up. "Aw right, but you have any trouble, jest call me. We're staying at the Holiday Inn in Daytona Beach, and will be there for the next few days. See if you can't get the poor lady straightened out enough so we can at least have dinner."

"I will, baby." Catherone gave him a hug and pushed him toward the entrance. She heard the screen door creak. She hoped Kelly and Neal didn't bound in spouting off about aliens. "I'll call you tonight," Catherone promised.

The door opened and Kelly shuffled in looking exhausted. Catherone sighed with relief, at least Kelly looked the abused part. The men gave the younger woman wide berth and hurried out the door.

"I'll call you, son," Catherone shouted from the doorway, waving. She watched until they turned onto the road. "Where's Neal?"

Kelly sank into a chair at the kitchen table. "I've been up all night and am so tired I can hardly move. Neal stayed behind … with other aliens … who have a ship. They're going to shut off the electric grid tomorrow."

"Ship, like flying saucer?"

"Yep, an honest-to-god UFO."

"The Aborigine is back."

Kelly said "Good," rested her head on her arms and went to sleep.

▼▲▼

Earth Orbit
June 14, 12:30 P.M. EDT

Frank took a bite of the green, curlycue concoction which looked disgusting though wasn't half bad as long as he fixed his eyes elsewhere; the sweet and pungent flavors vaguely reminiscent of watermelon and hot barbecue sauce. Pira sat across from him while Neal, Allison, and Massoud talked to Teinutta at the end of the long table.

Back on the ground they'd decided that Kelly would return to Florida, Ben would fulfill his obligations at the premiere, and Adam would try to keep the government's assassin under wraps until the mission was completed. With little to do until the new moon, they'd gone into high orbit.

"Not safe on the ground," Teinutta said. Technology provided by the Neboki which had been incorporated into stealth fighters was capable of disrupting the ship's operations. Pira and Teinutta agreed they must stay in orbit until late that night when they'd go to the old landing strip in Charlotte. Compatriots on the ground would meet the ship and take Frank and Massoud to the electric utility.

Frank gazed at Pira. "When did I leave you?"

"You've been gone close to fifty Earth years."

He was forty-nine; adding nine months for incubation meant he came to Earth directly from her planet. No time between lives as mystics generally claimed. "Fifty years? I thought souls rested between lives."

"Usually, yes. You left with the expressed purpose of taking your present incarnation."

"On purpose? Suicide?"

Pira drew back in revulsion. "We conducted the rituals—you merely assumed a new form to accomplish your purpose. We have preserved your old vessel; it is here on the ship."

Frank dropped the implement that served as a combo knife, fork, and spoon. "The old vessel?"

Pira was perplexed. "Your body, naturally. You could not return home in that form."

"What's wrong with this form?"

"It's too dense; you'd never survive on our planet. Your blood vessels would rupture, your small lungs would pant for air—"

Small lungs? "I can breathe this air just fine."

Pira was amused by his petulance. "We altered it to accommodate Allison. Teinutta and I are taking medication which enables us to cope. If you want to go home with us, you must return to your former physique."

"You have my old body here, on the ship?" Frank asked, conscious of eyes watching him from the end of the table.

"Yes, as we planned."

Frank shoved his plate away. "You have me at a disadvantage. I don't remember the plan."

"I should have expected as much—the scriptures say the veil is thick."

Pira was gorgeous, titillating, and Frank felt he'd known her before, yet the idea of coming from outer space was hard to swallow much less changing bodies like a suit of clothes. "Your people do this kind of thing often? I mean, change bodies?"

"*Our* people," Pira corrected. "It had not been done for eons, but the need was pressing. You did it for the greater good, to help this planet."

"Why?"

She was truly baffled. "The prime truth: *All that you give is given to yourself.*"

"What's that supposed to mean?"

"All things are joined, the Great One. Surely you remember that."

"No."

Pira and Teinutta exchanged bewildered glances. Teinutta responded, "We are all like drops of water in the ocean, each separate yet connected and part of a greater whole. This is the recognition that mankind must make in order to move into the new era. Man must see himself as part of everything and act accordingly. To paraphrase your prophets: As you do to the least, so you do to yourself, for you—we—are all one. Joined, inseparable, energy directed by intention."

Teinutta was getting dangerously close to religion, something Frank made diligent efforts to avoid. He'd been turned off to traditional doctrine at an early age, the constant ranting about sin and sinners seeming grossly out of sync with a message of peace and love. "Basically you're saying no man is an island?"

"Yes."

"I see that, but how does it explain my role on Earth?"

"As Kelly said, it is time for all of us to move to a higher plane. You came to help uplift this planet."

"Uplift how?"

Pira smiled. "I guess you're supposed to disable the electric grid."

"This is happenstance."

"Is it? Everything you've done in your life has led to this point."

"Pure chance," Frank argued.

"Call it what you will. However, it is a fortunate coincidence."

"Sure helps me," Neal said. "I didn't know how to do it and it's *my* mission."

"I'm doing this to save my pension," Frank grumbled.

"Whatever you say," Pira responded.

"So, where's my body?"

▼▲▼

Cheyenne Mountain, Colorado
June 14, 1:30 P.M. MDT

"Damned rug." Houston ripped the Navaho runner from his office wall and threw it in the trash. It mocked him; the geometric designs quivering, shifting, moving one into the other. There was no peace there, no peace anywhere. Things were crashing down around his ears.

Hanson had been picked up outside Charlotte wandering around in a daze. The agent couldn't remember who he was, what he'd been doing, or anything about Allison Winters and her whereabouts. Percy Damore had been taken into custody by the Savannah police for attempted murder. Dispatched to find Hanson, Damore and Sammy had followed Ben to Savannah. Next thing Sammy knew, Damore was being led away in handcuffs. So far Houston had had no luck springing him free and the police wouldn't even allow Houston's men to see Damore.

General Brandt had tried to exert pressure by calling in political favors, but the Savannah city judge had recently been audited by the IRS and was in no mood to cooperate with the federal government. The old coot seemed to get a perverse thrill from throwing every road block possible in their path.

Two pitches, two strikes, Houston thought as he sank into his worn leather chair. The telephone buzzed. What now?

"Sammy's on the line," his aide responded.

"Put him through," Houston barked. "Where the hell are you?"

"A little town in central Florida, Cassadaga."

"What are you doing there?"

"A long story. I've got good news and bad news. Which do you want first?"

Houston scowled. "I'm in no mood for games."

"The good news is I've located Neal Winters and Kelly Saunders. I followed the girl to a trailer here."

"What about Winters?"

"That's the bad news. He was picked by an alien starship."

"Shit."

"The tall peaceniks. The ship was south of Savannah. And, the Savannah policeman who arrested Damore is in cahoots with the aliens as well as Scortino, the Secret Service agent. Massoud Hassan, the Atlantergy employee, was also taken aboard, though I don't think he went willingly."

Houston banged his fist on the desk. "How did the Secret Service agent get involved?"

"Best I can tell, he followed the television reporter like we did, only Damore gets arrested and the alien woman takes Scortino under her wing. I watched them go onto the ship and he was not being coerced."

This was awful. The appearance of the ship meant the peaceniks were allied with the interdimensional visitors. Either group was a handful and working together they'd be impossible to stop. Houston had suspected something was up, UFO sightings had increased four-fold in the last few days. "Did you see the ship liftoff? What time was it?"

"About 5:15 this morning."

"Have you called for backup?" Houston asked.

"Two men en route here, three to Savannah."

"Who's in Charlotte?"

"Two men."

"Have one stake out the electric employee's home."

"Maybe we should pick up the TV reporter. I can get Kelly, the girl."

Kelly was the common thread between the two groups of extraterrestrials, and she'd returned to Florida where all hell had broken loose. Bizarre weather, UFO sightings, and magnetic fluctuations in the Bermuda Triangle. "Don't bother Saunders yet; I want to see what she does. Something big is cooking. I'll put Persman on, you can have whatever you need. Time's running out—we must get control of the situation." Houston pressed the call button and waited until his aide answered. Then he fished the Navaho rug out of the trash can, folded it neatly and laid it on the edge of his desk. Persman was talking to Sammy when Houston passed through the adjoining office on his way to Space Command's Missile Warning Center.

A good half mile away along the sterile halls and elevators that honeycombed the mountain, Space Command was responsible for the fleet of military satellites orbiting 22,000 miles above the Earth. Installed to monitor missile launches and nuclear detonations, they'd also proven handy for tracking UFOs. The aliens knew exactly what was going on; the peaceniks in the V-shaped ships would hover in front of a satellite for hours, as if daring the military to shoot it down. Of course, that would never happen—to do so would instigate World War III.

Houston found the section chief, Wayne Chang, talking to his staff in the middle of the bullpen. Chang caught sight of Houston. "Yes, sir," the young officer said.

"A bogey was spotted around Savannah at 5:15 this morning. Did you pick it up?"

Data from the satellites was beamed to the surface and stored on reels and reels of computer tape. While a technician monitored the information from each orbiting sensor, the flow of information was staggering, and a flash incident like a UFO could easily go undetected. In contrast to ballistic missiles, the aliens could turn on a dime, appearing as little more than an infrared streak to the sophisticated equipment. "Didn't get an incident report, sir. Let's check the tape." Chang led Houston to another work station. "Anything at 5:15?"

The technician entered a command into his terminal, bringing up a string of numbers. "Here it is," he said, pointing at the screen. The signature was typical of the peaceniks.

Houston said to Chang, "Can you redeploy satellites to search high orbit? I have a feeling our friend is hanging around."

"It'll take some work. We have to do it sequentially to avoid dead spots."

"Fine, do it."

By the time Houston got back to his office, Chang had located the vehicle. "It's in synchronous orbit over the East Coast."

"Keep eyes on it at all times. If it moves, I want to know."

His mother always said he had good intuition, and Houston's gut told him the aliens were about to make a major move. What? Why? It didn't matter; he would be ready. He buzzed Persman. "Get HAIR on the line, then the general. And find out where we have stealth on the East Coast."

Houston leaned back wearily and noticed the Navaho rug on the corner of his desk. It looked inert and harmless, the demons properly chastised and put to rest. Houston sighed and heaved himself out of the chair. The wall looked bare without it.

Chapter 28

Flagler Beach, Florida
June, 14 9:30 P.M. EDT

I'm glad you're here—he's waiting in the crystal room,"
Timothy said. "Been in there for hours, keeps saying the tall
sister will come. How anyone can stay in the crystal room
that long is beyond me."

Kelly dropped a knapsack by the stairwell and looked
around anxiously. Catherone pushed past them both into the
main room where Wally Christian was consulting a hand held
instrument. He nodded to the women.

"Energy's soaring—never seen it this high. The vortex is
expanding, centered in there." Wally pointed toward the
cubicle where the Aborigine waited. "We're on the threshold
of the next dimension." A hovering violet light blinked in
the corner. "That's bleed-through from the other side. It's
occurring more and more frequently."

Catherone went to the spot. "Always here?" At the instant
she asked the question a shimmering blue blob materialized
over Wally's head. He raised the meter to arm's length.

"Frequency's so high it doesn't register," Wally observed.

"What's causing it?"

"Our Aborigine friend says this place is the navel of Gaia's
body, the link to the cosmic womb. The energy readings would
seem to support that hypothesis," Wally said dispassionately.

"What about the other energy centers?" Kelly asked.

Timothy responded, "Natives, ancient people have descended on each site and started chanting."

"Chanting what?" Catherone asked.

"As far as I can tell each place is different—distinct mantras and pitch."

"The great chorus that Oooma mentioned," Kelly muttered, recalling Timothy's account of his meeting with the Aborigine. A rotating ring of green and violet lights appeared in the middle of the room. "I know I'm supposed to sing with Oooma, but I can't imagine what the chant is."

"It's the universal chorus Reese told you about. Meditate, hook into that Sirian message you talked about," Catherone said.

"I guess you're right." Kelly had reached the pinnacle of her life, her purpose for coming to Earth and the reason she'd met Reese. Neal and Frank were doing their part; it was time she did hers. She left the group and went downstairs to the healing room. Ten minutes later, she returned. "I know what to do. It's so simple."

"Do tell," Catherone prodded.

"The consciousness of the planet must be cleansed. It has become clogged by mankind's hatred and fear. Negative emotions are like a dark cloud which blocks the Light, and our connection to the Universal Source. Oooma and I must accept the Light for ourselves, then direct it to the planet. We are tuned to a particular frequency as the other natives have their own tone. The sum of all the frequencies will yield the white light of the Source. Alone we can do little, together we can heal the Earth." She hugged Catherone. "I guess I shouldn't keep our guest waiting." Kelly squared her shoulders and strode into the crystal room.

Catherone hung around with Wally and Timothy, trying to make small talk until she could stand it no longer. The atmosphere in the building was stifling, thick with expectation.

Although she'd given up smoking years before, Catherone suddenly craved a cigarette. "I'd give anything for a menthol," she said, pacing back and forth behind Wally who was meticulously recording energy readings. "Either of you smoke?" They both said no. "I knew you didn't; I normally don't indulge. Waiting is driving me crazy. How long has Kelly been in there?"

"Two hours," Timothy responded.

She listened at the crystal room door for the umpteenth time. "I don't hear anything. Do you think they're okay?"

"I'm sure of it," Wally stated quietly.

A flurry of violet flashes blinked about the room. Catherone started to pace again. "Whew, I wish I had a cigarette ... or a scotch. Say, Wally, do you have a flask?"

Wally glared, patience waning. "There may be some cigarettes in the guest house. A French scientist who visited last month was a smoker. I think he left a pack of cigarettes on the kitchen counter." Wally glanced at Timothy as if to say 'go along.'

Timothy nodded. "Why don't you check it out." He handed Catherone the key to the cottage next door. "You know Frenchmen, probably left a bottle of wine, too."

Catherone knew they were trying to get rid of her. Under normal circumstances she'd have planted her feet to spite them, but decided to let it pass—the tension of waiting was unbearable. She took the key and headed toward the small house reserved for visiting dignitaries.

The night was hot and no moon shone. As she unlocked the door to the darkened bungalow, she caught a movement from the corner of her eye. She hurried in and latched the dead bolt. Catherone flattened herself against the wall and peeked out the kitchen window. Two crouched figures were circling the GeoSphere.

▼▲▼

Outside Charlotte, North Carolina
June 14, 11:30 P.M. EDT

Teinutta brought the ship to earth in blacked-out mode. They dove straight in from orbit, landing at the abandoned airstrip on the outskirts of the city. Two of their *operatives* were waiting to ferry Frank and Massoud into town.

With Pira's help they'd built a descrambler that Frank would use to decipher the security codes. It was the same design used by the Service. Frank knew because he had once been forced to dissect a unit when it malfunctioned. In addition, they had two receivers, one for each mainframe. Utilizing information provided by Allison and Massoud, Teinutta fashioned communications devices that could access main memory if placed within a few feet of the company's computers. Frank was surprised by the aliens' understanding of Earth's computers. He'd asked how they acquired the knowledge, but Teinutta danced around the question.

The plan was for Massoud and Frank to enter the Atlantergy operations center and plant the devices. Once the instruments were in place, Massoud would go home while Frank returned to the ship. The electric transmission system would be disengaged from orbit. After that the ship would return, allowing Allison and Neal to leave while picking up other operatives ready to return to the homeworld.

Frank had the option of going or staying, whichever he wished. On that count, Frank wasn't sure what he wanted to do. He'd seen his other *body*, a strange experience, indeed. Held in stasis, the *vessel*, as Pira called it, looked much like her: tall, pale almost iridescent skin, broad shoulders, narrow hips and dark hair that fell almost to its shoulders. The long hair had turned him off, since Frank hated flowing locks on men—sissies, he'd always said. Pira explained that while the body itself had not aged in its fifty years of storage, the hair had grown. "You wore your hair very short when we were together." Frank was relieved to hear it.

The feeling he got from viewing the inert form was much the same as looking an old high school picture. You recognized yourself, yet at best, felt a weak connection. Although he'd had more memories of his life with Pira, there was still a sense of unreality or detachment. Earth was his home now, and Frank wasn't sure he was ready to give it up.

The van stopped on the street in front of the Atlantergy building. "Walk to the corner when you finish," the driver, Cathy Ann, instructed. "We'll circle the block. If anything goes wrong, go to the rest room in the garage across the street. If we don't find you on the street, we'll look for you there."

The upper floors of the Atlantergy building were dark, while the lower floors glowed. Switchboards were manned round-the-clock and the control center always boasted a full complement. The computers were housed on the third basement level. To get there Frank and Massoud would have to get past the security guard at the front desk.

"That will be easy," Massoud assured Frank. Massoud would simply sign in for his office, designating Frank as a friend. Bringing a friend or sibling along for a quick in-and-out was common practice during nights and weekends. Frank would have to show ID, which was fine because he always carried a fake driver's license. Once they were past the guard, no one would stop them as long as Massoud kept his badge prominently displayed. They'd go straight to the computer rooms where Frank would bypass the security system, plant the receivers and, with luck, they'd be out of the building in thirty minutes. Signals to shut down the computers would be broadcast later, at 3:30 A.M., providing a sufficient time gap so the interruption would not be linked to Massoud.

If all went as expected, the cause of the outage wouldn't matter anyway, Pira had said. Thousands of Sirians would slip in from the next dimension and authorities would be too preoccupied to care about the outage. The electric utility would eventually go out of business anyway, since the energized ley lines would provide all the energy humanity needed.

The exercise went like clock work, exactly according to plan. Within forty minutes, it would have been thirty if the guard at the front desk had not been talkative, Frank and Massoud arrived at the designated street corner. Cathy Ann pulled up seconds later. She drove Massoud to his apartment near South Park then headed out of town to the landing strip. At the moment the van appeared, the portal on the front of the ship opened and the purple light-ramp extended.

"Hurry," Cathy Ann said, "all is not well."

"What's wrong?" Frank demanded.

"Just go!"

He rushed to the ship where Pira was waiting. "You must go to your quarters. The military has discovered us. Planes are coming."

Frank felt a light-headed sensation and realized the space-ship had made a rapid ascent. "Let me come with you, Pira. I have a stake in this endeavor." Although she and Teinutta referred to him as a kinsman, they had pointedly kept him off the craft's bridge. Used to being in charge, Frank couldn't tolerate being cast aside.

Pira was perturbed. "Please, it is not allowed, and I don't have time to argue." She turned to leave.

He grabbed her arm. "I can't trade pleasantries with Allison and Neal while the ship is under attack. I might be able to help."

She looked doubtful.

"Am I your kinsman or not?"

Pira acquiesced. He followed her up a moving sidewalk and through a doorway on the upper level. The bridge was a pie-shaped room, the front corresponding to the point of the V-shaped vessel. A television-style monitor was built into the wall where a window might naturally have been. Teinutta and two crewmen were working when they arrived. Teinutta was obviously in charge, seated in an elevated chair in the bridge's center. She frowned at the sight of Frank.

"I insisted," Frank offered as way of explanation. Pira shrugged and proceeded to a console on the far side of the room.

"Sit there, and do not touch anything," the imposing woman commanded, motioning toward a chair at the side of the room. Frank bristled at the treatment yet complied without argument.

▼▲▼

Flagler Beach, Florida
June 15, 1:05 A.M. EDT

The moonless, star-filled night had taken a nasty turn. Clouds raced in from all directions, colliding into a churning, swirling mass. Sammy leaned against the side of the guest house, studying the sky. Everything else about the assignment had been screwed up, so a gully-washing thunderstorm would be apropos. The pager vibrated and he knew it was Houston. Who else would contact him in the middle of an operation?

Sammy sat on the back steps and pressed the redial button on his cellular telephone. He wasn't worried about being seen. He and O'Neil had circled the grounds four or five times and found nothing. Kelly and the old lady were in the GeoSphere. Peering through windows, O'Neil had determined two men—one old, the other in his twenties—were inside, too. Four occupants, two of whom were senior citizens, a piece of cake. Two agents could easily handle the situation; however, Sammy had ordered a third. There had been so many mistakes, Sammy intended to err on the side of caution.

"Persman, it's Sammy." He waited as Houston's aide routed the call.

"Status?" Houston demanded, sounding tense.

Sammy filled Houston in on the group and their whereabouts. "We can't tell what they're doing, the old man seems to be testing the air with some kind of instrument."

"Nothing out of the ordinary?"

"We followed the women here and have been watching ever since. No one has come or gone. Is something wrong?"

"Satellites have picked up a massive funnel forming in your vicinity."

Sammy looked up at the roiling sky. Storms were the gateways used by the interdimensional aliens, and Kelly was in league with them. He stood up, the stake-out taking on renewed urgency. "It *has* clouded up all of a sudden."

"I think you're about to have company," Houston warned.

Sammy's eyes darted, searching for O'Neil. He located the agent behind a hedge. "How do you want to proceed?"

"I want one of those aliens, alive. HAIR is standing by. This time we're going to disrupt the second vortex and capture one. The girl, Kelly, is their contact; use her as bait. Hold off until a whirlwind touches down, then nab her. A hundred bucks says the aliens will intervene and that's when you get one. This is important—no mistakes, no excuses. We've got to get a handle on the situation. The peaceniks have landed in Charlotte again; I've dispatched stealth to dog them."

"What's in Charlotte?"

"Damned if I know. The general and his *friends* are furious. They'll have our heads if we fumble again."

"Don't worry—they won't get away this time." But Sammy was worried. The wind had picked up, and there was a burnt, electric scent in the air. No moon, thick cloud cover. A tornado could touch down anywhere and he'd never see it. He pocketed the telephone and hurried toward O'Neil. It was going to be a long night.

Catherone moved away from the door on her hands and knees. *Old lady, indeed.* She crawled across the kitchen toward the living area, bones creaking and joints popping with each labored move. She'd felt anxious and jumpy for hours; now she understood why. A government S.O.B. had been following them.

Catherone knew the agent was capable of violence. His aura was black and murky, not evil per se—conscienceless; that was it, amoral. And he'd been talking to the man in stone she'd sensed earlier. This time Catherone perceived something else: *Stone Man* was scared.

She groped her way through the living room, finally locating a chair. One hand on the floor, the other on the chair's arm, Catherone levered herself up, joints shrieking from the unaccustomed movement. A little stiff—always had been, hated exercise—but she was not old. Catherone leaned back panting, her mind energized by the predicament.

The agent had mentioned Charlotte, which meant the Feds were wise to Neal and the other aliens. He'd also said 'Don't worry, they won't get away.' *Don't worry? Hmph.* "We'll see about that."

The room was pitch black but Catherone's psychic sight was on high beam. She ran her hand across the table next to the chair. A telephone—exactly what she needed.

▼▲▼

Flagler Beach, Florida
June 15, 3:10 A.M. EDT

A wail sounded from the crystal room, Kelly and Oooma had started to chant. *EEE—AAA—ah-ah-ah—eh-eh-eh—OOO—oo-oo-oo—I AM-M-M-M-M.* The sounds bounced around the room, one tone blending into another.

"All the other centers are on board," Timothy said, hanging up the telephone. "Everyone's chanting like crazy. Turns out there was no need to coordinate anything. The natives started on their own. Appears they know more than we do."

Wally stood in the center of the room with the meter held over his head. "Why does that surprise you? We're simply rediscovering what they never forgot." He turned slowly watching the instrument's display. "It's off the scale. Can you feel it?"

"The top of my head *is* starting to quiver."

"I'll bet Catherone—" Wally stopped, realizing he hadn't seen her for a long time. "Where's Catherone? She's been gone for hours."

"*Magosh*, you're right. I hope nothing's happened to her." Timothy headed out the front door, but only got as far as the parking lot when a karate chop to the back of the neck laid him out flat.

Sammy and O'Neil raced to the front door as the third agent dragged Timothy into the bushes. Sammy wasn't waiting any longer. The wind whistled ominously and Sammy thought he'd seen a funnel touch down beside the building. Guns held at ready, the agents flanked the door. With a nod from Sammy, O'Neil burst into the GeoSphere. Minutes later he reappeared with Wally Christian in a choke hold.

Catherone saw everything from the guest house. It was bad enough that poor Timothy had been flattened, but choking Wally? The man was in his eighties. Barbarians. She had to do something. Catherone flew from the house and ran down the narrow driveway toward A1A, arms flailing and screaming to the top of her lungs. Although momentarily startled, Sammy recovered fast and took off after her.

▼▲▼

Sky Above Charlotte, North Carolina
June 15, 3:25 A.M. EDT

Five stealth fighters were hot on the trail of the starship. Although the war planes posed no physical threat to the vessel—Teinutta could shed them in an instant by going into orbit—they did jeopardize the mission. The range of the receivers planted on Atlantergy's computers was limited, and stealth technology incorporated electronic countermeasures capable of distorting the signal the receivers used. Teinutta had encountered the problem before, she said. New starships utilized different frequencies, but, their craft had not been refitted.

"We'll take her into orbit to get these fleas off our back, then make a fast dive to emit the signal," Teinutta explained. "They won't be able to keep up and, with the element of surprise, we may break through their distortion waves." The vessel shot up among the satellites circling the planet. As it rose, suction from the chair gripped Frank's legs and buttocks. He grinned with surprise.

"The transmission must be made in four minutes," Pira said to Teinutta.

"Ready signal." Teinutta punched buttons on the arm of her chair and the ship plummeted toward earth. As the velocity increased, so did the suction from Frank's seat. He was pinned down, unable to move so much as a muscle. "Transmit."

The ship plunged to an altitude of 70,000 feet then leveled off. The stealth fighters appeared from the rear.

"We're not getting through; the airplanes have blocked the signal," Pira called.

Frank looked at the view screen expectantly. Charlotte shined below, ridiculing their efforts, thumbing its nose at the New Age.

▼▲▼

Flagler Beach, Florida
June 15, 3:25 A.M. EDT

Sammy pumped his arms, willing his feet to go faster. A few more steps and the old lady would be in reach. Waving her arms and screeching, Catherone lumbered down the road. Amazed the old bird could move so fast, Sammy lunged for her, missed, and stumbled. Then he realized she was no longer screaming; her shrill squawk had been replaced by a loud bass rumble. Sammy looked around, expecting to see a tornado but was blinded by a brilliant glow. He raised up on his elbows, the light was bearing down fast.

Two dozen motorcycles rumbled through, fanning out around the building. One ran up the steps of the institute. O'Neil flung Wally Christian aside and tore off across the field. Two bikers ran him down while four lurching Harleys pinned Timothy's assailant to the wall of the building.

Surrounded, Sammy lay immobile on the ground. Third strike, he was out. If these guys didn't kick his butt, Houston would. Yet, what difference did any of it make if aliens took over the planet? He rolled to his back and looked at the turbulent sky. The enormity of the situation descended like a lead weight. The world was on the brink of destruction ... and he felt an uncontrollable urge to laugh.

Kelly and Oooma were oblivious to the commotion outside as well as the ultraviolet intrusions from the next dimension that flashed inside. Carried on tones from their song, they'd entered an alternate world, an enchanted wonderland of undulating sights, sounds and colors. They saw themselves as they were together in Atlantis. Kelly recalled the pact they made in the final days: Oooma to stay behind, where he would work to maintain the planet's energy grid; while Kelly went back to Sirius to wait for the time of the second birth. She heard the Sirian message of truth and talked to a disembodied Reese. Their consciousnesses swirled in the ether, dancing merrily, happily—

▼▲▼

Sky Above Charlotte, North Carolina
June 15, 3:32 A.M. EDT

The stealth fighters broke into two groups of two with one singleton, moving to intercept in a star formation. Teinutta had no choice except to pull out of their range. The spaceship shot straight up at a death-defying speed.

"We didn't get through; no change in the electricity system," Pira said.

"I can't believe you're going to allow five little fighters to determine the fate of the planet," Frank said.

Pira responded. "We cannot intervene."

"You manufactured the transmitters."

"We helped execute your own plan," she corrected.

Frank racked his brain for a solution. "Reflect back the stealth fighters' signals, you'll blind them. Hit hard enough, and you'll burn out their electronics." He glanced at Teinutta, who had leaned forward, head buried in her hands. What the hell was she doing? Frank wondered. Was she overcome by fear or mourning their failure? "The airplanes—"

"Shh-h," Pira hissed.

After several minutes, Teinutta straightened, eyes glistening. "It will be done. Pira, prepare to transmit one more time. Pilot, set course for the center of the aircraft formation."

Frank looked around, confused. Everyone smiled serenely. A suicide mission? He started to ask, but was rendered speechless by the force of their descent. Plastered to his seat, he watched the view screen with bated breath. Initially looking like five dots against the bright lights of metropolitan Charlotte, the stealths grew larger and larger until they filled the screen. Frank braced himself, expecting to feel the force of a collision, but the starship shot through the middle of the formation. Taken by surprise, the planes veered off.

"Transmit," Teinutta ordered.

Frank prayed silently the lights in the town would go out. They didn't.

"Unsuccessful, we cannot penetrate the static."

Teinutta said, "Pilot, lead our small companions down to ten thousand feet."

"What are you doing?" Frank said.

"I am trying to save lives."

"Whose lives?"

"Theirs," Teinutta pointed at the stealths following them to the lower altitude. Moments later a brilliant flash filled the screen. The sky lit up as it had in Captiva, a magnificent aurora undulating across the sky.

"It's done," Pira called out, showing uncharacteristic excitement.

"What?" Frank asked.

"The electric transmission system is dead."

He looked at the view screen, Charlotte was dark. "How?"

"The antennas in the North."

Frank understood instantly. "HAIR. By God, Earthers did it after all."

▼▲▼

Flagler Beach, Florida
June 15, 3:40 A.M. EDT

Hank, Jr. yanked Sammy to his feet. "Tryin' to beat up on another woman?" Hank's buddy grabbed Sammy from behind, pinning his arms to his side. "You made a bad mistake when you took to fooling with my Mumma. Wanna fight? Let's see how you do with somebody your own size."

Sammy looked at Hank and giggled like a kid. "Careful, big guy. Don't make me mad, because when I get mad, the sky turns to fire."

The words had hardly left his mouth when the heavens blazed. HAIR had come to life, pumping the ionosphere full of energy.

A dazzling shaft of light shocked Kelly's senses. HAIR had been roused and the electric system blinked out.

Chaos temporarily silenced, the ley lines began to pulse. The native songs gained power as chants from all over the world united into a grand symphony. Wind whipped around the crystal room stirring Kelly from her trance. A throbbing cone of violet energy materialized in the middle of the chamber.

Oooma winked, pushed her against the wall, then stepped into the center of the vortex. He was gone in a glistening flare; a split second later Reese stood in his place. The alien stepped out of the funnel as another Reese appeared, and another one, and another.

... So the Sirians returned to the planet and the people they had wronged so long ago.

Dimensional ambassadors poured through vortices at other power centers while starships descended on sites around the world. And as each alien entered, the mass consciousness was raised another notch—pushing mankind closer and closer to the great leap forward, nearer and nearer to the Light.